PRAISE FOR
HALF-RESURRECTION BLUES

"Simply put, Daniel Jo[se Older is one of the most excit]ing voices in genre fict[ion...]"

"A damn good read. A[ll the best fantasy is] about matters of life and [death...] ~~Resurrection Blues~~ takes that to the limit. A hard-core, hard-driving fantasy."
    —*New York Times* bestselling author Simon R. Green

"In *Half-Resurrection Blues*, Older has created Noir for the Now: equal parts bracing, poignant, compassionate, and eerie. A swinging blues indeed."
    —Nalo Hopkinson, Andre Norton Award–winning author of *Sister Mine*

"Daniel José Older is here to save your soul. But he might just terrorize it first. *Half-Resurrection Blues* is the first novel of a fabulous talent, one who mixes the spectral and the intellectual with skill. This book kicks in the door waving the literary .44. Be warned."
    —Victor LaValle, author of *The Devil in Silver*

"*Half-Resurrection Blues* is so many things at once: a mystery, a suspense, a supernatural thriller. The world Older builds is familiar and alien, and it's so vividly imagined and rendered that the reader believes the contradictions. This is a fantastic beginning to what will surely be a fantastic series."
    —National Book Award–winner Jesmyn Ward

"*Half-Resurrection Blues* is not just a daring new mode of ghost-detective story; it's also a courageous effort to celebrate the diverse voices that surround us."
    —Deji Bryce Olukotun, author of *Nigerians in Space*

"*Half-Resurrection Blues* is a delicious urban fantasy paced like a thriller and scored like a fine piece of music. Daniel José Older hits all the soft, sweet notes of Brooklyn as well as its hard edges."
    —Andrea Hairston

HALF-RESURRECTION BLUES

A Bone Street Rumba Novel

DANIEL JOSÉ OLDER

A ROC BOOK

ROC
Published by the Penguin Group
Penguin Group (USA) LLC, 375 Hudson Street,
New York, New York 10014

USA | Canada | UK | Ireland | Australia | New Zealand | India | South Africa | China
penguin.com
A Penguin Random House Company

First published by Roc, an imprint of New American Library,
a division of Penguin Group (USA) LLC

First Printing, January 2015

ISBN 978-0-425-27598-6

Printed in the United States of America
10 9 8 7 6 5 4 3 2 1

To Iya Lisa Ramos and Iya Ramona Coleman

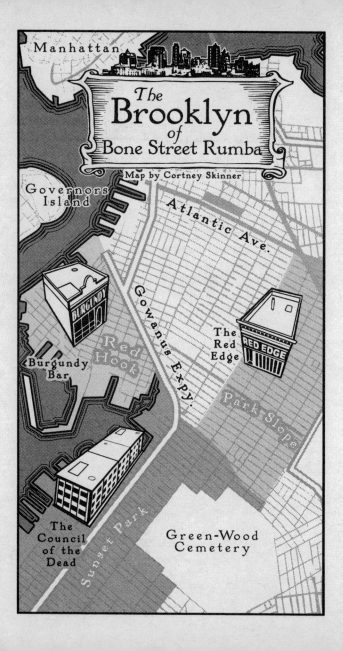

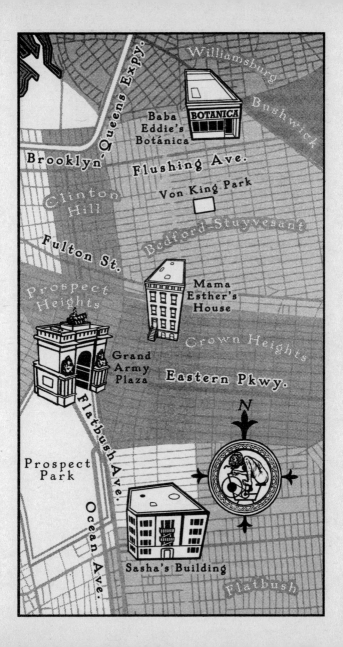

PART ONE

To live in the Borderlands means
   the mill with the razor white teeth wants to shred off
   your olive-red skin, crush out the kernel, your heart
   pound you pinch you roll you out
   smelling like white bread but dead;

To survive the Borderlands
   you must live sin fronteras
   be a crossroads.

—Gloria Anzaldúa

"To live in the Borderlands means you"

CHAPTER ONE

❧

It's just past eleven p.m. on December thirty-first—that dizzy in-between time when we're not quite here but not yet there—and hip, young white kids crowd the trendy streets of Park Slope, Brooklyn. Their pockmarked faces flash a theatrical array of expressions, everything from regret to ecstasy to total abandon, but I'm not fooled: they're bored out of their minds. I can tell because I'm dead— well, partially dead anyway. When you straddle a fine line like the one between life and death, let's just say you can tell certain things about people.

I dip into a brightly lit tobacco store for some Malagueñas and a pocket-sized rum. The rum goes into my flask and one of the Malagueñas goes in my mouth. I light it, walk back out to the street, and weave through the crowds. When I move quickly, no one notices my strange gait or the long wooden cane I use to favor my right leg. I've gotten the flow down so smooth I almost glide along toward the milky darkness of Prospect Park. There's too much information here in the streets—each passing body gives up a whole symphony of smells and memories and genetics. It can help pass the time if you're bored, but tonight, I'm far from bored.

Tonight I am hunting.

Music wafts out of a bar across the street—a kind of watery blues that evokes dentists' waiting rooms. The hipsters roam up and down the block in packs, playing out a whole mess of different daytime-drama plotlines. There's a few black and brown folks around, but they're mostly staying out of the way. And me? I'm a grayish off-brown—a neither-here-nor-there color that matches my condition. It would be a jarring skin tone to notice, but I tend to just blend in. That's fine with me. Whatever it is that's been causing all this static is out there tonight. I'm sure of it. The more I can disappear, the more chance I have of catching them.

It's been two weeks now. Two weeks of a vague and irritating twinge crawling up my spine every time I get near the crest of Flatbush Avenue. I've been walking circles around that area like an idiot, trying to sniff out the source. Stood for hours beneath the big archway with its soldiers' frozen battle cries and elaborate stonework; closed my eyes and just listened, feeling all the damn spiritual vibrations ricochet across Brooklyn. Major throughways shoot off toward Flatbush and into Crown Heights, but I narrowed it down to some indedamnterminate spot in the Slope.

When I took it to my icy superiors at the New York Council of the Dead, they nodded their old fully dead heads and turned silently in on themselves to conference. A few hours later they called me back in. Because I'm an inbetweener, and the only one anyone knows of at that, the dead turn to me when something is askew between them and the living. Usually, it's some mundane shit—

cleanup work. But every once in a while it gets really hairy, and that's when I go hunting. These are the times when I forget that I was ever even dead. Whatever shadow of life or humanity pertains to me—I know God put me on this fine planet to hunt.

Plus I'm good at it.

But the Council was all kinds of vague about this one. No explanation, just a photo of a man slid across the table with icy fingers. *We believe this is the source, Carlos. His name is Trevor Brass. Do your thing.*

"Which thing?"

An icy pause. *Eliminate him.*

And me: "Care to elucidate further?"

And them: *Nope.*

And what can really be said to that? They're dead. They don't have to elucidate shit. I don't mind though. Makes things more interesting.

Oh, and protect the entrada at all costs.

See, the dead are good for coming up with some last-minute oh-and-by-the-way type shit. Protect the entrada. An entrada is an entrance to the Underworld. There's only a couple scattered around the city, and they're supposed to be well guarded by a team of fully dead COD soulcatchers, impenetrable and all that, but really, it happens. Soulcatchers have other things to do, turns out, than stand around flickering doors to Hell. Protocols tighten and then slack again. The particular entrada they're referring to is in a shady grove in the middle of Prospect Park, not at all far from all this mess. It's not hard to imagine that whatever this grinning fellow in the picture is up to has something to do with breaching through. How they expect me to simultaneously track the dude down and keep him from getting to the entrada is another question, but that's not their concern. The Council hands out whatever garbled-up mandate they've regurgitated from their eyes in the field, and it's on me to sort through the chaos.

So I nodded, pocketed the picture, and walked out the door.

.

I swig on my flask and head for the park. I want to check on the entrada, and that swath of urban wilderness is the only place I can clear my head. I'd forgotten that this tremendous pockmarked flock of New Year's revelers would be here, jamming up all my otherworldly insights. A ponytail guy plows through the crowd to find somewhere to puke his guts out; I swerve out of the way just in time. He's wearing too much aftershave and looks like he spent three hours trying to make his hair look that carelessly tussled.

Then I see my mark. He's standing in the middle of all that hootenanny, laughing his ass off. He's caramel-colored but still somehow pale gray like an overcast day. He's got long, perfectly kept locks reaching all the way down his back and a goatee so carefully trimmed it might be painted on. His big frame rocks with laughter. Unquestionably, the cat is dealing with some supernatural . . . issues. Layers of grief, anxiety, and fanaticism swirl around him like ripples in a pond; they're peppered with a distinct aroma of, what's that? Ah, yes: guilt. And yet he's chuckling madly.

That's when it hits me: the guy's not dead. Here I was, assuming that because the NYCOD brought me in, I'd automatically have another faded shroud on my hands, some errant phantom trying to make it back or otherwise disturb the delicate balance of life and death. But this fellow isn't faded or translucent. He's breathing. His memories aren't closed books the way dead memories are. And yet, by the look of things, he's not fully alive either. I squint through the crowd at him, not even trying to conceal my intentions anymore.

He is like me.

Another inbetweener—and not just one of these half-formed, not-quite-here purgatorious mo'fos: Trevor is full-fledged flesh and blood alive and dead at the same time, both and neither.

I duck into the outdoor entrance area of another bar. The bouncer shoots me a look that says *why the fuck you movin' so fast, cripple?* I ignore it, tug on the Malagueña, and observe my prey. The smoke eases me into the excitement of the hunt. He is feisty, this one. I narrow my eyes. Just like the living, this man's head is full of plans—a map that keeps drawing and redrawing itself, a checklist, an incomplete letter. There's something else too: a solid chunk of his subconscious attention lingers on a scrap of thick paper in his pocket, probably some piece of whatever diabolical plot he's enmeshed in. He has all the makings of someone up to no good, and yet I can't help but feel drawn to this laughing wraith. For all his mysterious schemes and whatever chaos he's trying to let loose on my city, he's having a good time, and after all, it is New Year's Eve.

Anyway, I've never met anybody like me before, so instead of just ending him right then and there, I walk up and offer the dude one of my Malagueñas. Just like that. The very idea of doing this is so ridiculous that it shudders through me like the tickle of an invisible hand, and pretty soon we're both standing there smoking away and laughing like idiots.

We're definitely in the same curious predicament, but unlike me, Trevor's not at all concerned with blending in. In fact, he's determined to stand out. "Whaddup, douche bags and douche baguettes?" he hollers at the crowd. I'm mortified and fascinated at the same time. A few passing revelers chuckle, but most ignore him. A blond lady rolls her eyes as if she's being hit on for like the four hundredth time tonight. "Why so serious?" Trevor yells into the sky. I found the one other being like me in the universe and he is a total jackass.

Trevor turns to me, his face suddenly sharp, and says: "It's time. Let's go." His glare is penetrating and reveals nothing. A total blank.

We move quickly, with purpose. He either already knows I'm extraordinarily agile, or he didn't even notice the cane. I'm dodging a hodgepodge of hipsters and homeless rich kids, keeping my eyes on Trevor's paisley cap bobbing up ahead. He's still laughing and calling people douche bags, and I have no idea whether I'm giving chase or being led into a trap. Or both.

"What's your name, man?" I slur, playing up the rum on my breath.

He eyes me and then says, "Trevor."

"Carlos," I say, and I realize with a start that he's probably reading right through my every move just like I'm trying to read through each of his. The shock of this makes me feel momentarily naked; I quickly gather myself and cobble back the wall of deceit.

I have never dealt with someone like me before.

"Why so serious?" Trevor says again, this time at me. He's still laughing.

"Not at all," I say. Then I swig from my flask and he swigs from his.

He's meeting someone. The realization comes clear like

a whisper inside my head, and I can't help but wonder if the same voice is murmuring *he's onto you* in his.

We break from the crowd, cut a sharp right on Third Street, and end up beneath an ancient willow tree leaning out of Prospect Park. The wide avenue is deserted except for a few loping stragglers from the party on Seventh. It's a cool night. The light rain isn't falling so much as hovering in the air around us in a teasing little cumulus.

"This is the year, people!" Trevor yells at no one in particular. "The time she has come! People, get ready!" He kicks an empty beer bottle into a nearby bush, upsetting a family of night birds. I should just kill him now; that static filling the air hints at untold horrors. Also, I have no idea how hard he'll be to take down. I don't even know if I can fully die again. I'm bracing myself to make my move when a few figures emerge from the shadowy park.

"That you, broham?" one of them calls out as they get close. Broham? Is that Trevor's real name? I try to make myself as unnoticeable as possible, but we're a party of two, and we're both inbetweeners. "Who's the dude, man? Thought this was a secret and shit."

"It's cool, Brad," says Trevor or Broham, or whoever my new friend/prey is. "He's with me."

No one's ever said that about me. I'm flattered and repulsed at the same time.

Brad is tall and thick. His blond hair is close cropped in a military buzz cut. Of the crew behind him, three are basically Brad clones with different color hair, one is an Asian Brad, and another little guy is definitely Indian/Pakistani or maybe Puerto Rican. Or half-black. Whatever he is, he gets randomly searched every time he's within twenty feet of an airport. Finally, there's a hipster—the cats are *everywhere*—looking extraordinarily out of place and awkward.

"Okay, bros, let's do this thing," Brad says. Shady supernatural shenanigans in the Slope and it involves a bunch of frat boys? Curiouser and curiouser.

CHAPTER TWO

〜⚬〜

We make our way along the edge of the park. One of the Brads falls into place beside me. "Michael," he says, extending an awkward hand as I amble along.

"Carlos," I say. I nod, but don't touch his hand. People tend to notice how chilly and dry my skin is. And I tend to pick up way too much information about folks when we touch. Sometimes it's better not to know.

Michael's forced smile fades. "Are you going to, you know, help show us, uh, the other side?"

"Whose big idea was this, Michael?"

"Well, David, really." Michael nods toward the skinny hipster. "He gathered us together late one night at his house. He's Brad's homey. I don't really know him that well. Anyway, he said he had a big opportunity, a chance for us to see things no one else had seen. But only if we could be trusted, right?"

"Right."

"Said he'd met this dude—no name or nothing, just this dude—and that he was going to take us to, you know, the other side."

I make an ambivalent half grunt and Michael frowns, like maybe he revealed too much. He quickens his pace to catch up with the others. Darkened Victorians peek out from behind swaying trees across the street.

When we reach the wide-open roundabout at the entrance to Prospect Park, flickers of nervousness flare up from Trevor. Whatever it is he has planned, we're getting dangerously close to it. I wonder if these frat boys are unknowingly lining up to be the main course of some ritual sacrifice. Trevor seems just erratic and volatile enough to try to pull off such a stunt. But then, a few flatheads and a hipster getting glazed wouldn't warrant so much concern from the Council of the Dead—and they certainly wouldn't waste my time with it. Trevor checks his watch and then looks into the misty night. It's eight minutes to midnight. I try to tune in to the gathering storm of excitement that's about to explode all over the city, but it's just a faint glimmer to me.

We enter the park, move quickly through the fresh-smelling darkness. The Brads and David fall into a nervous silence. Trevor is a fortress—he gives up nothing to me, so I let my thoughts chase the ridiculous minidramas and power plays between our companions. We're moving toward the entrada, and of course, the timing is perfect: entradas are extra accessible to the non-dead at midnight, and this midnight in particular the air would be even more charged with culminating spiritual energy. The majority of Brooklyn's ancestral souls are out and about tonight, enjoying their own morbid festivities. You can almost taste the bursting molecules in the air.

As if to confirm my suspicions, we turn off the main road and duck down a narrow path through the trees. But what would an inbetweener be doing with a bunch of college kids at an entrance to the Underworld? *This is only the beginning*, the voice that knows things whispers.

*You who are neither here nor there keep the secrets of
both worlds.* And secrets are a valuable commodity. My
man has fashioned himself into a traitorous tour guide of
the afterlife. I close my eyes and imagine the Land of the
Dead overrun by oversized, pasty tourists, thousands of
bubbly Brads and Bradettes, snapping pictures and sipping frappuccino-whatevers.

Crap.

I really shoulda taken him when it was simple. Now
we've arrived; the entrada is a gaping void beneath droop-
ing tree branches. It's not black; it's just emptiness. The air
is crisp with new rain and a murmuring breeze. If Trevor
touches that void, it's game over—he'll disappear into a
relentless, hazy maze of wandering souls. David and the
frat boys would be shit outta luck, their magical romp
through the Underworld canceled, but Trevor would be
safe from my expert problem-solving hands.

I push my way up through the crowd of Brads. With
about ten feet to go before the entrada, Trevor makes a
break for it. My elbows shoot out in either direction, crack
into meaty midsections, splinter ribs. With a little added
encouragement from my shoulders, the home team collapses to either side of me, and I sprint forward in a ferocious, lopsided lunge, unsheathing the blade from my
cane as I go. It leaves my hand like a bullet. For a second,
all anyone hears is that terrible whiz of steel cutting
through air, and then the even more terrible renting of
flesh. That sound means I win, but for once it doesn't feel
so good to win. Trevor collapses heavily, an arm's length
from the entrada.

Without breaking stride, I pull my blade from Trevor's
flesh and launch back toward the college boys, cutting
the air and hollering gibberish at the top of my lungs.

They leave in a hurry, limping and carrying one another along like the good guys in war movies. I return to Trevor, who's bleeding out quickly.

If he can die, I can die.

It's a sobering thought. I have so many questions I don't even know where to begin, and his life force is fading fast. He makes like he's about to speak but just gurgles. All of his attention, all of his waning energy, is focused back on that little scrap of something in his pocket, but his eyes stare right into mine.

He knows I can read him. He's pointing it out to me.

I gingerly reach into his pocket and retrieve what turns out to be a photograph of a girl.

I can't remember the last time I said this. Maybe I've never said it. But this chick is fine as hell. Not just fine though—there's something about her gaze, the way she holds her chin, the shadow of her collarbone, that makes me want to find her and tell her everything, *everything*. It's just a silly snapshot. Her smile is genuine but grudging, like whoever took the picture insisted she do it. Her head's cocked just a little to the side, and something in her eyes just says, *I get it, Carlos. C'mere and talk to me and then let's make love.* Looks like she's in a park, maybe even this one; a few trees are scattered in the scenery behind her.

"Sister," Trevor gurgles, and I quickly wipe the hungry glow off my face. "She is . . . caught up in this too . . ." When he says *this*, his head jerks toward the shimmering emptiness beside us.

"This what, man? What is this?"

"Closing the gap," Trevor whispers. "The living and the dead . . . don't have to be so far apart. Like . . ." He takes a deep, death-rattle breath.

I manage to hide my impatience for about three seconds. "Like what?"

". . . like us. You and me and . . ." Another excruciating pause. "Sasha."

Sasha.

The hand holding the picture feels like it's on fire. I raise it up to his face. "Sasha," I say, failing to disguise the hope in my voice. "She's like us? She's in between?"

I almost break into a dance when Trevor nods his head. Suddenly, the park seems very luminous and beautiful at this hour. The night birds are singing, and somewhere, a few blocks away, Park Slope rocks to the New Year's revelry of two thousand wealthy white kids.

"Please," Trevor is saying when I return from my reverie. "Find Sasha. Keep her safe . . ." Done. No problem. How else can I help you today, sir? "From the Council."

"Uh . . ." I say, trying to slow my thoughts. "City Council?" Did you know it's possible to really irritate a dying person? Even an already mostly dead dying person. I don't recommend it though. Trevor looks like he might use the last of his life force to make a grab for my caneblade and cut some sense into me. "Right, right," I say quickly. "The Council of the Dead." He nods. "New York City chapter." My bosses. Surely he must know this. But whatever Trevor does or doesn't know quickly becomes a nonissue. He gurgles again, flinches, and then relaxes as death completes its finishing touches.

At least he won't have far to travel.

After gently placing Trevor's body into the entrada, I wander aimlessly around the park and work my way through the whole pack of Malagueñas and all of my rum. There's too many thoughts in my head right now. If I venture out into the city, it'll mean instant input overload. *The living and the dead don't have to be so far apart,* Trevor had said. Why are folks always so cryptic right before they croak?

Like us.

There's an us.

All I've ever known of the afterlife has been the rigid bureaucracy of the Council, and at first that had been relief from the cold disregard of the living. And then I just made friends with being the lone intermediary between the two, but now . . . When the Council's icy fingers slide the photo of Sasha's wry smile and sleepy eyes across the table, I will nod my head like I always do. Then I will find her. I will honor the dying wish of her brother, whom I murdered, and protect her from myself.

And then I will ask her out.

CHAPTER THREE

❧

Downtown Brooklyn in the middle of the day. No room for ghosts, too many damn living people clogging up all the inroads and walkabouts. There's rowdy teenagers, little old ladies, cops, businesspeople. At the feet of the skyscrapers, old men beg for spare change and young dudes in baggy pants pass out party flyers. Other cats are hocking their goods, everything from Bibles to porn to wooden giraffes to children's books.

I stand perfectly still and let the whole teeming masterpiece spin around me. I'm not sure why I'm here. The Council sent me. Sometimes they fuck up, and I'm pretty sure this is one of those times. *Go downtown.* Fine. They set me up in an apartment; they keep me doing what I do. I'll go downtown, then. And I'll pick a spot and be the frozen center of a messy human galaxy for an hour or two. Maybe some dead folks will show up. I don't care.

Well.

The truth is, since New Year's, there has been a growing murmur of discontent in the back of my mind. Used to be I could just say that I don't care, and it'd be truly true. Now I wonder. The feeling of Trevor's life slipping out of him, through my fingertips, it haunts me. It's not that I particularly cared for the guy; he was definitely about to unleash some nasty havoc. But he had a whole life I never knew about and then a half-life after that. We had something in common, and I've never been able to say that about another person. We could've, I don't know, compared notes. Been . . . friends maybe, if he'd have gone a different route. Yes, he was just some jackass to me, a mark, and still, somehow, I felt like it was my own life slipping away along with his.

"Carlos." Father Reginald's gravelly voice breaks me out of my reverie and I'm glad for it.

"How are you, Padre?"

"Can't complain. Another beautiful day." Father Reginald has a bushy beard covering most of his dark brown face. He looks grumpy as fuck, eyes and brow always gnarled up into some unaccounted-for grimace, but when he opens his mouth, it's always some "'nother beautiful day" type glory. They say he passed some tough years as a political prisoner in the Caribbean, but he never speaks of it. "People-watching?"

"Something like that."

Father Reginald nods knowingly. "Back to it, then, young fellow. I won't hold you up."

"Agent Delacruz!" some idiot ghost voice crackles through my head. The dead and their damn telepathy. *"Report immediately to Council Headquarters."*

Father Reginald regards my sudden flinching with some concern and then just smiles. "Take care of yourself, Carlos."

I nod and doff my cap at the priest. "Enjoy your afternoon, Padre."

I wonder briefly if I'm in some kind of trouble, and then I remember that I don't give a fuck. There's a bus up

Fourth Avenue that would get me there quicker, but I'm irritated these dipshits had me downtown for no apparent reason.

I walk.

I stop for coffee on the way, chat with some old guys sitting out on a stoop. Another cold front's moving in from up north. What else? Old Reggie's out of prison again, but probably just for a week or two, since he's already back to his old ways. Life tumbles onward, and eventually, when I feel I've wasted enough time to legitimately vex my superiors, so do I.

The Council of the Dead occupies an abandoned warehouse nestled between a sweatshop and a strip club on one of the forgotten backstreets of Sunset Park. There's a metal fire exit so desecrated by graffiti and trash you'd never notice it, but it's unlocked for us non–fully dead types. Well, for me. Inside, it's your traditional eerie empty warehouse: all rusted-out industrial skeletons and corroded pipes. Here there's an overturned wheelie chair, there a sea of shattered glass. A corner stairwell winds up to a catwalk that disappears in shadows. An awful mist hangs over everything; if you didn't know better, you'd assume it was the lingering fallout of some chemical disaster, but really it's just spirit shit.

They barely notice me when I walk in, all these trembling shrouds. They just go about their business. I head up the metal stairwell, my clanking boots echoing into the vast hall, work my way along a filthy, cobwebbed corridor to an empty room. It must've been the office of some middle-management troll at one time; there's a huge window overlooking the main floor and a corroded file cabinet.

"Agent Delacruz?"

"That's me."

Speaking of middle-management trolls: Bartholomew

Arsten. He appears in the doorway, a tall, translucent shroud. His shimmering, sallow face contorts with uncertainty. "You're here."

"You summoned me."

"I did . . ." He puzzles for a few seconds. "I did!"

"I know."

"We have a message for you."

"I'm thrilled."

"Riley wants you to meet him at the Burgundy."

"What?"

"Riley." He says it like I'm the incompetent one. "Wants."

"I heard what you said. I'm trying to figure out why you sent me a message dragging my ass across town to tell me a message to go back across town."

"Oh, it's a new protocol. We can't give locations for meeting points over telepathy."

"But you did that when you asked me to come here."

"Except for here."

"Bart, bruh, you know you full of shit, right?"

Bartholomew circles in the doorway and begins fading into the haze of shadows.

"You'd better go, Agent. The message was from two hours ago, so you're already late, technically."

CHAPTER FOUR

◦◦◦◦

Welp," Riley says, "that's basically what I told the dude." He scrunches up his face real meanlike. "'No, *you* back the fuck up.' Then I sliced him." He and Dro bust out into unchecked chuckles. Of course, it's easy for them to laugh with reckless abandon: they're just glimmering shadows to me and silent invisibilities to the drunks all around us. I have to be a little more conservative with my ruckus. As it is, the drunks see me speaking under my breath to empty seats on either side, occasionally smiling, swearing, or grunting. Anyway, we're in the Burgundy Bar—a joint that is full of enough fuckups and generally blitzed-out patrons that one weirdo talking to himself at the bar is not really a big deal.

Sasha's all-knowing smirk simmers across my mind for the eighty thousandth time today. I'm only barely here at all, just nodding, grinning, looking away.

"Carlos," Riley says. He's thick and translucent, bald headed and impeccably dressed, even in death. Riley and I share the common trait of having died so violently it shredded any memory of our lives, and in that we are brothers. When we're bored, we make up highly unlikely stories about what may have been. "First you show up later than your usual Puerto Rican late, and now you all sulky. *Kay tay pasa, hombre*?" I know he's emphasizing that silent *h* just to annoy me, so I ignore it. Besides, all his stories end with *Then I sliced him.*

I shrug. "Nada, man. Blame the Council. What we got for today?"

Riley leans over his Jameson and takes a sip. It looks stupid if you're not used to it—grown-ass man dipping into his drink like one of those damn plastic birds—but even the don't-give-a-fuck clientele at Burgundy would probably startle at a bunch of floating glasses. "Today's adventure, my friends, is a very special one."

Riley's was the first face I saw when I came back around. He was standing over me, grinning that grin of his, looking all proud of himself like he was the one who brought me back. He wasn't, but still, he found me, named me, brought me into the complicated fold of the Council, and has looked out for me ever since, in his own odd way.

Dro groans. "You say that every night, man." Dro doesn't drink. He's tall and remarkably well built for a dead guy. We suspect he's Filipino, but he keeps insisting on being Brazilian. Who can tell? Who cares even? Riley gets on him about it occasionally, but as far as I'm concerned, if Dro wants to be Brazilian, that's his business. Either way, the three of us are about as much color as the Council will put up with, apparently.

"I do say that a lot," Riley admits. "And I always lead you on a spectacular adventure."

"Sometimes," Dro says. "Sometimes no."

Riley turns to me suddenly. "Hey, how'd the business with the inbetweener go on New Year's?"

My pulse quickens to a slow-ass drag. I had just managed to push the whole thing out of my damn mind and then Riley went ahead and busted it back in. "Fine," I say. "Why?"

"I just heard it was quite a scenario: he was tryna bring a group of college kids into an entrada or something, no?"

I nod.

"Damn," Dro says. "And he was . . . like you?"

I make a grunty-affirmative noise. When they send me after a normal ol' fully dead ghost, it's usually to toss their translucent asses back into Hell or, when they're really acting out, slice 'em to the Deeper Death. That means they're gone-for-good gone, not just kinda-sorta gone. It takes some getting used to, yeah, but you figure, hey— they were already dead once. Not everyone comes back even as a spook, so they had got that second chance and jacked it up by playing the fool. The final good-bye ain't that big a deal in that sense. But this one . . . this strange, gray-like-me man with his wild schemes and last-gasp poetics . . . his death hasn't left me since New Year's.

Neither has his sister's perfect smile.

Anyway, should be pretty clear I don't want to talk about it, but my friends don't take well to subtle clues.

"Was that weird?" Riley says. "You clipped him?"

"No and yes." I really don't want to talk about this. I'm not even sure why, but the whole mention of it makes me feel like shriveling up inside this long trench coat and being gone.

Finally, Riley shrugs and rolls his eyes. "Anyway, as it so happens: today's adventure, brought to you by the illustrious Council of the Dead, involves the very house and home in which Carlos and I first became acquainted."

"What?"

"Mm-hmm."

"Mama Esther?"

"She's all right." Riley reads the concern etched 'cross my face. "But a house a few doors down from her has an ngk."

I blink at him. "A what?"

"An ngk." It's almost guttural, the way he says it. Like he's trying to speak through a mouth gag and then closing it off with a soft click.

"The fuck's an ngk? How do you even spell that?"

Riley nods at Dro, who's obviously been preparing for this very moment. "An ngk, Carlos, spelled *n-g-k*, is a small, rarely seen implike creature that is thought to be capable of vast unknown feats of sorcery and mischief. They tend to show up directly before tragedies of immense proportions, but it's still up for debate whether this is because of their ability to see the future or if they are the actual cause of the disaster."

"Damn."

"Yeah, they suck," confirms Riley. "It's very unusual that one'd show up at all, actually. They were thought to be extinct for a while, but have made sporadic appearances throughout the twentieth century. I dunno. I ain't never messed with one myself, but you hear weird stories."

"Like what?"

"Let's go have a look for ourselves, shall we?"

Sasha's smile stays on its broken-record rotation through my mind. A little challenge may be just what I need, even if it's in the form of some tiny unpronounceable freak from the other side.

It's been three years, but walking down this block always reminds me of that slow crawl back to life. It was days and days I lay there, listening to the cycles of street life sway by outside the window. The walls became my friends, if nothing else for the fact that they were perfectly consistent.

Everything was gone. I didn't even have a name, so being able to wake up to the same sun-bleached floral pattern became a small comfort in those first hazy days. I would slide from another sickly coma, see that faded ornateness and smile softly. Still there. Then the sounds of the street would find me: cars and buses grumbling past, the odd clicks and clanks of the city, yes, but most of all, the voices. The voices of life-living people, going about the business of being alive, all those tiny eccentricities, bothersome little errands, gossip on the corner, transactions, rebukes, come-ons. It was music to me, an endless chugalug of ambient humanity seeping through my pores as I healed.

When I finally got it together enough to make it outside, I felt like I already knew all the people on the block. I had learned to distinguish between the voices of my neighbors, imagined each one as a thread that'd reach up into the night sky and wrap around the other threads, their small dramas and schedules coalescing into a vast, chaotic quilt. And then I could put faces to the voices. I sat on that stoop for hours marveling at it all, surely appearing like some fallen-off crackhead, but content nonetheless. People nodded as they passed, and eventually nods turned to "all rights," which became small conversations, and then my voice mingled in the chorus. Another thread.

It's almost February, and a brisk wind shushes through the trees, flaps my coat around, whips a frenzy of dead leaves and plastic bags into the air. The kids are getting home from school, all puffy jackets, colorful hats, and cartoon-character book bags. Winter has driven most of the stoop sitters inside, and once the little ones tuck themselves away in their respective houses, things look kind of bleak, quite frankly.

Or maybe it's the ngk.

"Sweet, sweet memories?" Riley's beside me; his translucent body flaps gently in the wind like some luminous laundry.

"I suppose. Anything seem off to you? I mean it's cold, but still, there's usually more people out, no?"

"I think it's the ngk," Dro says. It annoys me that he sounds so sure of it, but I suppose he's already done his homework on this stuff.

"Shall we?" Riley makes an exaggerated after-you gesture toward the block that I used to haunt.

It's a pretty unremarkable building really, one more four-story row house on Franklin Avenue just south of Atlantic, a few doors down from Mama Esther's. There's a bodega, a liquor store, and a tiny church on the block. Atlantic is all auto shops and gas stations, traffic hurrying off to East New York and Queens. Farther south from where we stand, Franklin Avenue starts getting trendy: a brand-new sushi restaurant and some chic, nondescript boutiquey spots.

We walk in the front door, and immediately I know something's wrong. Can feel it through my body like a dirty sheet has been thrown over my heart. I just . . . don't even want to move. Also, there's a noise. It's barely noticeable, just an endless, irritating buzz and the sound of . . . I squint as if it will help me hear—little grunting gasps punctuated with . . . laughter.

I don't like this at all.

CHAPTER FIVE

❧

The old floorboards creak under my boots. Every step feels like a chore. All I want is for that buzzing to cease and that creepy little panting laughter to never trouble me again. I can't even tell you why it's so disturbing. Some otherworldly ngk magic, surely, that cuts right to the core of a man; my very soul is irritated.

It gets worse when I round the corner. The big old room, gray in the late-afternoon shadows, is completely empty except for a tiny figure in the corner. I don't want to get any closer, but I know I have to if I'm going to end this plague of hideousness. The buzzing, the grunting, the chuckle—it's all coming from this sinister little thing, this ngk. It only reaches up to just above my ankle. Pale, greenish skin stretches in wrinkly folds across its bony little body. That face—an alarming grin reaches from one side of its head to the other. The frail lips are parted slightly, and its wormy tongue reaches out between tiny, uneven teeth. And, perhaps most unnerving of all, the ngk is riding what appears to be an exercise bike of some kind. It just cycles and cycles and cycles and pants and chuckles and grunts, not even registering that a tall half-dead Puerto Rican has entered the room.

It irks me that the ngk doesn't look up. I want to scream at it, but what good would it do? Riley and Dro float up beside me, and I don't have to look at them to know they're experiencing the same shriveling discomfort that I am. They're both diminished, their iridescence reduced to a feeble, blinking glow.

"The fuck?" I say. The words feel like they're ricocheting through an echo chamber in my head.

"The ngk," Dro announces unnecessarily.

"Esther must be miserable with this thing nearby," I say. Each time I open my mouth is a new dimension of hangover. I decide to save nonurgent conversation till the ngk is safely disposed of. "How 'bout I just cut its head off and then we leave?"

"Can't," Riley says.

"Why not?"

"You can't kill an ngk," Dro informs me through gritted ghost teeth.

"Why . . . the fuck . . . not?"

Dro shakes his head. "No one knows."

That's not good enough. My hand's on my blade and it's taking all I got not to free it from its cane covering and make a quick end to this feverish little bastard. I just want it to stop. "What are we doing here, then?"

"I needed you guys to see it," Riley says, more somber than usual. "I don't have an answer for how to get rid of it, but Esther's saved all our asses in one way or another, and we owe it to her." The thought of Riley needing his ass saved startles me; I've never even seen him ruffled.

Then a horrible shrieking sound blasts through everything else. I cover my ears, but it's useless. The shit's tearing me up from the inside out.

"What the hell?"

"That's the ngk call," Dro says. We're all backing quickly toward the door. "It's lethal as fuck."

In seconds we're out on the street, panting.

"All right," Riley says. "I wanna check in with Mama Esther."

The feeling follows us down the block, even lingers as a dull whisper while we trudge up the creaking steps at Mama Esther's. Then we enter the library, the only room in the entire house with any furniture, and everything's all right again. There aren't even shelves, just stacks and stacks of books from floor to ceiling. You'd think it'd be a chaotic mess, all packed in there like that, but somehow there's a harmony to it; the books seem almost suspended in midair. They're everywhere, and the room is wide and tall enough that it doesn't feel cluttered. If I don't clean my little spot in more than a week, it starts to close in on me, so how Esther keeps this utterly full room spacious is beyond me. Some ghost shit, I suppose. Either way, it's oddly comforting.

Esther's floating in her usual spot right in the center of the room. That's where her head is anyway. Beneath that great girthy smile, her wide body stretches out into invisibility in a way that lets you know she's got the whole house tucked within those fat ghostly folds. "Boys." She nods at us; the warmth of that smile is a sunbath after the grimness of the ngk.

Mama Esther was the second face I saw after I woke up.

Once he figured out I was gonna make it, Riley chuckled and went on his way, promising to be back later. Next

thing I knew, this large smile was looming over me like
the moon. Esther. Scared the shit out of me at first. I
thought I was dead anyway, so one more grinning shroud
just added to the confusion. She didn't speak that night,
just let me know by her presence that I was safe, that I
wasn't alone, and it was true. Even when she was back up
in her library, which was most of the time, the very walls
radiated her smile, kept me from sinking back into the
abyss of despair that death had shrouded me in.

Today, though, I can tell the ngk is getting to her. The
smile's still shining with all that loving ferocity, but her
old face seems creased; her glow is dampened like Riley's
and Dro's. It makes me hate that little cycling minifreak
even more. We trade pleasantries and banter, and then
Riley gets all serious-looking.

"Do you know where it came from?"

Esther shakes her head. "The motherfucker just showed
up one day. I could feel it like an itch, then a dull, pulsing
ache, and finally, this festering disaster has taken over
that whole building." Esther looking like she's about to
break down is one of the worst things I can think of. I
look away.

"Ah, I'm all right, Carlos. Don't worry about me. You
know a stupid ngk isn't going to fuck up Mama Esther's day."

I look back at her and nod, trying to dig up a smile.
"We'll get rid of it for you, Mama. Don't worry."

"I know you will, Carlos. I know you will."

Even if it kills me again, I think, cringing as we return
downstairs.

"Where you going?" Riley wants to know.

To hunt down that hipster kid and his frat boy fan club
and see 'bout this fine lady. "I dunno," I say. "A nap?"

"Well, hang on, Carlos. We gotta chitchat on this a second. Damn." The ngk left us all a little irritable, and Riley has the unfortunate ability to know me very, very well. I can't even lie to the dude in any kind of satisfying way. Dro is looking at me with eyebrows raised, and he has a point. It's not really a time to be running off. I walk back to the two hovering shades, and we settle into an easy saunter down Franklin Avenue.

It gets dark so damn quickly these days. Night just drops out the sky with almost no warning, and suddenly the whole city is just those ugly streetlights and deli signs and flashes from passing cars. I see my breath congeal into a little cloud in front of my face and then dissipate. "So we can't kill it," I say. "What can we do?"

"This is the thing," Riley says. "There's not much precedence for getting rid of ngks. They pretty much just show up and either become an infestation, the opening act to utter disaster, or it's just one, and it does whatever sick little magic it has to do, then goes about its business. Maybe it's a spy and whatever it found out was unsatisfactory; maybe it's just a loner. Nobody knows."

"Therein lies the problem," Dro points out.

"Indeed," says Riley.

"So what? We wait?" I say, trying not to let my impatience out. "Hope it's just a one-off and disappears?"

Riley scowls. "That's not the Riley Washington way."

"So you have an answer?"

"I didn't say that either. All I'm saying is, just because nobody's ever figured out how to deal with an ngk in the past doesn't mean it can't be done. And I plan to do it. Or at least make life very unpleasant for the little guy."

"Well, that shouldn't be too hard for you," I say encouragingly.

"Har-har. I gonna need both y'all's help. Dro, research.

Everything. Follow all leads in every which way possible. Interview experts, pore over texts and scrolls and
whatever other bullshit you gotta do. You need to be my
brainiac numero uno on all things ngk. Dig?"

Dro nods. You can tell he's excited about this. The dude
loves nothing more than to hole up in some barely there
biblioteca and disappear for hours, nerding out on an
extreme obscurity. And now he's been given a mission.
He's in Dro heaven.

"And Carlos."

"Hm?"

"There's gonna be some living people angles of this, I
surmise, that I'll need your help with. See all these FOR
RENT signs?"

I hadn't noticed it, but he's right: an inordinate amount
of apartments seem to be available in the couple blocks
we've walked.

"Could be coincidence," Riley continues, "or could be
something to do with the ngk. Or ngks." We all frown at
that. "Tomorrow I want you to hit up the botánica, see if
Baba Eddie got any info for us, and then go real estate
hunting."

CHAPTER SIX

L ittle David the hipster lives in Clinton Hill with two beckys named Amanda. One of them has a . . . python. Or something. Hipness has taken this once-downtrodden neighborhood by storm; it became so suddenly swank that folks still walk around looking whiplashed from the sudden influx of wealthy whites.

David leaves to get a pack of American Spirits at the grocery spot. He walks with a quiet urgency, whips his head around before crossing even the smaller streets. He's got on those same 'nad-constricting jeans. He looks terrified and he keeps dabbing a wad of tissue against his eyes and nose. The terror that Trevor and I put him through a few weeks back still hangs there like an old jacket he can't take off. I wonder, briefly, if he'll ever recover.

When he leaves the bodega, I'm circling behind him, cutting a wide enough berth to stay clear of his periphery. Really though, it's all a little extra. He's so caught up in his dark thoughts, this doesn't even count as hunting. I'm just walking behind someone. His mind is so cluttered with boring roommate drama that it's spilling out in waves. One of the Amandas fell in love with him, but he loved the other one; then they all switched, some frenzy

of postadolescent musical sex chairs that I'd rather not
know the details of, but there they are, suspended in the
air around his head like a stupid halo.

I ignore all that, try to keep focused, slide my cane
into the front door of his apartment just before it slams
and wait for his footsteps to disappear up the stairwell.

I'm a patient man. I don't know a damn thing about my life
before I died, but I suspect this ability to sit still for hours is
a new quality. Maybe it's because I get a little flush of pride
every time I manage to do it, like a part of my old antsy self
is echoing forward to approve of how calm I've become.
Either way, it comes in handy at times like this. I don't
want the Amandas to be awake when I make my move. It's
too complicated, too much explaining, especially considering I'm not even on a real Council mission and can't resort
to their usual cleanup tactics. Tonight I'm a free agent, so I
find an out-of-the-way spot at the top of the stairwell, just
before the roof entrance, and settle in, taking occasional
sips of my bodega coffee.

Night turns into late night. The sounds from the street
slow from steady stream to occasional passerby. Inside the
apartment, where the heat is cranked up way too high, the
three roommates have finished cooking an organic, taste-
less meal and are settling in for the night. Some cranky
folk music gargles up the stairwell at me, accompanied by
the starchy smell of gluten-free pasta.

I wait.

The CD ends. Footsteps plod from one end of the apartment to the other, then back again. Some casual words
are exchanged. I slide into a meditative trance and let
another hour slip past. Then I put away the last sip of cold

coffee and head down the stairwell, on fire with that calm confidence wrought from sitting still for hours on end.

Inside the toasty warm apartment, the sounds of three slumbering souls intermingle with the clanking of old pipes and wall heaters. My feet barely touch the ground—that's how smooth I am right now. I lurch silently down the hall, slide David's bedroom door open without making one goddamn sound, and then stand there in the darkness. This is the tricky part: if David wakes up screaming, the Amandas will surely be here in a flash. If I play it too low-key, the boy'll just be unpredictable, so I opt for the sudden menace that will gradually lead into the tell-me-everything-and-we-can-forget-all-this-happened.

I put the edge of my cane a half inch away from David's neck. His chest rises and falls in quiet snores. He's dreaming of one of the Amandas, but she's not naked or anything. It's one of those emotional dreams. She keeps bringing him his slippers and yelling at him. I touch his neck gently with my cane, and when he opens his eyes and gasps, I say, real calm and slow: "Don't say a single motherfucking word or I'll cut your fucking head off."

Five minutes later, we're on the roof. He's shivering, still in his pajamas, and I'm doing the grim and menacing routine, even though he's already so flustered it's pretty much unnecessary.

"I'm sorry, mister. I'm really, really sorry," he blubbers. "We won't be f-fucking around with the Underworld anymore. I p-promise."

"I'm not interested in your promises, David." He shudders when I say his name. "Tell me how you linked with the inbetweener."

"Who, Trevor? He came to me. At the—at the—at the bike store I work at. And he said to bring some people.

So I took it to Brad. And his buddies. Trevor came to me though. I didn't find him."

"Did he tell you how to reach him ever? An address, a phone number? Anything?"

"No!" David's teeth are chattering. A gust of wind blows past, and I feel a little twinge of sympathy for the kid. "He just kept coming by the bike shop and talking to me, and so we went for beers one night at the Red Edge in the Slope. And we got wasted, and he started talking about the Underworld, and at first, you know, I just thought he was freakin'. I thought he was crazy, you know? The Underworld. But I was drunk, too, and I just kept nodding and yessing him and he kept going and somewhere in there I realized he was dead-ass serious. He wasn't fucking with me at all. And, I mean . . . the Underworld. Jesus. I just . . . so I, you know, I was interested. I wanted to know. I wanted to see it. I mean, death! That's, like, that's the final fucking frontier, man. Death."

"Go on."

He wipes his eyes with the tissue and snorts a booger back into his nose. "So then I got Brad and a few of the other guys in on it, and pretty much the same thing happened: we all went out for drinks, you know, got shit-faced, and they were all incredulous at first and it was like, no! But then, you know, the night progressed, and Trevor kept talking and talking and making sense in that freaky way . . ." David's story comes to a crashing halt. "Trevor's dead, isn't he? Dead, dead. You killed him."

Why this information is hitting home right now is anyone's guess, but I don't like the sudden manic look in David's eyes. "He was already dead," I say. "Mostly."

"I don't understand any of this!" David yells. "This is fucked up."

"You ever see anyone else with him?"

"Look, I'm sorry! Okay? I'm sorry I broke whatever cardinal rule of life and death or whatever the fuck it is that we trampled on. I didn't fucking mean to! I swear. And I will not tell anyone. Not a single person." This is clearly a lie. It doesn't take magic powers to figure out that at least one of the Amandas has been blubbered to already. And, depending on how slow the reality show pendulum swings, the other one'll probably be enlightened to it in another week or so. If I were on the job, I'd give a damn, but I'm not, so I don't. Let the kids have their little campfire fairy tales. I'm here for information.

"David, I'm not going to kill you, but if you don't stop rambling and tell me what I want to know, I will hurt you." This snaps him back into the present tense nicely. "Now: did you ever see Trevor with anyone else? A girl, perhaps?" I didn't want to take it there, but when I say it, he immediately squints his face up and nods.

"There was a girl. Well, I noticed her. She didn't say anything, but every time I met with Trevor at the Red Edge, she was there, always at the same table in the corner, always drinking a glass of red wine. And it struck me, you know, because I never saw her there before, and she was, you know . . ."

"Hot?"

"Yeah, definitely. And also . . ." He waves around looking for the word.

"Black?"

"African-American, yeah."

"Did you just correct me, David?"

"No! I mean—"

"Anything else about her?"

He has to think about how to answer this for a second.

"I always had the feeling she was like somehow with Trevor or something. Cuz I go to that spot pretty frequently . . . well, I did, and I'd never seen her before."

"Anyone else?"

"Uh-uh, not that I saw. I mean, I could be wrong. You know . . . I don't really know. I just . . . yeah."

I'm about to send him back downstairs when he gets this real concerned look over his face. "The other thing is . . ."

"Yes?"

"I've been, um . . . off, ever since."

"How so?"

"Well, I feel like shit, and . . . I'm bleeding."

"Bleeding?"

He shows me the wad of tissue. It's bright red.

"From where?"

"Everywhere. My eyes, nose. Ears sometimes."

"That's not good. You seen a doctor?"

David shakes his head. "Nah, I'm gonna wait it out, see what happens."

"Probably not the best move, considering you're bleeding from your eyeballs."

He shrugs. "Yeah, well, thanks for your concern. Can I go back downstairs now?"

I picked up a habit at Mama Esther's once I'd slipped far enough from death's icy claws to see clearly again. Every night I'd lope up the stairwell to that massive attic library of hers, retrieve some random, ancient hardcover, and then go back to my room and read it till I passed out. At first I was all the way lost, all the time. Gradually, pieces began fitting together, shards of history, warfare, science, magic all clicked into place. Reading any book from that library became like following a single endless story with infinite tentacles. Through all the tumultuousness of healing, reopening wounds, sliding back and forth between the edge of death and helplessness, I found peace in that unending story. It was a place I knew I could always return to. Solace.

So I carried on the tradition when I got my own place. I have a modest couple of shelves—nothing that could shake a stick at Mama Esther's collection, but it does the job. Tonight I'm on Herodotus's *Histories*, a copy that Esther perma-lent me when I left, but it's not holding my attention at all. Instead, disparate scraps of the day catapult back and forth across my mind. The ngk, the fucking ngk. I can still taste that filthy dread in my mouth. The fact that it's in Brooklyn, so close to Mama Esther's library—the only truly sacred place I know—makes things all the worse.

And then there's Sasha. I retrieve her crumpled photo, feeling somewhat stalkerish, and check to see if that certain oomph is still there.

Yes.

With a vengeance. Something lurches in my gut. It's like fear but . . . yummier. How can a single moment, captured on a tattered scrap of paper, cause such havoc on my insides? I'm stoic, steady-handed. I've died, dammit.

This is unacceptable.

I'm wide-awake and irritated. I toss the picture off to the side, grumble for ten seconds, and then collapse into a dreamless, unpleasant sleep.

CHAPTER SEVEN

∽᎒᎒∾

The first time I met Kia I realized I could never hide anything from her. She was only fourteen, and by the way she worked the counter at Baba Eddie's botánica, you'da thought she owned and operated the joint single-handedly. She bounced back and forth between customers, arguing about how much yerba buena to use in a spiritual cleansing and helping an old man who wanted to get his wife back from her new lesbian lover. When she saw me, there was a momentary freeze in her confident frenzy. Her big green eyes bored into mine, and I knew she could tell there was something not quite right. She raised one eyebrow and pursed her lips. I was startled. Most people have to touch my skin to realize I'm a little off and then they're all freaked-out. So I was even more startled when she said, "I'll be right with you," and kept it moving.

Now she's sixteen, and I'm pretty sure she handles most of the online business and advertising for Baba Eddie. And possibly runs the entire business as well. She's perched on a stool, clackety-clacking away on the desktop computer, when I walk in. "Whaddup, Carlos?" she says without looking up.

"Kia." I nod. "Taking over the world again?"

"Mm-hmm. One online customer at a time."

"I hope Baba Eddie's paying you well for all the good work you do for him."

Kia scoffs. "You're damn right he does. Well . . . let's put it this way. I get paid."

I raise my eyebrows.

"I do payroll. So . . . I get paid. And so does Baba Eddie. So everybody's happy."

"I see."

"Anyway, Baba got Russell and his big corporate paycheck taking care of him, so it all works out."

"You getting your schoolwork done in the midst of all this?"

Kia looks up at me for the first time and narrows her eyes. "How 'bout Carlos worries about Carlos and Kia worries about Kia, m'kay?" She turns back to the screen.

I just frown and say, "'Kay." Kia looks up again, probably because I didn't zing back with some slickness, and now regards me more carefully.

"Whatsamatta—lady trouble?"

Ugh. Omniscient teenagers are the worst. "No."

"What's her name?"

Now I wish Kia would go back to her computer and leave me alone. Sometimes I think she has the same third-eye vision that I do. I try not to imagine Sasha's smiling face dancing around my head.

It doesn't work.

"She a weirdo like you?"

She is! I want to yell it from the roof of this crummy little building, shatter the storefront windows with my raging joy to have found another weirdo like me. Instead I say: "How 'bout Carlos worries about Carlos and Kia shuts up and does her homework?"

Kia rolls her eyes and submerges back into whatever social networking site she's ruling. "Okay, Carlos." *Clackety-clackety-clack*. "Have a wack afternoon with your heart full of lead, dipshit." *Clackety-clack*.

"Thank you, Kia. Baba Eddie 'round?"

"The back." *Clackety*. I make my way through the narrow aisles full of potions, soaps, and candles. "With a client."

Fine. I drop into an old easy chair they have set up next to the bookshelf and liberate a Malagueña from its wrapper. Before I can light it, a commotion erupts from the back room and then a perfectly round woman in her late sixties bursts out of the curtain. "¡Coño!" I jump to my feet, hand clutching my cane-blade, and then remember where I am. A screaming Latin lady is really no kind of anomaly in Baba Eddie's place. "Gracias, Baba! ¡Gracias! ¡Ay, coño . . . ! ¡María de los aguas infinitas! Se me va acabar mañana . . . ¡Mañana, carajo!"

Eddie's voice drifts out from behind her, a gentle sussuring of affirmations.

The woman explodes through the store in a flurry of jangling jewelry and thick perfume. She blows kisses at Kia, waves dramatically at the three of us, and exits. The bells and wind chimes on the door jingle away as she rumbles off, still chatting ecstatically to no one in particular.

"Well, damn, Baba."

"Don't ever let them tell you Baba Eddie don't know how to please a lady." He's a little guy with a big mustache. Also, he dresses more like a dorky suburban dad than a Brooklyn santero. Today he's got on an old beige baseball cap and a plaid shirt that hangs from his ponchy potbelly over slightly stained khaki pants. "C'mon, Carlos, let's go outside for a smoke."

I don't get cigarettes. It's like all the worst parts of cigars—
stank breath, yellow teeth, slow and horrible death—but
none of that warm invigoration. Baba Eddie, on the other
hand, adores his menthols with religious fervor. Smoking's
the last poison left for him since the retrovirals kamikazed
his liver, and he relishes that shit like it's the first drop of
Mother Mary's tit milk, each and every time. I gotta say,
repellent as the habit is to me, I respect a man who can
enjoy a simple, cancer-filled pleasure. So I wait while Baba
Eddie ceremoniously produces a single smoke from the
gold cigarette case that Russell gave him for their twentieth
anniversary. He smells it, closing his eyes like a good little
connoisseur, and then places it between his lips. I can see
the excitement building in him. He actually enjoys teasing
his body, triggering those little addiction demons that roam
through his bloodstream. He brings the lighter up to his
face, flicks it to life, and then holds it inches away from the
tip of the menthol. I roll my eyes. This routine used to
annoy the shit out of me until Riley and I got smashed and
made fun of it for about fourteen hours straight. Since then,
Baba Eddie's cigarette appreciation ritual has only been
comedy to me.

Finally, it's lit, and the first luxurious drag has been
released into the chilly afternoon air and the little priest
looks up at me and smiles. "What's troubling you, Carlos?"

"It's not me. I mean, it's not what's troubling me that I'm
here for. That's not . . . It's another. What I mean is . . ." I
pause, but my thoughts still won't collect into rational sentences. Baba Eddie puts on his patient face and enjoys his
cigarette. "I mean nothing's troubling me."

"Mentira."

"True. But that's not why I'm here."

"Fair enough."

"I'm here because Riley, Dro, and I are dealing with an ngk on Mama Esther's block."

Baba Eddie's eyes get big. "You saw it? A true ngk?" His pronunciation is exquisite, like he's been saying "ngk" all his life. Must be part of the training to achieve Baba-status, which, from what I gather, must be pretty rigorous.

I nod.

"Shit."

"You know how to deal with 'em, Baba?"

The santero shakes his head, still wide-eyed. "Carlos, this could be disastrous. Is Mama Esther okay?"

"She's managing. It's a few doors down from her."

"But if it spreads . . ."

"I know."

Neither of us wants to say the next part, so we just let it hang there unspoken. I borrow Eddie's lighter and spark up my Malagueña. "Any idea what we can do?"

"I . . . I'll have to check on some things." I've really never seen him this flustered and I hope I never do again. Even when we don't need spiritual advice, Baba Eddie's is where we come just to hang. It's nice to be around folks who get it, and Baba will keep his head on through any kind of fuckery and come out smiling.

"Thanks, Baba," I say. He nods, and then we stand out in the cold, coveting each thick tug of smoke and not saying anything for a long time.

CHAPTER EIGHT

〰

I'm almost six feet tall and Moishe the real estate guy
still towers over me. When he smiles, it's not the please-
be-my-friend grin of a man trying to sell me something. Instead his mouth creases outward and opens
slightly into a true, from-the-gut smile. When he asks me
how I am, I believe he really wants to know. Moishe's
dressed in the standard all-black Hasidic trench coat and
hat. He's only twenty-five and his beard is still a little on
the wispy side. He laughs energetically when he shows
me pictures of his triplets—I have no idea how it even
got to that so quickly, but there it is—and then we get
down to business.

"There are many apartments for rent in this area, Mr.
Delacruz. We have a wonderful selection, and very af-
fordable."

"I noticed. It's more than usual, no?"

Moishe shrugs and drops the edges of his mouth into a
pensive frown. "Eh, in some ways." He's Brooklyn born
and raised, he proudly informed me earlier, and his
speech is thick with Yiddish intonations. "But you know,
real estate is a complicated type of business, hm? The
market is a changing animal, very different from one day

to the next, you know? It's never"—he searches for a longer word and fails—"the same . . . from day to day."

"Okay."

"But let's start with this beautiful two-bedroom on the second floor." He gestures to a brownstone three doors down from Mama Esther's. "Very classy. All brand-new renovations. Eat-in kitchen. Well, come. I'll show you." He laughs again, I'm not sure at what, and leads me up the stoop steps and into the building.

It's a little ragtag, but we're still in a middle zone of gentrification, not quite here nor there, so I'm not surprised. We head up a dingy flight of stairs, all off-color carpets and slow-mo dust tornados, and then walk into a pristine, sun-drenched modern apartment.

"Well, damn," I say almost involuntarily. The place is nice. It puts my cranky little loft of shadows to shame. Moishe nods and ushers me around, making little clucks and shrugs as he points out various appliances, views, closets. "Why'd the last residents move out?"

"Eh, people, they move." He hunches those big shoulders and waves his hand back and forth. "These people, they moved."

"I see." Useless.

Then that horrible feeling rips through my body like an earthquake and I have to steady myself on Moishe so I don't collapse. The towering Hasid looks at me like I've lost my damn mind. His mouth moves within that wispy beard. He's speaking, I'm sure, but all I hear is that screeching: a thousand trains trying to brake, all at the same time, all too late.

Then it's gone.

A moment of awkward silence passes as I catch my breath. "Mr. Delacruz?" I stand, spin, plant my cane hard on the ground, and hold my balance, but only barely. "Mr. Delacruz? Are you okay?"

"No. Yes. Yes. Yes, I'm fine."

"You sure? You don't look . . . too good, you know?"

I never look too good, really, but I guess now I look worse. Something is gnawing at my subconscious, more and more fiercely as my balance returns. The ngk. It's that feeling, but . . . more so.

There's one in this building too.

"The basement."

Moishe's still trying to process my near-syncope, so it takes him a second to catch up. "What?"

"Can I see . . . the basement?"

"Um . . . yes. But are you sure you're okay?"

"I'm fine." Bullshit, and he knows it, but I seem to be able to walk. The wretchedness has dimmed. I follow him down the stairwell to the first floor. The screech comes back while Moishe's fumbling with his massive key chain. It's worse this time, but I'm ready for it. Prickly waves of nausea radiate up and down my body. I plant my cane on the ground and lean hard on it, determined to wait out the anguish. Moishe toils away, oblivious, and then says something, might as well be in Yiddish for all I know, and pops open the basement door.

I'm relieved he doesn't glance back, because I'm sure I look like even more shit than I did a few minutes ago. Still, I've steadied myself and manage to make it down the stairs without collapsing.

I want to find the thing, but my vision's blurred and I'm having trouble walking a straight line. The basement is what you would expect: a long dank room, all cluttered with dust-covered furniture. Two of the four overheads are busted and the two left are uncovered; sharp shadows clash with sudden fits of brightness. The ngk could be anywhere—all I can do is stumble toward wherever the horrible is more horrible. Hopefully, Moishe won't decide I'm nuts and haul me out of there first. Also, hopefully, I won't drop dead in the thick of it.

I make my way through a narrow aisle, squeeze my body between an old file cabinet and some wooden chairs, and then the screeching-nausea-death feeling stops altogether again. Which I suppose is good—my body is certainly grateful—but I don't know how I'll find the thing without my rapidly decomposing soul to use as a compass.

"Mr. Delacruz." It sounds like he's been saying it for a long time. He's not pleased. I can almost hear his salesman's need to be nice clash against his irritation that this particular customer is stumbling around the basement in a deathlike frenzy. "You may need medical attention. And, either way, we should really leave this basement, okay? Come."

I would like to. I really would. I've just about had it with this wild-ngk chase, and I don't like pushing Mr. Moishe's kindness further than necessary. But I also have to see this thing. I need to confirm, with my own eyes, that there is in fact a second ngk here. I turn toward Moishe, and I'm about to spit out some bullshit explanation, when something, something that I was absolutely sure was just a piece of furniture, detaches itself from the shadows in front of me. I don't have time to unsheathe my blade. I barely catch my breath before the thing bursts past me, rushing toward where Moishe stands on the stairwell with his mouth open.

He can see it. The thought flashes through my mind as

I watch the Hasid hurl his massive frame over the banister and clutter into the shadows. The thing moves too fast to make it out. It's just a pale flash of something vaguely humanoid with long black hair, definitely upright but somehow hunched over, and then it's up the stairs and gone. Moishe yells a barrage of what I have to assume are the vilest of Yiddish curse words. It's enough to let me know he's alive and relatively unhurt, so I make for the stairs. Maybe I can at least get a glimpse of the thing. I might've made it, too, if the damn ngk's screeching didn't start searing through me just as I was lunging toward the doorway. I'm caught off guard this time and collapse on the steps in a heap.

Things get dim. Those stupid Cheerio-shaped bubbles float across my view of the open door in front of me. For a second, I think I'm gonna make a comeback. The ngk's screech still shreds from inside, but I'm strong. I'm trained for this. I'm—

CHAPTER NINE

⟨◦⟩⟨◦⟩

Someone is wailing. It's an intense, reverberating howl, then a yelp. It surges out from just above me.

I'm lying on my back. There's a slightly chubby Latino guy looking down at me. He's holding a metal scythelike tool a little closer to my face than I'm really comfortable with. "Oh!" he says when I open my eyes. I wrap one hand around the arm holding the scythe and the guy gets the point and puts it down. He slides two fingers against my neck and frowns. Then we hit a bump and the guy cascades forward, grabbing something for support at the last minute before he utterly crushes whatever's left of me. He settles back in and takes my pulse again. "You're . . ."

"What's the deal, Victor?" someone yells from behind him. The driver. We hit another bump. Victor's face disappears for a second, and I just see the plain gray ambulance ceiling. There's a clear bag of fluid dangling from it that's probably attached to me somehow. I try to shake the bleariness out of my head, but it turns out I'm strapped down hard to something.

This can go nowhere good.

"I have to go." I rip the taped contraption from my

forehead and pull myself upright, straining against all the crap that's holding me down.

"No!" Victor yells, maneuvering around the stretcher and trying to push me back down. "You shouldn't even be alive, man!"

"Well, I am." I undo another strap.

"You have no pulse! How is that even possible?"

This is exactly why I won't be going to no hospital. I cannot abide by all these ridiculous questions. Anyway, I have no answers. It just is what it is. "I have to go," I say again, putting a little growl into it this time. Victor sits down on the bench and just looks at me. The driver lets out a few yelps of the siren and keeps barreling down the street.

"What . . . the fuck . . ." Victor says. It's not a question, just a general observation.

I shake my head, sit up all the way. "I don't know, Victor. But I won't be accompanying you to the hospital, so you can tell your friend to pull this deathmobile over and I'll be on my merry way, thank you very much."

Victor's having a lot of thoughts right now. They're tangled and confused, a briar patch of curse words and years of street experience coming loose in his mind. "Can I just . . . ?" He reaches out to take my pulse one more time, and I let him, if nothing else because I'm still woozy and he seems like a decent guy.

"It's there," I say. "Just very slow."

He nods, staring at me.

"But look, I'm okay. Okay? You want me to sign something?"

He does, but he can't find the words to express that, so instead he shakes head slowly and then, without taking his eyes off me, says: "Rudy, pull over."

"Huh?" The siren stops wailing.

"Pull. The fuck. Over. Rudy."

Rudy swerves the ambulance to the side of the road and slows to a halt, mumbling a few curses along the way. Victor and I hop out, and Victor immediately puts a cigarette in his mouth and lights it. He could learn a thing or two from Baba Eddie about appreciating his vices. I guess I need to get my bearings, because instead of running off, I just stand there next to him. Then dizziness sweeps over me, so I sit my ass down on the bumper of the ambulance and light a Malagueña.

"Five-seven William," Victor says into his radio. After a scratchy reply, he spits out some numbers that I assume mean their patient went AWOL and then sits on the bumper next to me. It's surprisingly peaceful here, after the madness of the basement and then the rush of the ambulance.

"The Jewish guy called?" I say after a few minutes of quiet smoking.

"Mm-hmm. Said you collapsed. That's why we hadta tape you to that backboard, in case you broke your neck or something."

"Right."

"But basically"—he takes a drag and lets it out—"you were dead. You had no pulse. You were unresponsive. I was about to put a tube in you that would not have been pleasant to wake up with."

"That was what that blade was for that you were poking at my face?"

Victor grunts an affirmative.

"I see." It's turned into an unseasonably warm afternoon, and I suddenly remember I'd been planning to go to the Red Edge to see about Sasha tonight. Also, I have to let Riley know we're dealing with more than just one ngk, that something foul is lurking.

I stand up.

"Wait," Victor says. "What are you?"

I shake my head.

"What happened?"

"It's hard to explain. But I don't do hospitals. Too many stupid questions."

Victor frowns.

"I mean, they're not stupid. But you know. I don't have answers."

He nods like he understands, which is endearing even though he obviously has no clue what's going on. He stands up and shuffles through his pockets for a moment before handing me a business card. "Take this. My girlfriend, Jenny, does natural healing. You know, herbal crap and all that. Doesn't stand up too strong when you're in cardiac arrest, but she's pretty good at what she does."

"Thanks," I say. I don't really know what the hell he's talking about, but he seems genuinely concerned. I pocket the card, nod at Victor, and trudge off to find Riley.

CHAPTER TEN

༄~ঙ্কুৎৎ

There's what?" Dro doesn't look too good. He's the guy who's always got that unshakable thing about him—pretty much glides on through whatever shit may come. He must still be shook from the ngk, because the fact that he can raise his voice above a calming whisper is a novelty to us. "Get me another drink."

I signal Quiñones, the surly one-eyed bartender at Burgundy, and he places three more shots of rum in front of me. We exchange a nod that might mean all is understood and might mean he thinks I'm out of my fucking mind. Doesn't matter either way. I put one down my throat and place the other two in front of the empty seats on either side of me for Riley and Dro to sip.

"The way I see it," I say as the alcohol runs burning circles through my bloodstream, "it's still not an infestation. We can't panic yet. I mean, sounds like these guys do show up here and there and it still doesn't wind up as a full hive of them."

"You don't understand," Dro says. He's straining the way some drunks do when they're convinced no one will ever grasp the simplest possible concepts. "The shit I've been reading . . . The ngks don't just precipitate disaster:

they *are* disaster. There was this plague, one of those nasty European ones back in the fifteen-whatevers, right?"

"Mad meticulous with your details, huh, Dro?"

Dro plows past Riley's comment without noticing. "The numbers of *little people* sightings right before and in the early days of the outbreak were startling. Even this local pastor commented on it in one of his journals. And then I started looking . . ." He waves his hands and widens his eyes to dramatize "looking." "It wasn't the only time. There was another one, Amsterdam, I think, and it was the same thing: people see these strange little men and then horrible Black Death shit happens. Bubonic and whatnot."

"Brooklyn's full of strange little men," I point out. "But ain't nobody gone bubonic yet."

Dro narrows his eyes at me. "You know what I—"

"Look." I cut him off before he can go into another rant. "I'm just saying, it's not like every time an ngk shows up, shit goes haywire." I say it, but his disorganized little presentation has given me something to think about. "Anyway, what I'm more worried about is whatever that thing was that was down there with us."

"You didn't get a good look at it?" Riley asks. He's been pretty quiet this whole time, mostly scowling and grunting as I relayed the past few hours to them.

"It was fast and caught me off guard. Plus the basement was pretty dim."

"Dead or alive?" Dro asks.

I've been tussling with this one since it happened and haven't come up with a good answer. And I'm the one who's supposed to know these things. "I'm not totally sure." Riley grunts irritably, and I ignore him. "The Realtor saw it, so either he's got the Vision, or the thing's alive."

"Or the third possibility," Riley says.

I get all cold and uncomfortable. I hadn't wanted to

think about that possibility, so I hadn't. But I knew it'd come up one way or the other.

"That it's a Carlos?" Dro says unhelpfully. Riley nods.

"I don't think . . . I mean . . ." Words are not my friend right at this moment. I want to express that that's probably not the case, even though it very well might be the case. Instead I just shut the fuck up and order another shot of rum.

"It's a possibility we need to explore," Riley says. "Especially considering you just bagged a halfie on New Year's." I can't stand that he's being so professional and quiet right now; it's really bugging me. "Might be related." He's not even bothering with his shot.

"Fuck," Dro says. He's bothering plenty with his shot, and I'm a little worried some of the less completely demolished drunks will start to notice.

"Either way," I point out, "there's no need to get all shook."

"Yeah," Dro says as if I were talking about someone else. "True."

CHAPTER ELEVEN

❧

Thing is, I dress pretty slick. Comes naturally to me, actually. I like the way the crease in my pants feels, the certain swagger that goes with knowing everything fits just right, the perfect puzzle. All that. No matter what kinda supernatural fuckshit is going on, I take my time getting dressed in the morning. Not to the point of obsessing over it all, mind you, certainly not in any kind of teenybopper way at all. But I relish sliding each button into place, feeling the whole package that is me come together.

Tonight I take special pleasure in it. I'm a little extra slick from the three rum shots taken straight to the head. A sultry rumba blazes from my little stereo. My shoes are shiny; my hat fits just right. Each element complements the other, and when I hit the street, the weirdly warm end-of-winter wind seems to carry my dapper ass along down the block. When you come dressed correct, the whole world moves with you on whatever divine mission you set out on, even if that mission is making time with some fine forbidden piece of ass that you should really know better than to mess with.

The Red Edge is a classy spot. True to its name, the

inside is all varying shades of dark crimson; it's mostly candlelit and full of long, flowing curtains and surly bar maidens. Fortunately, David's not here—probably will never come back again, now that I think about it. I strut in feeling good, great actually, and there's Sasha, perched like a sad and gorgeous little bird at a table in the corner. I order a rum and Coke and a red wine and sit at her table, ignoring the little rumbling of uncertainty in my stomach.

She looks down at the wine and then up at me. She's more beautiful than she was in the picture. The smile has been replaced with a pout, and a miasma of sorrow is on her like a fancy perfume. It stays there for about two seconds after we make eye contact, and then there's nothing, and I remember: she's like me. She immediately knows what I am. And she knows I can see her, see all the spinning satellites of her fears and pleasures dance through the air. And what's more, she can see me and mine.

For half a beat, I trace the tangled web that stretched between us before we even met—the one that begins and ends with me murdering her brother. Then I come to my senses and suck it all back inside me and it's gone.

I search her eyes, hopefully not with the frenzy I feel, to see what she has seen, but she gives me nothing. Or perhaps that glow that I want to drink into me and succumb to has blurred my senses. Either way, the next thing that happens is we both smile. It's a true smile, an admission of the explosive awkwardness that just passed between us, and it makes me happy in a way I'm not even sure what to do with. The bar spins around us: bad nights and mediocre nights and epic life-changing nights—they all play out like tiny television shows, sending their scattered bursts of light into the atmosphere.

I could give a fuck.

This woman, this *woman,* is looking back at me and truly seeing me. Even if it is in a way that requires both of us to put up all of our guards and retreat into our innermost sanctums—what a feeling: *to be seen.* Acknowledged. Finally, the pulsing between us settles into a more manageable kind of awkward, and she takes a sip of her wine and says, "Mmmm, why, thank you, sir."

I raise an eyebrow in a bid to look dashing and nod. "It is my pleasure."

I want to tell her everything.

I want to swash it all onto the table and let it do what it does, all the unruly, troubling information, because I can't bear the thought of holding on to it for another second. But I also can't bear the thought of this moment right here mutating into some horror show. I can't. There will be trouble ahead; this is certain. But I want this right now to be what it is: two people find each other in a crowded room, in a crowded world, and connect.

I let the moment pass, allow the confession to die on my tongue, and then I smile at her.

Sasha rests her chin on one hand and says, very slowly, like she's weighing each word as it comes: "Maybe . . . we should agree . . . not to . . . look too deep . . . for now?"

Yes. I chose correctly. This is not the time. Plus, she clearly has her own secrets to keep, which gives me some sense of balance at least. I nod. "Agreed."

Another silence follows. It's one I could just sit and simmer in for days. A warm glow may or may not be emanating from our table, and I wonder if other people will start to notice. She's wearing a loose red top, one of those amoebaesque female fashion thingies that somehow hangs just right, revealing just enough but never enough. Seems to flow with her movements—a mostly solid, teasing little cloud more than an article of clothing. Her skin is a few shades darker than her brother's with only the slightest hint of gray. Her mouth starts small, when she'd had it squeezed into the mourning pout, but when she smiles, the damn thing expands all the way across her face and looms large like the moon. Her black hair is pulled back beneath a headband and then explodes out and down to her bare shoulders in twirly strands. A blue necklace wraps around her slender neck and dangles between her breasts. Her breasts. The top slopes peek out from behind her swirling shirt, and I imagine them bouncing in front of my face while she rides me.

"Are you looking at my breasts, sir?"

I look up at her. She's smiling. "I was, yeah. Were you looking at mine?"

"No!"

"Because you can if you want to." She laughs and swats me off. It's stupid, really, and I'm pretty terrible at flirting, but somehow, it doesn't matter. We're flowing along like two leaves in a river. It's a corny river, but I don't care. I'm just happy to be here and that she's my other leaf. The twisted universe has conspired to give me this moment and this night and those eyes looking back at mine, all amid the hurricane of infestations and betrayals and possibly imminent doom, and I will take what's mine. I'll be Baba Eddie and this'll be my death stick, and I'll milk it for every sweet, lethal drag.

Sasha's looking at me more seriously now. "How did you find me?" I open my mouth, but she throws up a single finger and stops me. "No. Don't answer that. I don't want to know."

I make a fair-enough face and wait because she looks like she has more to say.

Sasha sips at the wine again, looking like she's enjoying

making me wait. "Let's instead talk about something utterly mundane and ridiculous, shall we?"

"That's the best idea I've heard all night."

"Let's pretend, for a moment, that we are just two normal people who met in a bar."

"Do we like each other or are we just passing time?"

"That remains to be seen, I suppose."

"I see. Well, fancy meeting you here."

"Ugh!" she moans with an exaggerated eye roll. "You're terrible at this!"

"All right, all right. Give me a chance to get the hang of it, jeez! What do you do . . . for a living?"

She puts her serious face back on. "I am a contract . . . negotiator."

"What's that?"

"I don't know! I just made something up. Stop! Let me try again." I nod at her to go ahead. "I am a construction worker."

"Me too!" I say.

"No!"

"Yes! I construct."

"You're not even taking this seriously at all."

"What's your name?"

When she says it, everything gets quiet again. The bar, Park Slope with its boutiquey avenues, the trembling night and all that fresh winter air—the whole world around us takes a breath. Also, I'm pleased she didn't lie. "And yours?"

"Carlos Delacruz." I wonder if the universe performed similar acrobatics for her. Probably not, but women seem to roll in a whole different slipstream of flirtation from men, so I don't give it too much thought.

Her eyes narrow like she's telling me a secret. "From the cross."

"Ah, you speak Spanish?"

She smiles and makes a guilty little *mezza-mezza* wave with one hand. "Un poquito. ¿Y tú?" The accent's not a native speaker's, but it's not bad either.

"Sí. Do you know where you're from?"

She looks downcast, shaking those curlicues back and forth. "Not a clue. You?"

"The folks who found me . . ." I slow down, realizing I have to tread carefully here not to give away too much. ". . . decided I was Puerto Rican. And it feels right. But, honestly, no."

Now we both sit for a few seconds in the sadness of our own torn histories. I imagine each of our sorrows hanging over our heads, and then I see them merge into one and disperse away like a puff of smoke. I'm just thinking that it actually worked, and a swell of pleasure seems to descend, when Sasha looks up with almost tears in her eyes. "I have to go," she says, and then she's gone and the converged cloud of despair settles over me like a bad dream.

Once again, Herodotus is not cutting it. All those damn weird stories just can't force out the single burning question: why (the fuck) would (fucking) Trevor send his own murderer to protect his (gorgeous fucking) sister? I find that I'm actually angry at the guy for the utter illogic of his decision. And he, he's safely off in the deeper-than-death netherworld, probably some blissed-out cloud of ether mingling with the cosmos, and I am here, burdened with this irrational, inexplicable quandary.

That asshole.

I switch to poetry. Perhaps one of the Nuyorican masters will do the trick. My eyes glance over the dancing stanzas of delicate and ruthless indictments, tragedies, revolutions, love affairs . . . but my mind returns to Sasha. And then, less pleasingly, to her damn brother. I've found my job is so much easier, moves so smoothly, when I don't get into questions of right and wrong. The Council wants someone to be ended, I end them. It's usually pretty clear why—basically if an afterlifer is minding theirs and staying out of trouble, they won't be dealt with. If they start acting the fool, begging for attention, well, they know the Council will come calling in the form of some long-legged, blade-carrying motherfucker like myself. And really, bringing a bunch of college kids into the Underworld? Who does that? It's an ignorant-ass move that's bound to attract attention one way or the other.

There's a little voice, somewhere in the back of my mind. It's tiny, really. But it's gnawingly aware of how ridiculous all of this is. Who's the Council to decide what's the proper amount of shenanigans a ghost can participate in? Why should they get to regulate that delicate line between the living and the dead?

This is why my job is easier if I don't think too hard. These questions lead nowhere productive, obviously, because now I'm thinking about the inevitable moment when some minister up in the Council realizes Sasha's an errant soul, an unacceptable ambiguity that must be brought in and destroyed. And then to the inevitable moment when Sasha realizes that I am a deceitful bastard who has no right whatsoever to woo or even speak to her. Does she even know her brother's crossed over into fully dead status? Her whole countenance spoke of mourning, but that could be at his disappearance, not necessarily his death.

Too. Many. Questions.

I toss the poetry book and pick up a mystery novel,

read three lines, and realize that's not gonna cut it either. Finally, as dawn whispers in through my windows, I give up and just settle into a confused, star-crossed stupor until sleep comes, and then I dream of killing Trevor, again and again and again . . .

CHAPTER TWELVE

〜❦〜

"Talk to me, Dro." We're strolling down Franklin again. Well, I'm strolling. Riley and Dro are floating in long, fluid strides that approximate a strut. Riley seems to be back to his old genial self today, which I'm grateful for, because my underslept, overthinking ass is not.

"Okay, well, I was up at the Council Library all day yesterday."

"Yes, we got the inebriated, unhelpful version last night."

"Can I talk, Riley?"

Riley nods graciously.

"Thank you. They got a whole section on imps."

"Imps?" I say.

"Yeah, like those annoying little naked guys that fuck up people's gardens and shit."

"Thank you, Dro. I know what an imp is. I just didn't know NYCOD had a Dewey decimal number for them."

"Oh, well, yeah, there's an imp section, and there's some whispering that the ngks have a certain relationship to imps."

"Like distant cousins?" Riley asks. He doesn't look like he's feeling this thought line any more than I am.

"More like evil stepbrothers."

"Oh?"

"Oh, indeed. The whispers say that imps are like the less lethal, mentally challenged relatives of the ngks."

"I'm quite sure," Riley says, "that it doesn't say imps are mentally challenged."

"You know what I mean though. And whereas the imps show up in scattered randomosity—"

"That's definitely not a word," I point out.

Dro ignores me, which is probably for the best. "And apparently have no greater purpose, other than to make a mild nuisance of themselves. The ngks, on the other hand, come in quite strategic clumps, usually, and serve a very specific purpose."

"And what purpose would that be?" says Riley.

I notice a throng of kids chasing one another up and down the block, immersed in some wildly complex game they seem to be making up the rules for as they go. Every few seconds they switch directions as one, just like a flock of birds, and then fall out into fits of laughter. Two old drunks enjoy the show from a nearby stoop.

"Well, of course it's all very shrouded in—"

Riley gets curt again. "Cut to it."

"Annihilation of the dead."

All three of us stop short at the gravity of those words. "Come again," Riley says.

Dro repeats himself, looking quite solemn indeed. "One very old Welsh text stated that it was commonly known that these creatures are summoned with the express purpose of annihilating all the spiritual activity in a given area . . ."

"Must have something to do with how they precipitate tragedy," Riley finishes eagerly. "Fuck."

"You said, 'are summoned,'" I point out. I can tell that

phrasing will haunt me for a long time, with all those passive hints of some hidden hand at work.

"Did I?"

I don't like it when Dro gets sloppy with language like that. His shit needs to be impeccable, considering how serious things are right now. "You did. Made it sound like *someone* is doing the summoning."

"Hmm, I'll have to check. I read through hundreds of books, Carlos."

He has a point. I'm probably just tired.

"You thinking 'bout the thing you saw?" Riley says. I nod, frowning.

The kids have scattered off to their respective houses, and a nasty winter breeze sweeps through the city around us.

"But did the two ngked houses even have spirits in 'em?" Dro asks.

Riley shrugs. "Who knows? There's hundreds of loose spirits flitting around, taking up residence in places they shouldn't. If there were, they're surely gone now."

"If there weren't," Dro points out, "what'd be the purpose of putting a ghost annihilator where there's no ghosts? Who'd get got?"

"Us," I say. "And it's already almost worked twice."

I'm surrounded by Estherness. The old ghost has a way of taking up space and not at the same time. She's everywhere, fills the aging room with her jovial old self and yet never overwhelms or suffocates. It's a skill. I feel safe just being near her, let alone immersed in her. A very simple thought occurs to me: maybe everything will just be all right. I doubt it, but still, the thought is there and I decide to go with it for now.

"You look tired, Carlos."

"Haven't been sleeping much." I want to hold on to that thought, tattoo it to my mind, but it's like trying to grab water. "Rough week."

"You're worried about the infestation."

"It's not an infestation. Not yet anyway. Just two." Mama Esther's look reminds me that she's not stupid. "You're not worried about it?"

"Nah," she says, but I don't believe her. "I've seen this neighborhood through so many changes. You wouldn't believe some of the ghoulish monstrosities I've watched come and go. Some of the horrors I've withstood. Ah, Carlos, when you're young, every new travesty seems like the last. You shouldn't trouble yourself so much."

I want to believe her so badly that I almost do. The ngks just being any old passing spirit would be such a blessing, but I know that's not the case. Deluding myself won't help now anyway.

"There's something else," Mama Esther says. She could always see right through me. Seems everyone can these days.

I nod. The story waits hungrily at the edge of my tongue. Speaking it into existence would be like taking off a jacket made of chains. My suddenly unburdened soul would float up into the darkening sky. I want to say it so badly it aches. Esther can see it all over my damn face anyway. "Ah, I'm fine."

"Right." I didn't lie because I thought I could deceive her, just to signal that I couldn't talk about it. She looks disappointed. "You know, I'm very good with matters of the heart. I had eleven children and twenty-three grandkids. They all came to me with their hopes and fears about love, Carlos. And they always left knowing what to do. Esther knows things."

"I know." I'm alarmingly close to breaking down, so I scan the shelves for something to change the subject with.

"Oh, *Richard III*. Haven't read this one since I lived here."

"What's her name, Carlos?"

"Esther . . ."

"What a beautiful name! I like her already."

"Esther."

"Carlos?"

I shake my head. "No."

For a full minute, we just stare at each other. Esther's old even by ghost standards. Her smile, always a little whimsical, has diminished in these past weeks, and the strain shows in other ways too. Little flickers have begun to erupt in her voluminous shining girth. Now it seems she's not just old, she's aging. I wonder briefly if something else is wrong with her, some ancient ghost disease no one knows about, but quickly banish the thought. I don't need to make things any more complicated than they already are: Mama Esther is stressed.

"It must get lonely," she says. She doesn't have to finish the sentence. Anyone else would've gotten some lip in return for the condescension, but the old house ghost manages to say things in just such a way that you can't be mad at her. Plus, she saved my life.

Ever so slightly, I nod. I hadn't ever thought of myself as lonely until Trevor came along with his diabolical plans and beautiful sister. I was just an awkward intermediary, and for the most part, I was okay with that. Now I'm here about to get all gushy in Mama Esther's library.

No.

Not right now, anyway. I'm afraid if I start to blubber I'll never stop—some ever-present dam I've had up since my resurrection will burst and there's no telling what's on the other side. This is not the moment to find out. Not with ghost annihilators popping up on the block and God-knows-what-else running around the basements. "Must get lonely being in a big house all by yourself."

Esther takes the hint. "Ah, you know, folks come by and use the library often enough. It's not so bad."

A strange thought occurs to me, and then it seems even stranger that it'd never occurred to me before. "Folks come by . . . that don't work for the Council?"

"Of course, Carlos!" For no clear reason, Esther is chuckling. "All variations of dead come through my doors to do their research or to find a good mystery to keep them up at night. It's not odd."

"Right." My mind is moving fast now. *All variations of dead.* I wonder. I wonder . . .

"Agent Delacruz." The staticky explosion of telepathy tears through my thoughts. The Council's so damn annoying with their damn transmissions at all the wrong damn times. I cock my head at attention so Esther realizes why I'm not speaking. *"Agent Washington requests your presence urgently at Franklin Avenue and Bergen Street."* Crap. So much for their no-locations policy. That's right down the street, but still: crap. *"He says to inform you that there's been a sighting of your . . ."* The ghostly voice pauses and then says cautiously: *"Your naked friend."*

"Crap." I thank Mama Esther and start heading down the stairwell. She doesn't have to ask to know what happened; it's written all over my face.

CHAPTER THIRTEEN

ⱺ⤳ⱺ

"Sorry 'bout the page," Riley says. "I didn't have time to fuck around with a messenger, and I didn't know if you'd get the telepathy blast." All that supernatural mind-talking stuff doesn't work two ways for me. I can receive the messages, usually, but can't send anything out. If I know Riley's trying to reach me, I can get one-on-one messages, but it's not a sure shot. And we avoid going through the Council to reach each other if we can help it, so when Riley wants to get at me, he usually sends one of the wandering lost souls that zip here and there through Brooklyn looking for something to do.

"It's cool," I say. "I was around the corner at Esther's. Whatchu got?"

"Had soulcatcher patrols movin' up and down the block for the past day or two. One of 'em just saw an unusual-looking character streak past, and by *streak* I do mean *streak*, and disappear into this building. He called for backup like a good little newbie, and here we are."

"Thing is?"

"Thing is, then he went in after it and hasn't been heard from since."

"I see." Ghostly forms swirl around us in a controlled
frenzy. The Council soulcatchers wear thick, shimmering helmets shaped more or less like horseshoe crabs
without the pointy tail. Their bodies and faces are hidden beneath flowing robes. Overall, they cut an imposing
image, but today their nervous energy fills the air till it's
almost hard to breathe. I wonder if the living folks around
pick up on all this disturbance.

Suddenly Dro's beside us, panting. "What'd I miss?"

Riley runs it down for him, and we walk to the building—
an old brick four-story on Bergen between a clinic and
an abandoned car lot. Behind us, the soulcatchers fall
into position. I feel their swarthy ferocity carry me forward like a gust of wind. They're ready to die the final
death to help their brother. They're furious and determined and afraid.

I walk into the dingy hallway and draw my blade. At a
signal from Riley, the soulcatchers flood around us in a
torrent, burst up the stairwell and into the various apartments. They howl as they rush forward, a desperate and
bone-chilling battle cry that never fails to unsettle me.

I nod toward the basement, and Riley draws his own
blade, a shimmering shadow in the dim hallway. We walk
forward side by side, and I feel the long night of confusion
blow off me in the fevered charge of the moment. Riley is
the most ferocious motherfucker I know. Something sinister and freakish awaits us. Whatever it is threatens not
just him and me, but this whole neighborhood, Mama
Esther, and possibly the entire natural order of the afterlife. Everything else becomes blissfully petty in the face
of all that. No wonder Riley seems to have gotten his
swagger back too.

I open the door slowly, hear nothing, sense nothing from

below and sidestep, blade first, down the basement stairs.
It's dark as fuck, but the ickiness hangs in the air like a
chemical cloud. From out of the emptiness, someone yells.
It's a living human yell, at once terrified and triumphant.
The urgent shriek of someone who has absolutely lost his
mind. Beneath it all, there's another voice, a softer one,
blubbering and whimpering.

I flinch and then flail for a dangling light chain. The
voice is sobbing now, sobbing and gurgling, and that
thickness in the air keeps getting thicker. I finally swat
the chain and then catch it in my hand and pull. It takes a
second to sort through the tangled tableau in front of me.
The naked man stands on top of something, lifting one
pale foot and then the other. He's hunched forward like
he's about to pounce, and his mouth opens and closes
around a series of shouts, sobs, and cackles. A black tangle of greasy hair hangs down over his face and shoulders. His long arms stretch to either side; one hand is
wrapped around the face of a soulcatcher, who's hovering there miserably. Then I realize that the thing the
naked man is standing on is actually a person—the one
who'd been doing the whimpering. A very tall person.
"Moishe!" I say, more out of sheer surprise than anything else.

"Mr. Delacruz," Moishe whimpers. "Please . . ."

Soulcatchers flush down the stairs and form a circle
around where the naked man is howling. In about five
seconds, Riley will give the signal and they will burst
forward like a single death-dealing machine and end this
whole horrible situation. Just before they do though, the
naked man gets eerily quiet and turns to me. His beady
little eyes glare out from the squinched-up gray face, and
instead of the fermenting hysteria of a madman, I see

something much worse: intelligence. He seems somehow familiar, a junky I've bumped into a few times around the way, I think. The guy smiles, a horrible, toothy grin, and I see the muscles flex on that long pale arm and I know what's about to happen right before it does: the soulcatcher writhes and then spasms and collapses. That shadowy glow diminishes and then fades completely; he's gone.

The other soulcatchers don't need a cue from Riley anymore. They take the first step in, but stop in their tracks when the horrific shrieking of the ngk tears through all of our minds. It caught everyone off guard, and I see a few soulcatchers stumble and collapse from sheer shock. They won't last long. Beside me, Riley gives the pullout signal. I know he's cringing, hating himself for it, but it's the right move. This ngk, wherever it's hiding, is either stronger or angrier than the other one; its screech is twice as grating.

The soulcatchers retreat, but I figure I have a little longer left in me. I steady myself, try to block out all the terror and screaming, and let my blade fly. It cuts through the air, a little harder than necessary perhaps, but the aim is on the money. I hear that telltale *sploitch* sound and watch with satisfaction as the point enters the naked guy just below his rib cage. He stumbles backward, looks down at it. I wait for him to collapse, but he doesn't. He looks back up at me, and now he's smiling. His beady eyes drill into mine as he pulls the blade out of himself and then puts the tip against Moishe's head and pushes down. I close my eyes, cringing, as the sound of tearing flesh and bone and that final scream fill the air.

Dark red blood stains the basement floor. Moishe's head has vomited its contents in a chunky, steaming mess. The naked man is still staring at me, still smiling, still holding my blade.

There's nothing more to be done here. The ngk shrieks again, nearly doubling me over. I take a step backward, then another. Then I do something I haven't done since my resurrection: I turn around and run for my life.

CHAPTER FOURTEEN

∽∾⊙∾∽

Late at night, after all the wildness of the street had finally simmered to a scattered call-and-response, and the hustlers, families, gossiphounds, stoopgoons, hopscotchers, beatboxers, and little old people had wandered off to their respective houses or hovels, all that was left was the city and the swelling tide of life returning to my broken body. You could hear Brooklyn breathing through Mama Esther's windows in that quiet four-a.m. ecstasy. The rush of an occasional passing car, a gust of wind, the leaves outside brushing against one another, a delivery truck backing up a few blocks away. Somewhere, even farther, an ocean liner's mournful call would sound as it pulled into the harbor. Construction on the Brooklyn-Queens Expressway. An ambulance howl in the night, and then another, their calls sounding out across the city.

I took it all in. Let it sink into my pores as I lay there feeling each cell of my body blink back awake, one by one, night after night.

There is no such peacefulness to be found at the Burgundy Bar tonight. The soulcatchers have congregated

here to seek shelter from the relentless memories. All
that heavy spirit crap has scared off the regular customers, so it's just my half-dead ass, Quiñones—he doesn't
seem to be fazed by anything—and a bunch of shook-up
ghosts. When we arrived, I bought some rounds and left
them at the empty tables around the bar for the soulcatchers to devour at will.

"I've never seen anything like that in my life," Dro
says. He's more together than I was expecting, given how
shook he'd gotten over the first ngk run-in, but he's also
talking too much. "You ever known the COD to retreat
like that, Riley?"

Riley grunts a no and slurps down a shot. I follow suit.

"I mean, what happens now? We're not just gonna let
that freak get away with taking one of our own."

"We regroup. There's a squad watching the house, but
'long as the ngk is in there, we can only go in for a few
minutes at a time. We lick our wounds and bury our dead,
so to speak, and figure out what to do next."

"Oh." You can see Dro's not so satisfied with that
answer. He wants a grisly revenge to level out the playing
field, overwhelming force and a brutal showdown and all
that. Fortunately, he's smart enough not to go on about it
just now.

"I think he's . . . like me," I say.

Both Riley and Dro look at me. I suppose they're startled because I don't usually talk about what I am, and it
obviously bugs me that something so hideous could share
a title with me. But fuck it. It's going to be said; I might as
well say it. Plus I'm five shots deep and well past giving a
damn what anyone thinks. Put it on the table. "Put it on
the table!" I say, slamming a hand on the bar. Quiñones
takes it for a sign that I want another round, and I decide
not to disabuse him of the notion.

"What do you make of it?" Riley asks. He's humbled, our glorious leader. He's asking me as an equal. The tragedy seems to have leveled us all out some.

I shake my head and then stop. A few seconds later the room stops too. "I don't . . . know. I hate it. Two months ago I met the first person who was like me and I killed him. Now perhaps I've met another, and he's a sick fuck who murdered a soulcatcher and a nice Jewish man in front of my eyes." And that's not even to mention the one I can't stop thinking about. "I'm not very happy right now."

"Understandable," Riley says. I clink my glass against theirs and drink.

"Hey," a voice behind me says. It's a soulcatcher, unbelievably smashed and wobbling a few inches from the back of my head.

"Can I help you?"

"One'a yer fuckin' people took out one'a our fucking people tonight. You know that, right?"

"Excuse me?"

"I said . . ."

"Angus," Riley says, stepping between us. "You're out of line. Back up."

Angus considers for a moment. Riley is definitely his superior and able to make his life irretrievably miserable. On the other hand, we're all drunk, and Angus saw his buddy get murked and wants to take out his anger somewhere.

Apparently, the big stupid half of his brain wins, because then he slurs: "I oughta fuck you up on general printhipal. We all oughta." The line is obviously designed to elicit some kind of rowdy response from the other guys, but only a few people nod and go "yeah." Most of them know me pretty well and aren't anxious to vex Riley on an already tense night.

"Tough talk from a guy who's one letter away from being an asshole," I say.

Angus has to pause and think about this for a second, and this is the second in which I would cut off his idiocy with a quick uppercut and then level him with a jab to the face. Instead I stand there, waiting for him to subtract the *g* from his own name while everyone around us chuckles.

I'm in no mood to fight, not after what I've seen. And I don't need any more side-eyes coming my way. Finally, he either gets it or pretends to and growls at me. "You're gonna get some of your own medicine, halfie!"

I don't even think he knows what he means by that, but it doesn't matter; he starts swirling his arms around like he's about to try to jujitsu me. Then Riley's there, between us again. His thick hands catch Angus by each wrist and pull, hard. Angus buckles forward, gasping. "What'd I do?" he moans, suddenly the victim.

"I said back off," Riley growls. "Which means you back the fuck off." He pulls Angus forward to get him off balance and then shoves him hard, and the soulcatcher flies backward into the crowd and disappears.

"You all right, bro?"

I laugh. "I'm not the one you just tossed, Riley. I'm cool." We drink another round in silence. Around us, ghosts seek solace from trauma in the sudden camaraderie of the damned.

CHAPTER FIFTEEN

❧❦❧

Iknow I shouldn't be doing this, but I am.

My feet propel me forward, ignoring all my mind's mumbling protests. I sweep through the rainy streets, leaning hard on my now-bladeless cane. Brooklyn becomes a blur of bodegas and dark houses. I'm navigating through my drunken haze and the steady drizzle, a crazed geographer, mad with memories—this intersection where I cut down a lovelorn haint who wouldn't let his ex alone, and that corner where I tracked down a nest of infant spirits who'd died in a building collapse decades ago. The memories of ghosts become ghosts in their own right. They follow me along through the misty twilight, crowd in on my drunkenness in a rowdy throng.

I know I shouldn't be doing this. Because if I make it to the Red Edge and Sasha's there, I'm gonna tell her everything. I'm not going to hold back, because it's all right here, pulsing through my veins with a languid thump, tickling the edge of my tongue like a fireball I need to spit. I have truths to tell, and this alcohol-soaked frenzy provides a perfect excuse to shun reason and hurl it all out into the night.

I wonder where I should start. How do you begin to

tell such a ghastly tale? I hang a left off Flatbush Avenue and wander into the Slope. It's late, and only a few night cabs and barhopping stragglers flit back and forth through the streets like exiled angels. After a couple wrong turns, I stumble into the Red Edge.

She's not here.

Fuck.

It's probably good though. I station myself at her table and order a beer. I've arrived, after all. Might as well celebrate. When I close my eyes, the blobs of light spin circles around me. It's time to go. The hipsters glance at me like I stepped out of one of their nightmares. Maybe I did. Or maybe we dreamed each other up, and the Red Edge is just where everyone's nightmares come to drink together. Surely, once Sasha figures out who I really am, I will be the stuff of sleepless nights and sudden wake-ups for her too.

It's definitely time to go.

I close my eyes to ready my body for motion again, and when I open them there's a white girl sitting in front of me. It takes me a second to break through my delirium and realize she is in fact really there. Then I realize it's one of the Amandas. I open my mouth to say something and then close it again. I have no reason to know her name. As far as she is concerned, I have never seen her before in my life. Then why is she sitting there staring intently at me?

"Hello," she finally says, as if it were the most natural thing in the world.

"Hey."

"I've never seen you in here before."

"I've never seen you in here before either."

She laughs and does a pretty good job of making it sound real too. "Well, I come here all the time." This conversation is going nowhere. "You, sir, are the stranger."

I'm not even sure what I say back, something mostly unintelligible that makes her laugh again, and that's when it finally kicks in: Amanda wants to bone. Or at least get my phone number. I squint at her and allow the tiniest sliver of her thoughts to materialize in the air. Yes, she definitely wants penis. The hunger lurks around her in unmistakable torrents. And me? I'm a new face. A dapper, tall fellow in a room full of mostly scrawny unkempt dudes.

It's just never happened to me before. I don't really go out besides to the Burgundy. I have no idea how any of this works.

"What's your name?"

"Carlos."

She smiles. For a grim moment, I can see it all play out—the frenzied taxi ride home, the scurry of clothing being peeled off, the magnificent entrance and then the untold wonders of a night of passion—and I want it. I can even taste the chance of total mediocrity and still: I want it. If nothing else, because it would cap off a terrifying day with a dash of ruckus pleasure. But even through my drunkenness, I know better.

"What do you do, Carlos?"

"I'm a contracts analyst."

"Ooh, sexy!" She says it mockingly, but it rings true anyhow. Half of me is about to leap across the table and take her right here and now. She's not bad looking, a little odd perhaps, but the sheer sex radiating from her body is working its magic on me. All those crude fantasies heavy up the air between us.

"Why don't we get out of here?" I say, even though I'm pretty sure that's not such a good idea.

She looks down at the table, then raises her eyes to meet mine. It's a little forced, but still cute. Or maybe I'm just drunk. There's a sadness around her that I can't put my finger on. Once I notice it, it becomes even more intense, and I wonder how I could've missed it. She's devastated. "Yes," Amanda says with a crooked smile. "Let me just tell my friends."

I wait for her to get up, but instead she just pulls a little calculator-looking thing out of her purse and starts clacking away at it. A few seconds later, a bunch of girls at the bar all pull out their calculators and start giggling. "Okay," she says with a smile. "Let's go."

We get a taxi, and she's all over me, trying to burrow away from her sorrows. Desperation. Our lips never meet, but she drapes herself across my lap like a wilted flower; her fingers toy idly with my lapels. I remember to ask her where she lives before just blurting it out to the driver, and then she turns to look up at me. "Carlos?"

"Hmm?"

"Hi."

"Hey."

She rolls back over and slides her fingers down my chin, along my neck. "Oh," she says, her carefully trimmed eyebrows creasing with concern. "You're so cold! My goodness."

"Mm-hmm."

"We might have to do something about that." Her hand moves from my neck down to the relative comfort of my shirt and stays there for the rest of the ride.

There's something different about this place. It's emptier; certain things are missing from the wall, and a heaviness hangs in the air. You can feel it the second you walk in. Then I realize it's all David's stuff: gone. Amanda takes my hand and leads me down the hallway past David's door. It's ajar and his room is empty, stark-naked empty, not even a bed. "C'mon," Amanda says, beckoning with one finger. "This is my room."

It's a mess: papers and textbooks all over the floor, clothes piled in the corner, half-full coffee cups on the bedside table. A paperback copy of *The Alchemist* lies open on the bed next to a rolled-up sock and a small pile of receipts. She displaces all that to the floor with a single, drunken swipe and plops down, leaning back on her elbows. "Hey."

I'm standing over her, looking down as she squirms herself around, trying to be seductive.

This is all wrong. Terribly wrong.

I open my mouth, about to make some ridiculous excuse for leaving, when she sniffles and then breaks down completely.

"Um." I step back and then forward again, caught between two no-good protocols. "You okay?"

"I'm fine," she sobs, wiping tears away and snorfling. "I'm sorry. I'm totally fine." Ask a stupid question. "I just . . ." She sighs and horks a booger into a tissue. "It's just been hard, is all."

"What?"

"My roommate," she says, her voice quivering. Then she bursts into tears again. I sit on the bed beside her and pat her back. "He . . . he died last week. Just . . . died."

"That's terrible. How?" Probably not the right question, but I need to know.

"Just . . . he was s-sick. He was, I don't know, no . . . He was fine, well, no." She takes a deep, shivery breath and collects herself. "He'd been acting weird since New Year's."

"Weird how?"

"Just . . . off, you know. Like sometimes he was cool, but sometimes he just wasn't himself. He'd fall into this darkness, like there was a rain cloud around him that he couldn't shake. And then suddenly he was sick. Ugh . . ." She blows her nose again and rallies some of her composure back. "And we thought it was just the flu or whatever. Finally convinced him to go to the ER. Called nine-one-one for him and everything, but the stupid paramedics were assholes, talking about 'Oh, why'd we call nine-one-one if all he has is a fever,' or whatever. Assholes."

"Jeez."

"And then they sent him home with just some antibiotics, but he didn't get better." And she starts bawling again, this time dropping her head against my shoulder, her tears and snot soaking into my suit jacket. "He just kept getting worse. It was like he was gone, like he wasn't even there, you know? Just gone. And he kept having bloody noses, all the time. Just filled up trash can after trash can with those bright red–stained tissues." She lets out a gaspy sob. "And then the next morning he didn't get out of bed, and we went to check on him, me and Amanda . . ." A long pause. I wonder if maybe she fell asleep. Then she says: "And he was deeeeeeaaddddd," and breaks down sobbing again.

"Wow."

"They didn't even take him, those fucking ambulance pricks. There was blood all around his body and he was pale as a sheet of fucking paper, and they didn't take him because they said there was no point; he was too far gone."

"Had he been stabbed?"

"No!" Amanda yells, suddenly furious. Then she rolls her eyes and exhales a heavy breath of vodka and something artificially fruity. "Sorry . . . no. It just came out of him somehow. I don't know. I don't understand. No one would tell us anything."

"How . . . horrible." Words are such pitiful stupid things sometimes. Like when I speak them. To people who really need to be comforted. The fuck good does a word like "horrible" do anybody? I resolve to shut up, but then I just feel cold. And then, without warning, it doesn't matter anymore, because Amanda has managed to pass the fuck out on my shoulder. I gently lay her onto the bed and quiet-walk out into the hallway.

David's room isn't only empty of absolutely everything; it's been scrubbed down. I close my eyes, imagining his last moments: blood gushing out of who knows what orifice, a whole mess of coughing, vomiting, fighting for air, and then finally that slow descent into nothing. I can see the sudden burst of motion as the cops and paramedics show up, take a long, unnerved glance at his empty body and call it a done deal; I can see the screaming Amandas, the quietness of the crime scene until it's ruled a medical death, the final deep cleansing and scrubbing of the room, and now this: total silence. A shiny hardwood floor. A fairly·decent view of the backyard grotto.

I shake my head, realize I'm still drunk, and swagger out into the night.

I don't even fuck with Herodotus or the Nuyoricans. Nights like this . . . well, there's never been a night like this. But on those wretchedest of nights, when the fury of the day still pounds through my head with no sign of letting up, I seek refuge in the *Barrow's Guide to North American Birds*, 1978 edition. Got it for eight bucks from one of those old guys with a foldout table on Eastern Parkway.

Wrens. Blackbirds. Starlings. They're so alive in these nice full-color pictures. A little foggy maybe, or maybe that's me. Their little names are so simple. Wren. What could be more straightforward than something called a wren? Build a nest. Feed your young. Find another wren and fuck it. Start over.

Sleep is a friendly way of telling my head to shut up.

CHAPTER SIXTEEN

I wake up already tussling with the problem of the ngks and their lethal naked benefactor. The whole situation seems to just be sitting there as I come around, an ugly, uninvited houseguest. Also, I'm hungover, but that was expected. All the way through my morning routine, out the door, and down the street, I'm pondering how the little cretins do what they do and how we can stop them. In my mind, there is the one homicidal halfie, killing a soul-catcher and Moishe in one fell swoop. He's surrounded by a grim constellation of ngks, all panting and biking away, and those horrible shrieks bursting through the air like sparklers. Somewhere nearby is Trevor and his weirdo plot to bring some college kids into the Underworld. Sasha's a little farther off, all sleek and fragrant and sorrowful at that table of hers in the Red Edge. Surely lines stretch between them all, but I have no idea how.

I find Riley in a similar mood. He's standing over an ancient wooden table on the second floor of Mama Esther's place, puzzling over some papers. "What I can't . . . quite . . . grasp," he says by way of a greeting, "is what the fuck kinda sick magic that naked halfie was dealing in."

It warms my heart actually. Besides hunting, this is

when Riley and I are at our best. Seems yesterday's defeat has thrown us both into strategy hyperdrive. That, plus the Council's probably all up in his ass about it. "Been working the connection with the one I took out on New Year's," I say.

Riley looks up. "Anything?"

"Only that the one was trying to bring the living and the dead closer together and the other seems to be trying to take out the dead one by one."

"Is he? Or is it something else?"

"Like what?"

Riley shoves some papers aside and unfolds a map across the table. "The three ngks so far have been within a four-block radius. Here, here, and here." I unsheathe a Sharpie and dot the little squares he points to.

"Not unusual for ngks though, right? If it's an infes—"

"Right, right, but what if that's why he's using them? If that's not an incidental feature of the little creepy guys but the whole point?" Riley thinks he's onto something, but I don't see it yet. I'm not even sure if he does. He's just plunging forward on gut instinct and teasing out the idea as he goes. I'd roll my eyes, but it usually works for him.

"So you think there's something special he wants to do and he needs the ngks in a cluster to do it?"

"What better way to get into some nefarious shit without the Council being able to touch him? Think about it: he's got some very old, very nasty magic working for him, yes, but even with all that, certain things take time. And powerful though he may be, he probably can't hold off a patrol of soulcatchers *and* complete his secret science project at the same time."

"So he builds an impenetrable barrier against ghosts."

"Exactly."

"But what's the project?"

Riley shrugs. "No clue. Was hoping you'd get that part worked out."

"Great."

We ponder in silence for a few minutes, shuffling papers and sipping corner-store coffee.

"Is it weird?" Riley says out of the blue.

I know exactly what he means, but I say, "What's that?" anyway.

"You know, you're this one and only for three years, and then all a sudden there's half-dead guys popping out the woodworks. And they're launching plots, being freaky, declaring war on the dead and all kindsa fuckery. Just wondering if you got feelings on it."

"I do." I almost leave it at that, but then the words slip out of me. "I feel caught between two worlds I don't understand."

Riley nods and sips cold coffee.

"I mean, that was always true. But now it's even truer. And yeah, I don't really know what to do with it. It'd help if the one guy weren't a homicidal freak."

"Amen. And it was all so deliberate, the killing. One ghost and that set off our boys, and then the Hasidic guy."

I put some coffee in me and mull it over. "And the fact that he was looking right at me when he did it is just . . ." I shudder. "You know I don't get icked out easy."

"It's true."

"But this . . . yeah, it got to me some."

We settle back into a working silence for a few minutes and then Riley curses. I look up at him. "I don't know why I didn't see this before."

"Hm?"

"If you triangulate the ngked houses"—he drags the Sharpie in thick lines between the three dots—"you get an unpleasant surprise."

"Mama Esther's house."

"Damn skippy."

"Right in the center."

"Correct."

"Damn."

CHAPTER SEVENTEEN

❦

I light a Malagueña to ward off this hangover as I trudge along toward Bushwick. It's a brisk afternoon, the kind you can really get lovelorn over. Today I'm keeping it professional though; my mind still teems with ngks and halfie plots. I'm fast, so there's still some cigar left by the time I reach Baba Eddie's.

"You can't smoke in here," Kia says when I walk through the jingling door.

"Bullshit."

She indicates a brand-new NO SMOKING sign hanging above her head. "I'm a growing child, and y'all's nasty secondhand smoke is fucking up my uterus and lung capacity."

"Your uterus, huh?"

"If I say so, then yes."

"Fine." I head back out the door. "Would you tell Baba Eddie I'm outside?"

"He's with a client."

I growl something at Kia, but it gets voided out by the clamor of bells and the slamming door. She smiles and flips me off over the heads of the saints in the window display and then gets back to work.

———

"Carlos!" The thing about Eddie's boyfriend, Russell Ward,
is he really looks like your average white dude. He's pale
and has thinning salt-and-pepper hair and a big white-dude
grin that comes at you outta nowhere. He's not white, of
course; he's Indian—like Indian from upstate, not Ban-
galore—and he used to be on some real hate-whitey shit
back in the sixties, from what I hear. He's some kinda big-
deal lawyer now and, according to Baba Eddie, milking the
corporate bastards for every cent they have from the inside.
I ain't mad. "What you been up to, man?" Russell says. "I
haven't seen you in forever!"

He gives me a firm handshake and settles in beside me
in front of the store. "Life is good," I say. "No, that's bullshit.
Everything's a mess."

Russell frowns. "I'm sorry to hear that, Carlos." He
sounds like a used-car dealer, but I know he really means
it. "You want to talk about it?"

"I can't, really. But thanks."

We stand there for another minute, and then I say:
"You ever feel trapped between two worlds?" Then I face
palm. "Sorry, that was a stupid question."

"No, it's fine, Carlos. And yes, every single day that I put
on this suit and go to work, actually. And every time I walk
down the street and someone mistakes me for something
I'm not. Also, anytime I step foot back on the rez and get
called a sellout. And during certain arguments me and
Eddie have had. Yes. Quite a bit actually."

"Damn."

"But I'm all right with it."

"Oh?"

"I'm gonna be fifty-three years old next week, Carlos."

"Happy birthday."

He shrugs it off. "Yeah, yeah, whatever. The point is, I could give a fuck what people see me as now. Does it still vex the shit out of me when someone calls me a cracker? Of course, especially if I haven't gotten my mochaccino yet."

"I'm sure the mochaccino does wonders for you not looking white."

Russell rolls his eyes. "You know what I mean though. There's moments, sure. There'll always be moments. But in the grand scheme of things, I know what the fuck I am. The one man I truly give a fuck about knows what the fuck I am, and the Creator on high *definitely* knows what the fuck I am. So what the fuck do I care about anybody else?"

He makes a good case for not giving a fuck. I'll give him that. "You ever feel like you might one day have to pick sides?"

"Oh, like the apocalyptic race war? Let me tell you something, Carlos: that shit's been going on every single day since the country was born and long before that too. People walking around waiting for it like it's gonna be some moment, us and them, but no: war is the constant state of things. Slow fucking death. We're just trying to squeeze out whatever little slab of peace we can find. You feel me?"

I nod, regretting slightly that I unleashed the rampage. But instead of going on, Russell just stares at me for a few seconds.

"What is it?" I ask.

"This is usually the part where, having listened to what I have to say, you then share something."

"Oh." I forget how these things work. I think for a second, then shrug. "I really have no fucking idea what's going on.

All I know is: I ain't really this and I ain't really that. I don't know if I believe in God, but if there is one, I feel like he or she or whatever is fucking with me right now."

Russell nods. "Sounds about right. God's good for fucking with a man. We get our britches in a wad about it, but usually? That shit ends up pointing us exactly where we need to go."

"I guess . . ."

"And you wanna know something else . . ." It's a demand, not a question. "They took me aside one time, when I went back to the rez and I was all fucked up. I was a complete alcoholic, to tell you the truth, and a fuckup in general at life. And that's not even to mention the fact that I had one foot in the closet and the other on the dance floor." He belly laughs. "Anyway, yeah, they took me aside, some of the elders. We call them elders, you know, not senior fucking citizens, where I come from, because they're people and not cheap boxes you check off to get a discount on your car insurance."

"Okay."

"Anyway, they were like, 'Look, Russell, this can go one of two ways: you can continue to fuck up your life and die in a sniffling pool of your own self-centeredness'— I'm paraphrasing, of course."

"Of course."

"'Or you can embrace that wild enigmatic complicated bitch that is your destiny and ride it into the motherfucking sunset.'"

"Damn."

"Again, paraphrasing."

"Right."

"They said the Creator made certain ones of us look white for a reason, that we had a mission: to infiltrate the white man's world and find out what we could, right? Because the fact is, a white dude will tell my pale ass some shit he won't even tell your pale-but-brown ass, just on the sheer fact that I pass much more than you do, Carlos. It's just a fact of it. And I can complain about it, because it's easy to fall into bitterness when you got white people in your ear talking about all their twisted fears and fantasies, trust me. But now it's ordained as such. There's a reason for it. The Creator wants us to use our complexness for the good of our people. Reconnaissance. You feel me?"

I nod because I do, I really do. I'm not sure how it applies to my life yet, but I definitely feel him.

"And I was like, fuck: I have a mission. A divine motherfucking mission, no less. All right." Russell struts a few times and adjusts his slick blue suit like he's just now coming into the glorious realization of who he is. "That's some shit I can deal with. Let me tell you something." As if I could stop him at this point. "I never drank again. I sold all my coke."

"You sold it? Most people just flush it."

"I'm a businessman."

"Understood."

"And I never looked back."

"Damn."

Russell nods endearingly and swoops into the store on the wings of his own self-generated momentum. I stand there for a few seconds trying to puzzle out whether the dead are the white people or the Indians and then Baba Eddie pokes his head out. "You wanted something, Carlos?"

"Oh, yes! No. Wait . . . Hang on." I'm all turned around from Russell's speech.

"Hanging."

I see Eddie make for his pack of smokes and stop him. "Wait—let's go inside."

He looks disappointed but shrugs and leads me to the back room. Baba Eddie divines with a bunch of cowry shells, a piece of chalk, and a pebble, from what I can tell. I've never actually gotten a reading from him, but I get the feeling he knows what he's doing. His reading room is tiny, possibly a converted broom closet or bathroom, with a little foldout table and a chair on either side. A Ferrari calendar from 1993 hangs on the wall as if it belongs there, and there's a little shelf with various spiritual knickknacks in the corner. That's about all that could fit in the place anyway.

"You want a reading?" Baba Eddie says with a mischievous grin. Maybe one day I'll get one, but this isn't the moment. Part of me just doesn't want to know what kind of spiritual mess is going on with me right now; I think it'd be too depressing. Part of me just can't be bothered.

"I'll let you know." I take a seat in the client's chair. "Things've gotten hairier."

"Hairier than ngks in Mama Esther's hood? Do tell." Baba sits in his spot and listens attentively as I run down the events of yesterday, glazing over certain details around the Amanda situation. When I finish, Baba just sits glumly for a few ticks of the clock and ponders.

"That is hairy," he finally says.

"Indeed."

"Riley thinks the guy's building something?"

"Well, plotting. Maybe building. We have no idea, to be honest."

Baba Eddie lets out a sustained *hmmm* and unconsciously fondles his cigarettes. "I wonder."

"Do you wonder something in particular or just wonder?"

"I wonder . . . I wonder if this character, this naked

fellow, is actually trying to get your attention more than anything else."

"Excuse me?"

"Yes. You said his massacre had an air of performance to it, no?"

"Well, he waited till we were all there, certainly. And"— I shiver a little somewhere deep inside—"he looked me right in the eye when he did the real estate Hasid."

"See. He could've killed you, no?"

"Well, I wouldn't say that necessarily."

"He certainly could've tried. Had ample opportunity. But instead he killed someone in front of you."

"I suppose so, yes."

"He was showing off," the santero says with finality. Then he puts a menthol in his mouth.

"If you light that, Kia will fuck us both up on behalf of her uterus."

Baba Eddie nods, showing a generous amount of restraint toward his young office manager, in my opinion.

"And this other partially dead fellow—Trevor, you called him?"

"Yes."

"A minion of some kind, perhaps. Maybe even a reluctant one."

"Why reluctant?"

"He also could've at least attempted to kill you, save his own life. Was he even armed, Carlos?"

That hadn't really occurred to me in the frenzy of the moment. I'd just been glad the kill was clean. "No," I admit.

"There's a missing piece to this equation."

Sasha. "You think?"

"No doubt."

"Eddie! You comin'?" Russell calls from the front. "Reservation's for eight. I don't wanna be fuckin' late."

Baba Eddie rolls his eyes and stands. "Such a poet, that one. The trials and tribulations of a domesticated santero, Carlos. I swear . . ."

"True love is a feisty bitch."

"You have no idea."

"I really don't," I say and follow him out through the curtain.

CHAPTER EIGHTEEN

❦

She's here. Sasha. The missing piece. Looking sullen again, but she lights up when she sees me. Which causes pangs of fear and delight to supercharge through my veins. I sit at her table like that's just what we always do, and then I put all the good things I think about her into a smile. I don't smile much, so I try to make them count.

She blushes. "Happy to see me?"

"I am." And so glad she wasn't here last night to absorb my drunken truth-telling. "Always."

She rolls her eyes. "No drinks this time?"

"I'm . . ." *Still hungover.* "Taking a break."

"Ooh-la-la." A mischievous smile.

"But you want one?" I make to get up, and she stops me, putting a chilly, perfect hand on mine.

"No, it's fine. Stay."

I sit, and she leaves her hand there for a blissful second before retrieving it. Her eyes are glued to my face though, probably trying to make sure I'm not suddenly repulsed by her coldness. That's what I'd do anyway. Makes no sense, because obviously I'm cold too, but petty insecurities don't politic with reason. I know as well as anyone.

Less than twelve hours earlier, I was sitting where she is and blathering back and forth with Amanda. I send up a little prayer of thanks to whoever's listening that grieving and coolheadedness prevailed.

"You want to go somewhere?" I say. I realize that sounds like a complete come-on, which I hadn't totally meant it as, so I add: "A walk or something?"

She relaxes a little and nods. "Sounds lovely."

I don't mean to, but we end up veering toward the park anyway. I swear the place has a gravitational pull to the less-than-living. Anyway, it's a beautiful, fresh night; the air is crisp and perfect like some divine hand was feeling meticulous about putting each piece into place. Sasha's wearing a black peacoat that adds a pleasing militant element to her otherwise debonair swagger. Sproingy black curls bounce out from under a knit cap and surround her face in an inky ocean of hair. I want to take that face in my hands and put my own face against it and let our connecting faces be the fulcrum that swings our two bodies together and let the winter night guide our combined life forces into an intimate tangle that obliterates all our fears and regrets, but instead I just smile and offer her my arm.

Riley says ladies like it when you go slow right up until this one particular moment in time—Point Zero, he calls it—when everything changes and you gotta switch into hunting mode. The idea being that there's a diminishing series of digital numbers that speed toward Point Zero and from there they zoom back upward toward the Insertion Moment. "It's all about the motherfucking timing." Clearly time is one thing Riley has way too much of.

Regardless though, I'm pretty sure Point Zero has not arrived yet for Sasha and me, so we stroll along the avenue, chatting amiably.

"The only thing I remember," she says without an over-abundance of sadness, "is standing next to my brother, surrounded by strange faces. I'm glad he's there, holding my hand, but I'm nervous about something. I see an oil-covered dead man with a mustache. And then we die."

"Wait—what?"

"I know. It doesn't really make sense. But that's the best way I can describe it. He was frozen and shiny and all black like oil had been dumped over him and crying out into the night, silently. That's the last thing I saw."

"You don't remember how you died?"

She shakes her head. "Must've been quick, whatever it was. Or I blotted it out."

I like how matter-of-fact she is about death. Not devoid of emotion, but not ruled by it either. It's a comfortable balance that most living people could never understand. "You?"

I shrug. "There's not much there. I think you have more than I do. I was murdered. That I'm pretty sure about. I'm looking up at three faces, well, not faces: they're wearing ski masks. I know it's all over, but it's been a real fight and I can see they're winded and one's bleeding, so at least I didn't give up easy, I think to myself. Then one of them moves his arm and it's over."

"Damn." She raises her eyebrows and looks up at me with an endearing blend of concern and curiosity.

We walk a while in silence along the edge of the park. Classy old buildings line one side of the street. The block we're on is shadowed by the darkness of trees and under-growth stretching toward Flatbush. I can almost feel it breathing, beckoning me, but I don't want to retrace the steps of Trevor's murder. Who knows what thoughts and emotions would spill out and poison the night air?

"Where do you live?"

Sasha gasps. "My good gentleman! How very forward of you."

"Well, I meant it . . . What I mean is . . . Hm." It takes a second to register that she isn't really offended and then I just shut up.

"Flatbush."

"May I escort you home?"

"You may escort me to my door and no further." She eyes me to see how that settles in.

"It would be an honor." Point Zero is many miles away, but it's a beautiful night and I enjoy long walks.

The night ended like this: we stood outside Sasha's huge prewar apartment building on Ocean Avenue, our faces so close together I could count the hairs in each swirl, and we let the conversation wind itself down. In the comfortable silence that followed, I went in to kiss her. She turned her face so I landed on her cheek instead of her lips and then held very still. For a few moments, we just stood there with my face barely touching the side of hers. Breathing in, breathing out, the winter night wrapping around us, the passing traffic. Breathing in, breathing out, trying to memorize the moment in case it never happened again.

And then she was gone.

An ecstatic stroll home, through the park, the once dark and foreboding park, now all illuminated with the sparkle of late-season snowfields and the glorious palpitations of my motherfucking heart. Drunk on only the moment, I make it home, blissfully stumble out of my clothes, and immerse myself in the warmth of New York's Puerto Rican poets before pleasuring myself and passing out at sunrise with a smile on my face.

CHAPTER NINETEEN

◦⟨∞⟩◦

There's a small ghost at my door.

It can't be too important, so I fall back asleep.

There's a small ghost at my door. Still. His irritating little telepathy twitters around my bedroom like a stupid fucking bird that I want to kill. Instead I fall back asleep.

And wake back up, semialert with the knowledge that there is a small ghost at my door.

And that all this has already happened. Once or twice. Ah yes, ten minutes ago. Shit. I stumble out of bed, open up, and then look down where the little guy is hovering just a few inches over the floor, looking up at me.

"Sorry to disturb you."

"It's fine."

"No, I'm really sorry. I tried to be subtle with the telepathy. I didn't know if you were sleeping or not, so I was really trying to be respectful of that."

"It's fine. What time is it?"

"Four fifteen."

Ugh. "Four fifteen in the what?"

"Afternoon, sir."

"Christ. What do you want?"

"Unfortunately, I was asked to interfere with your alone time to deliver a message." The little guy is so deadpan I have no idea if he's being sarcastic or not, but I don't really care.

"Yes?"

"The message is from Agent Riley Washington with the New York Council of the Dead."

"Thank you. What is the message?"

"Agent Washington asked me to deliver the message to Agent Carlos Delacruz at this residence."

"You want a tip. Is that what this is about?"

"Gratuity is a privilege and not a right, sir. I am simply being thorough with the procedure and assuring that the message is delivered correctly and to the correct recipient."

"What's your name?"

"Elton Ellis."

"Okay, Elton Ellis. Tell me the message. Now." I say it sweetly, but there's no doubt that I'm done playing.

"Dro went home."

I like Riley because he doesn't waste words. Probably because he knows the messengers will, so he keeps it right to the point. Dro went home.

"What do you think it means?"

I narrow my eyes at the little guy. He's looking up at me, salivating for some gossip for the ghost world. I shake my head and shut the door.

Sometimes I'm glad that I don't have more than that single snapshot of a memory from my life. It's freeing, in a way. I couldn't find anything out, so I don't try. It's a fool's mission and I don't have time for that. Instead I slide into the comfort of perpetual ignorance and go about the business of living. Or half living. Whatever.

Dro is not so fortunate.

He was a family man. Cut down by cancer just like that, in the prime of his life. He's mostly moved on, he really has, but every once in a while something will trigger him and he'll find his way back to the house his wife and teenage kids still live in.

And he'll wallow.

I can't judge him for it. The very thought of a family is so foreign to me—I couldn't even begin to imagine what emotions he's having. But this is no time to wallow. There's too much at stake right now, and Dro has been unsteadier than I've ever seen him. He seemed all right at the bar the other day, but this . . . this can't be good.

The house sits on a pleasant residential block in Flushing. It's a simple two-story type deal, pretty much identical to all the others around it. Dro's hovering outside the kitchen window, and I can feel his poor dead heart disintegrating from across the street. Inside, his wife, Ginny, is taking dinner out of the oven, and Beatrice, now almost seventeen and finally leaving behind the gawky preteen look, sets the table. Delroy is in the living room doing homework. It's so simple, and I'm pretty sure that's what makes it so hard. In the thick of things, it's easy to get caught up and ignore that somewhere there's people having a normal life, day in day out, that you were once a part of. Then it slows down. Your mind has time to catch up and fuck with you and there you are, levitating outside the window of a house that once was yours, watching a family to whom you're only a memory and a picture on the mantel.

I walk up next to Dro, careful not to make any noise whatsoever, and stand there with him for a few minutes, watching.

"Riley sent you."

"Mm-hmm. Sent word with this slow-ass little courier ghost."

"Oh, Elton?" A smile creeps over Dro's face, but his eyes are oceans of sadness.

"That's the guy. He's a little procedure maven, that one."

"He is." Dro hasn't taken his eyes off his family, and I wonder if he's going to go easily or make a fuss. The last time this happened, he stayed for a full day, but it was a less drastic time and we didn't really need him around, so Riley and I agreed to just wait it out.

"I'm coming," he says. Probably wasn't hard to guess what I was thinking. "I'm done here."

It's a little too easy, and I almost ask if he's sure. But that would be counterproductive. "Okay." When he doesn't move for another full minute, I take the initiative and step backward, very quietly, away from the window. Dro's shoulders hunch over, and for a second I think he's sobbing. His glow flickers, then strengthens. Some invisible act of regeneration has just happened, and it was probably too personal to let me see, but part of me wishes I could've. It's a whole other kind of sorcery—pulling the pieces of a shattered heart back together, and it's one I know nothing about. When he turns around, Dro looks fine. Okay, his eyes are still sad, but his half smile is real. "Let's go," he says softly. "Now."

There's a little urgency in his voice, like if we don't leave this very second he may be trapped there eternally, so I fast-walk out of the driveway and we head down the quiet block as the darkness grows around us.

CHAPTER TWENTY

✦

Riley greets me with a curt nod and hands me a blade, handle out.

My eyes widen. "Y'all got it back?"

"Recovery team went in after things calmed down, before PD and EMS swarmed the place. The ngk was still there, so they moved fast. Guess the dude just dropped it, but it's clean."

I nod. Sheathe it in my cane. It feels good in my hand, an old friend.

Riley looks at Dro. "You good, bro?"

Dro smiles, says he is, and we settle around the paper-strewn table. "All right, guys," Riley says. "I'm sure it won't come as a surprise that another ngk has shown up." He points to a new dot on the map. "This one is closer to St. John's and still fits within the overall pattern that Carlos and I were working out yesterday. Still wraps around the central location where we're sitting right now, unfortunately. But I want to try something new."

"You have a plan?" Dro asks.

"Of sorts. Well, something I want to try anyway. Was talking it over with some of the big heads upstairs. They want us to check into the possibility of disabling the ngks, since we can't kill them."

I immediately don't like this idea. "You want us to break their little legs? 'Cause I don't see them taking very well to that either."

"Not their legs," Riley says seriously. "Their machines."

"The stationary bikes?"

"Yes. Whatever they are. No one's too sure, but as far as we can tell, the machines are somehow integral to their ability to poison the air for ghosts. The idea being if we disable the bikes, it'll stop them without us having killed them or tried to kill them."

"Which we're not allowed to do under any circumstances," I grumble.

"Right. So this is the next best thing."

I raise my eyebrows. "The Council came up with this plan?"

"They did," Riley says. "But I think it's worth a try. We probably have about seven to ten minutes, if we fortify ourselves, before the ngk shit overtakes us. Carlos might have a little bit more on account of having a body or whatever, but you get the idea. The hardest part obviously will be getting the little bastard off his bike. Once we get it, we get out of there and figure out how to break it."

"That's not a plan," I say. "That's a let's-try-this-and-hope-it-works fiasco."

"It's what we got right now," Riley snarls. "And it's what we're gonna do. We leave in a half hour, so do what you gotta do to get happy with the idea till then. Class dismotherfuckingmissed."

"Balance."

I close the book I was reading and frown up at Mama Esther. "What?"

"Balance. Life and death is all about balance, Carlos.

We dead like to think we're so independent of the living, that we got our own thing going and those flesh-and-bone folks just get in the way. But all of our actions, even the petty stupidities we participate in, have repercussions in both our world and theirs. The universe is an echo chamber, and the echoes have no regard for that boundary between who's alive and who's not. We help them out; we mess with their lives; we pretend to ignore them, but they're a part of us. And they do the same."

I don't know where this sudden lecture came from, but I don't want to mess up her flow, so I just nod to show I'm listening.

"The Council thinks they're the regulators of that balance. That without their mighty soulcatchers, all would dissolve into chaos. And sure, there's some truth in it, but the living and the dead have found their own odd harmony since the beginning of time. The Council doesn't realize it's just another one of the universe's tools to maintain balance. One of many."

"Sounds about right."

"The ngks and whoever is working with them are trying to upset the balance."

"How you figure?"

"That's what the ngks do. That's the only reason you'd bring something so drastic into the equation. The tour guide you sliced on New Year's. The ngks. This character running around basements. I don't claim to know the details . . ."

"No one does."

"But if you ask me, someone's trying to bring upheaval to the balance of life and death."

"The balance of life and death, huh? Sounds like one of those existential novels about nothing."

Mama Esther half laughs and then looks concerned. "You worried about tonight, Carlos?"

"A little." Something's picking away at my consciousness and I can't put my finger on it.

"What's wrong?"

It's something she said. The Council's just another of the
universe's tools . . . one of many. "Ah!" I yell. "It's what
I've been meaning to ask you since the other day. You said
other people come here? Dead people. Non-Council dead
people?"

Esther nods. "Of course. Loads of people, Carlos. You
think the Council are the only . . . ?"

"No. I know there's tons of ghosts around. But ever see
anyone . . . like me?"

The big house ghost looks away. "Every once in a while."

"Recently?"

"I think of myself like a priest or a lawyer, Carlos. I don't
like to—"

"I know, Esther. I know what people look up in your
library is private, but this is about saving your house right
now. Not to mention all the rest of us. I need to know."

"I suppose since he's deeper than dead now, it doesn't
matter."

"Trevor!"

She nods sadly. "He was frantic."

"Frantic? Over what?"

"Wouldn't say. He was like you in that sense too." That
wry Mama Esther sense of humor. I fold my gut reaction
away for some other time. "Just searching and searching
like his life depended on it."

I feel an involuntary twinge of guilt and then shake it
off. "Any books in particular?"

"Old stuff. Sorcery. Forest people. Conjuring." She taps
the list off her big shining fingers. "Um . . . what else?
Little people."

"Shit. Like imps?"

"Imps, gnomes. All of that." She gestures distastefully at the air like she's flinging a little person off her hand. So Trevor was caught up with the naked cellar dweller. His research assistant, perhaps. A reluctant minion, as Baba Eddie put it.

"He ever mention who he was working with?"

"He had a sister, a halfie like him. Never met her though. And . . ."

"And?"

"Someone else."

"Who?"

"He only said the name one time, and I'm sure it was by mistake, barely even mentioned him out loud, in fact."

"Out loud . . ."

"It was all over him, Carlos. You couldn't miss it. Fear. Well, fear mixed with something else: a certain admiration almost, or an eagerness to please, better put. Like the guy was a messiah of some kind, some great prophet."

I control the urge to interrupt Mama Esther. When she's finished, she just looks at me, a challenge.

"The name?"

She sighs. "Sarco."

Sarco. It doesn't mean anything to me. I shrug and shake my head.

"I don't know either," Mama Esther says. "The name pops up here and there in some old tomes, but nothing useful. One of these archaic old souls that vanishes and reappears throughout history."

"Like an overgrown ngk. The research was for him?"

"Seemed like some of it was. But I couldn't tell how much. He was definitely following his own intuition for part of it."

For an uncomfortable moment, I see Trevor immersed in Mama Esther's library, poring over ancient tomes,

scribbling notes. This man was more like me than I want
to think about. A moment returns to me, unsolicited and
obnoxious: Trevor out on that chilly Park Slope street;
his eyes suddenly becoming sharp and focused, he looks
at me and sees me exactly for who and what I am.

He recognized me.

It's time. Let's go.

He wanted to show me what was going on. Maybe
wanted my advice. He knew what I was and he wanted to
bring me in. The whole stupid setup with the Brads and
David could've been a ruse to lure me in and then talk to
me about whatever the hell they were working on.

Or kill me. Or worse . . .

I wonder again if in some other version of this universe, one where I didn't take the Council so seriously,
Trevor and I would've been friends.

"Carlos?"

I shake off the thought. It's too awful. "Esther, why
didn't you tell us this before?"

Her shining bluish hue flashes toward crimson. "You
think you and the Council the only ones out there, Carlos?"

"No! Of course not . . ."

"I know things are tight right now. I know things've
spun out of control. But what I don't know is who to
trust." I've never seen Mama Esther's rage. Never known
her to be anything but overflowing with affection. Nothing I can say makes any sense, so I stay quiet. "Mama
Esther doesn't take sides. Not for the Council, not for the
free-swinging spirits out there. Not for halfies or fullies
or nobody. The dead want to come take shelter in these
stacks, revive their weary souls within the protection of
my warmth, that's what I can offer. But don't demand of
me that I pick sides . . . Don't do that."

"I wasn't. I mean . . . I didn't mean to."

Her whole giant frame sags. "I know, Carlos. I know. There's so much you don't understand. You can't. Hell, there's plenty I don't understand."

"Do you . . . know what's going to happen?" I'm kind of cringing while I say it, because I don't want her to get all fiery again, but instead she just sighs.

"No. I wish I did. I really do. I knew there was trouble brewing, but quite honestly, sometimes trouble can be a good thing. The world needs a little trouble to keep moving forward. Seems this trouble may have gone a little above and beyond that though."

"It does seem that way."

"Carlos!" Riley calls from downstairs. "Getchyo shit together! We movin' out!"

Fuck. I don't like any of this. Too much swirling through my head to focus on this fool's mission we're about to go on.

"I suppose," Mama Esther says wryly, "it just doesn't make much sense keeping a dead man's secrets anymore, and I know you're doing everything you can to deal with those creatures."

"We are, Mama Esther. We are."

"Here." The old ghost gestures to a pile of ancient books sitting on the floor. Post-it notes and scribbled-on scraps of paper stick out of the pages at unruly angles. "Trevor's stack. You can take them if you want." She's frowning at this breach in her own rules about privacy.

I load the books into my satchel. "Thanks." Doesn't seem like quite the right word, but it's all I got.

She gives me the saddest smile I've ever seen and then quickly turns away.

CHAPTER TWENTY-ONE

∞

It's worse. Like it knew we were coming. Or maybe each new ngk builds on the strength of the previous ones. The second certainly came in fiercer than the first. Whatever it is, I seriously doubt anyone's gonna make it seven minutes, let alone ten. Five would be impressive.

This building's a littler cleaner and better kept than the other two. There's a newly installed door-buzzer system and fresh doormats. But the noise, the feeling of fast-forward deterioration deep down inside, the utter degradation of being near that little screeching, panting monster . . . It's almost too much to bear as soon as we walk in.

"Jesus," Dro says, throwing his hands over his face as if that would do anything to relieve the feeling. "What the hell?"

"I know." Riley's playing the reluctant lieutenant, stifling his terror through gritted teeth. "Let's get this . . . the fuck . . . over with."

The ngk is in a shadowy corner of the basement, cackling and panting away on his little bike just like his brothers. Again I have to stifle the urge to draw and slice the damn thing into a million pieces.

"I gonna make a grab for the machine," Riley says.

"You two cover me." Better him than me. Dro and I draw
our blades, mine vividly steel and solid compared to
Dro's shimmering ghost blade. I don't even know what
we're preparing for, since we can't . . . whatever. The
screeching had stopped for a minute, but as Riley goes
in, it comes back strong, almost knocking me to my
knees. The ngk, ever focused, keeps its squinty little eyes
straight ahead as it pants and chuckles to itself on that
stupid stationary bike. Little patches of hair dot its pale
shriveled body like weeds on a vacant lot. I steady myself
and watch out the corner of my eye as Riley reaches for
the bike. The shriek gets noticeably worse as he closes
in. I check the stairs, squinting through the pain to make
sure no one's coming.

When Riley gasps, I swing back around, blade poised
to strike. There's no one to strike at though. Riley's skid-
ded away from the ngk, shaking his hand like he wants
to fling it into a corner. "Fuck! The thing burned me!"

"You okay?" Dro yells.

"I think so," Riley says. Then he collapses. He's lying
there, flickering and fading like ghosts do right before
they cease to be. I go to grab him, but Dro gets there first.
Only instead of getting Riley, he lunges at the little grinning creature in the corner. I open my mouth, but the
words haven't come out by the time Dro brings his sword
down full force on the ngk, slicing a clean, maroon lac-
eration into the thing's head.

For maybe a half second, nothing happens.

We both just stand there, staring like idiots at the ngk as
its dark blood pours freely from the brand-new gaping
mouth Dro made in its forehead. Then it falls over itself
like a sack of potatoes that just realized it was an inani-
mate object. There's a moment of peace; the screeching
stopped the second Dro's blade hit its mark. Relief flushes

through me. I'm reaching down to grab Riley, who's looking slightly better, when the screeching returns in force. Not only is it twenty times worse, but it's coming from all around us. Carrying Riley's trembling, barely there form, I turn and stumble toward the stairs. It takes all my inner strength not to come crashing down and give up, but I can't. There's no Moishe to call nine-one-one this time, and Riley's unconscious ass is depending on me.

I'd figured Dro was right behind me, but then I hear him scream. At least six ngks are on him. I have no idea how they moved so fast or where they came from. All I know is, they're swarming over Dro's translucent body like maggots on meat. I take a weary step toward him, almost pass out, and then realize it's useless anyway. What am I gonna do—slice them and get myself eaten too? If that's what they're doing. I see one reach a tiny hand *into* his ghost flesh and twizzle its fingers around. Dro screams in agony, but I can barely hear it beneath the ngk shrieks. And then he's quiet. Because he's gone. The ngks finish whatever sick cleanup ritual they have and then turn their hungry eyes to me.

And I'm gone. I don't know if I've ever moved so fast in my entire short, weird half-life. The stairs are a blur beneath my uneven legs. The door slams behind me. I'm through the hallway out onto the street, Riley a quivering pressure against my back. I'm surprised I didn't go straight through the glass windowpane on the way out. I keep going, tearing around the corner in an oblivious frenzy, up the block, 'round another corner, and then straight on into the night.

I pause at Eastern Parkway, where cars are still bustling back and forth. It's a comfortingly large thruway. There's trees, big apartment buildings. A little up the way, I can see the Brooklyn Museum, brightly lit on this

cold, cold night. I collapse on one of the benches lining
the shadowy jogging path beside the service road. Every
breath reignites the fire into my chest. Riley lies flickering beside me: still there but only barely. He doesn't have
much left in him.

There's only one place I know where he'll be sure to
heal, and unfortunately, it's back in the direction I came
from. I exhale a frosty curse into the winter night, hoist
Riley on my shoulder, and slump back down Franklin
Avenue toward Mama Esther's.

PART TWO

At the crossroads
where her spirit shocks
she comes sweeping
through the night,
spirits and hounds
baying behind her.
her wings keep me warm.
three jackals
watch with me.

    I am the gate
  demons and vanquished gods invade
then pass into this world to get to you.

—Gloria Anzaldúa

"Canción de la diosa de la noche"

CHAPTER TWENTY-TWO

❦

After the sounds of the city night faded to ambience, the predawn creaks and cracks of this old house kept me company. Some plaster would crackle above me and to the left; then a few dozen seconds would slip by and a clack would sound out across the room. I used to trace imaginary lines between each tiny beat, draw constellations in my head from pop to clank. Then an old engine somewhere would sigh to life, fans spinning, belts whirring past. Its entrance was always a grand pronouncement, but in a few minutes it would blend with the scattered night orchestra.

The best, though, my all-time favorite, was when someone in the adjacent building would take a shower. The piping was connected to Mama Esther's, so as soon as they turned on the faucet, you'd hear the torrent of water race up one wall, across the ceiling, down another side, and then rush off toward the neighbor's. You could imagine the water joyously swooping across the building, up and down pipes and finally exploding out of someone's silver faucet. I thought about how the building was very like a living thing, how a whole system of ticks and tocks and whirring sounds and circulating fluids kept it all in working order, flushed out the garbage, spread life through the pipes. The clicks and clacks and murmuring rush of water became a song, a call-and-response with my own slow-beating heart and the fluid rushing through my pipes, and the song was about life.

But now I'm too worried about Riley to fuck around with found-sound symphonies. Mama Esther plays her part, the old ghost, carrying on and dithering over Riley's depleting shadow. I play mine too, waving off her concern for me, slumping glumly in the corner while she works on him. I gaze on with dazed interest as those huge, see-through hands slide over my partner, working that ancient magic, pulsing life back into him.

And Dro. Dro is gone. I can't linger in that emptiness too long or it will swallow me.

At some point in the night, Mama Esther rouses me from a half-assed nap to send me on my way. "There's nothing else that you can do for him, Carlos. You already saved his life." A flicker of doubt in her old eyes: *provided he lives . . .*

And it's true. After she leaves, I just stand here in this room that I know so well and try to chart the odd progress of my life up till this point. It's mostly been a series of encounters with the dead, a few wild drunken nights, and many long walks across Brooklyn. And now the man who pulled my mostly dead ass off the street and brought me here to become whole again is on the brink. And all I can do is pace the room. "Go home, Carlos," Mama Esther had said. "Rest yourself. You've had a long and terrible night."

She was right, of course, but I don't go home. I've had a long and terrible night. Home means nothing to me. I have no interest in wallowing, and I know Herodotus and the poets will never eclipse the image of Dro falling to the ngk swarm. And then the ngk swarm turning to me as one, those myriad hungry eyes glaring through the darkness of the basement.

No.

Home is not the place for me. My mind knows where it wants to go, but I let my feet carry me on their own. It's easier that way, not allowing the conscious desire to surface. Do what you have to do, feet, and soon we're ambling through the park, and the thousand late-night spirits and birds howl their creature songs and the songs mingle with my crooked heart and its off-tempo scampering, my swirling fears and the regrets and wonders, my aching head. I'm just a park spirit too, at the end of the day. Housed in this crooked body with its crooked heart, off-tempo gait, and deathlike swagger. But inside, I'm just a ghost like the rest of them. Don't be fooled.

It's so dark here. I'm sure I'm a holy terror to any late-night sojourner, this limping half phantom fleeing from a long and terrible night into the arms of some unknown disaster. Fuck. I haven't even drunk anything and my mind's moving too fast for its own good. I forsake the path for those blessed with the full breath of life and trundle through the underbrush, upsetting a family of birds. And then I'm out in the sudden clutter of Flatbush and then I'm on Ocean Avenue and my finger's on the buzzer of her door and I'm slumped against the wall, waiting, trying not to think too hard.

"Carlos?"

She's in pajamas. A light. She's probably not really glowing—I just haven't seen anything that could make me smile in what seems like years but is really only hours. I find I don't know what to do with myself, how to carry this strange body. Fortunately, my face says it all. Sasha takes one look at me and opens the door. It's startling, how instantaneous her decision is. I see it flash across her face. It's not that she didn't think about it at all, but . . . she brings me inside, leads me to an elevator, down a hallway, into a cozy little dim one-bedroom. She helps me out of my jacket, collapses me into an easy chair that seems to have been waiting there just for me, and puts on some water to boil.

I'm doing everything I can not to look like a complete zombie when she comes back in the room. "Do you want to talk about it?" she says very softly. I have no words for what happened. And I'm not in a storytelling mood. And the more I say, the more likely I'll fuck up, and this night will come crashing around me even more than it already has. I shake my head. She nods and goes back in the kitchen to fuss with the tea.

"Milk and sugar?"

"Uh-uh."

She returns with two steaming mugs. "I hope peppermint's okay. It's all I got." She's wearing flowy pajama pants and a tank top. You can just make out the shadow of her nipples through the shirt. Her clavicles slide beneath the straps and meet at her neck, where the tiny shadows of her jugular veins triangle up and away toward her ears. I stand and take the teas out of her hands. She reads my expression and, with the slightest of smiles, says: "No." I give one of the teas back to her and sit.

"You can show up at some ridiculous hour of the morning with death etched across your face and I'll lend you my couch. I don't even know why I trust you that much, but I do. But don't overplay your hand, Carlos."

"Fair enough." I'm elated just to be here and not in some delirium of sorrow. I sip at the tea, which is pretty bland, and allow contentment to displace confusion. I don't know how we settled into a conversation, but we did. She knew I was lost and took the initiative, talking about the park and how different it was at various hours of the day. I was quiet at first, but she ignored it like a pro. We stick to larger universal topics—the smell of coffee, waking-up routines, and soon it feels natural, like what normal people do. Our eyes say plenty more, but soon even all that gets lost in the winding conversation. And then I find I'm fading; the night with all its longness and terriblosity, has caught up to me. I'd've been perfectly happy sliding into unconsciousness on this comfortable-ass easy chair, but instead Sasha lays me down on the couch—me mumbling total nonsense like an old man and her cooing and shushing me, covering me with blankets till everything becomes dim, and then there's nothing at all.

CHAPTER TWENTY-THREE

〰️

It's snowing when I wake up. I have no idea what time it is, a few hours from dawn maybe. The heater's clanging incessantly like some angry troll got trapped in there on the way to his cave. Sasha is apparently quite the movie buff; stacks and stacks of videotapes and DVDs crowd around her television like a fragile entourage. Besides that, you've got your standard van Gogh coffee shop painting, a portrait of Frederick Douglass looking surly, a few dangly plants and some framed photos that might very well be the same sample ones they use in picture frames all over the place. It's a nice spot, altogether, and seems to be keeping my demons at bay.

Something moves in the corner of my eye. She's standing in the doorway to her bedroom, watching me. I have no idea how long she's been there, but what's important is she's still wearing those flowy pants that look like they could be gone with very little effort, and her nipples are still insinuating themselves through that tank top. That's what's important to me anyway. Her mouth is frowning, but somehow I can tell she's smiling in some deeper place. Her eyes meet mine and she nods her head. It's the smallest of gestures: Point Zero. I send up a brief silent prayer

of thanks to whatever omniscient force has guided my
life to this point and a quick silent shout-out to Riley for
a speedy recovery, my dear brother, and then I stand, let
the sleep slide off me as I rise out of the covers, and follow her into the room.

When I was lying completely still in that room in Mama
Esther's house, life tiptoeing back into my body, I heard
the flutterings of a coupling. Through all that back talk
and smack talk, all the tiny and gigantic legends that
unraveled, there was one that you could pick out above
the rest. A singular, crisp ray of emotion: unmistakable.
It was a simple thing—two teenagers. A young dark-
skinned girl with big eyes and a Dominican kid, all shiny
curls on his head and baggy pants. The other kids'd be
rollicking through the motions and these two would join
the fun, but there was something else going on. I don't
think it was just me who could sense it; the other young'uns
picked up on all that electricity too, with that unerring
adolescent radar they have.
   He lived in Bushwick, a few neighborhoods over, but
they went to the same school and he started showing up on
the block and fell in well with the other kids. You could tell
he wanted her by his quietness and his stupid boy teasing.
In my room, I imagined her shy smile as she punched his
arm for saying something stupid and him contorting with
joy at the attention. I couldn't tell you what separated it
from any of the other flirtations that played out up and
down the block that summer. It was just something you
could taste in the air whenever they got within a block of
each other. It was easy: a force greater than either of them
wanted that union to happen, and the world sent that great
magician of the inevitable, gravity, to make it so. Once

gravity enters the picture, all bets are off. Those kids were hurtling toward each other like two asteroids that traveled bajillions of light-years just to cross paths at that one fatal instant. Who knows what endless cause and effects spiral out of those gravity-inflicted collisions? There's something different about them though. They burn harder, and the fallout can shake the whole city on its foundation.

The day they finally did it—a rainy afternoon toward the end of summer—the shit woke me up from one of those deep-as-an-abyss type naps. They were quiet; don't get me wrong. I think her old grandma was only a few rooms away in her rocking chair, so they had to keep it down. But the vibrations. You could feel 'em tumbling through the air like tsunami after tsunami, a relentless, joyful series of explosions that momentarily collapsed the natural order of things. A giddy kind of chaos burned among the exploding molecules around me. I knew it was happening and smiled. I'm sure even Grandma's dreams simmered with those colliding, gravity-stricken teenagers. I'm sure she woke up smiling and confused, hopefully none the wiser.

The drumbeat kept up all through the afternoon—I was impressed, actually—and simmered into a gentle caress as night fell. The whole block burned with it, pulsed with it, and when the lights came on to fight off the coming dark, they glowed brighter for the ferocity of that loving, that true sheet-grabbing throb that emanated from the sweat-soaked room on the third floor.

Gravity.

Outside, the snow keeps falling. I take the back of Sasha's neck in my hand and put our faces together. The sky is dark blue and flecked with white. I'll move slow, because

I feel the momentum as it wraps around her. The promise of all that's about to come slides up her legs, weakens her knees, caresses her thighs, and really—there's no rush.

We have arrived.

My other hand is on her cheek; her arms reach up, encircle my neck. She brings her face up to mine, her lips up to mine. Her skin is cool; my skin is cool. The place where our lips meet is on fire. I'm taller than her and broad where she's slender, but still: we mirror. The word *finally* swims through my mind, and then our tongues find each other and do battle and there are no more words. Her hips find mine. I'm rock-hard and let her know with a nudge. Her legs spread and I lift her up into the air, wrap her around me.

The snow's in no hurry. It'll always get where it's going. When it moves fast, clamoring over itself to cascade in all those frantic rivulets, it's not rushing, just following the pattern the wind has set for it. Teasing gravity, and gravity plays along because they both know, in the end, gravity always wins. Her skin is off-brown against white sheets as she lies back and slides easily out of her clothes. My arms are on either side of her; I'm a shelter above her. I press forward against her and stop, allowing the gravity to collect around us, the sheer, impossible joy of standing on that precipice, her juices flowing, inviting me inside. I wait for her to moan with blissful impatience and then inch forward, and she plays along because we both know, in the end, gravity always wins.

"You want to hear a song?"

I do, but I'm still groggy and delicious-feeling from those two rapid-fire orgasms that blew through my body like nuclear explosions. I rub my eyes and say, "Yes, please." She grins, excited like a little kid, and shuffles out of the blankets, reaching across me to the stereo beside her bed. It's one of those old-fashioned deals with a record player on top and a million buttons. The bedside table actually is one of the speakers, I realize. It's huge.

A sad piano progression chimes out over some rumbling bass notes. It's got an old barroom blues feel, all jangly and almost dissonant, and then the drummer kicks in with a modern march, smooth but insistent, and the whole thing comes together: a rickety old soldier stumbling through the rain. It's just a pretty song until the singer starts. Then something happens. I don't know shit about music, so I couldn't tell you if it's the key she's singing in, or the way her voice slides in between the notes like she's flirting with them, or just the simple truth of her sorrow, coming straight out of her mouth, but whatever it is, the song lays me down and eases all my blissfully aching muscles. It creeps inside my heart, circulates into my bloodstream.

"You like it?"

Apparently I do, because I'm smiling pretty hard and I don't really do that a lot. "What is it?"

She shrugs. "I dunno. Trevor brought it home one time, something he dug up in some archival library when he was researching some shit."

"There's no label on the tape or nothing?"

"It's hand-written. Just says 'PLEASE' in all caps."

"That's kinda sad."

"Or beautiful."

"Both."

Then we shut up, because the woman's voice hits this particular note that is everything and just hangs there while the band trundles their cool blues beneath her. You can tell they all know they're making magic, got that

divine swagger like nothing matters but each single note
as they play it and then the phrase and how they all wind
together and become one.

Halfway through the song, the woman drops out and a
trumpet takes over. Sasha puts her head on my chest, and
I can feel my slow heartbeat against her face. The trumpet blurts out a note, stops, blurts another, swings into a
melody something like what the woman was singing and
then takes off into a wild, burgeoning improvisation that
leaves me breathless. "Damn," I whisper.

"Right?"

"Mm-hmm."

The woman comes back, resanctifying the space, and
Sasha's moving against me. I'm hard again, and I know if
I just lie here, her slowly gyrating body will find what it's
looking for.

CHAPTER TWENTY-FOUR

The Council will blast one of their stupid messages through my head any second now. I can feel the vibrations of imminent ignorance like an oncoming freight train. Sasha smiles in the blissed-out sleep of the fully fucked, I notice with satisfaction, and I'm enjoying a few quiet moments before my mind and unartful employers catch up to me. I slip out of bed so as not to pervert the peaceful air with their bullshit, and the transmission comes as I'm walking into the kitchen.

"New York Council of the Dead to Agent Delacruz. Your presence is required immediately at Council Headquarters for a hearing in regard to yesterday's events, the extinguishing of a Council agent and the injuring of a soulcatcher prime during the course of duty. Please respond posthaste to room 849 in the headquarters main offices immediately."

Respond posthaste immediately? Dickheads.

"End transmission."

She wakes up while I'm sliding my belt on; blesses me with a groggy smile as she watches me lace up my boots.

I take her face in my hands and kiss it, once on the lips,
once on the forehead, once on each cheek. A rumbling
inside lets me know that if I linger any longer, I'll be here
all day, all week probably; so I stand, nod, and stroll out
the door into the snow-covered morning.

Bureaucracy's got its own special language. It's trifling,
of course, the lowest order of poetry, and manages to divest
words of all meaning and still weigh them down with extra
banality. After a while, you get good at it. Riley's reached
legendary status the way he spits that shit out like it's
scripted in him. Makes it look so easy.

I'm not there yet.

I still gotta bounce my mind back and forth along the
highways of implications that burst out of each sentence,
so my rhythm's off and I come a little clunky with it. But
I'm getting better.

In a chilly, mostly dark room up in some corner of the
Council's industrial warehouse headquarters in Sunset
Park, I lay down the story in the best bureaucracy-talk I
can muster. The committee is a semicircle of shrouds
around me, indistinct in the foggy gloom. Somewhere,
the ever-watchful eyes of at least one of the seven ignoble
chairmen must be watching us.

"At this point in time, I withdrew from the premises
with Agent Washington."

"Why," an icy voice cuts me off, "Agent Delacruz, did
you not make an attempt to intervene on behalf of Agent
Arroyo?"

You see that? Poetry. The most overindulgent, self-
important use of language ever. I stifle a curse-out and
then say, "The situation with Agent Arroyo had deterio-

rated beyond any point where intervention would have been . . . useful."

Where's Riley when I need him? The motherfucker has a way with words. I can only imagine how he knocked 'em out after the last basement debacle. But Riley's unconscious somewhere, recovering from the ngk poison. And I'm floundering.

"And by that you mean?"

"The ngks had already dealt mortal injuries on Agent Arroyo, and he was, by my estimation, in a state of Deeper Death. Unsalvageable." I cringe at the word because it makes Dro into an object that must be thrown away.

"By your estimation." I sense precise intonations being recorded forever in that endless ghost memory.

"Also, I had no idea what possible intervention I could've performed to release Agent Arroyo from the ngks, seeing as his own assault on one of them was the inciting incident that led to the attack." Now I sound like I'm blaming him for his own death. I want to get out of here so badly it hurts.

An uneasy silence follows my words. Then the voice says, "I see. Continue."

"Upon withdrawal from the scene, I absconded to what I deemed to be safer territory, namely Eastern Parkway on the corner of Franklin Avenue."

"At this point you were with Agent Washington?"

"Correct. I was carrying him, actually."

"He was unconscious?"

"Honestly . . ." I take a breath and then start again with less growl. "I wasn't able to determine Agent Washington's level of consciousness because I was too busy"—*not getting my ass murdered*—"absconding."

Fuck.

"I see."

"When I paused at the specified intersection, I then had time to check on my superior and discovered that he was in dire need of medical attention, having sustained an unknown injury from his contact with the ngk machinery." *Which was all y'all's brilliant idea, jackasses.*

The shroud in the middle of the semicircle steps forward, and for the first time I can make out his features: a hyperaggressive chin, sharp eyebrows, and the fakest of smiles. It's Chairman Botus, the only one of the Ignoble Seven High Council chairmen to ever let his identity be known. I hate that grin he's wearing like a cheap suit after a bad date, and I hate that he's towering over me, immersed in shadows. "And here, Agent Delacruz, is where things get murky, so to speak."

"Hardly," I say. I'm doing everything not to take the bait, but the whole conversation is so infuriating.

"Ah. Do explain." Botus leans forward like he really wants to hear what I have to say.

"Agent Washington's condition was such that, as I stated"—*easy Carlos, easy*—"he required immediate medical attention. So I . . ."

"So you brought an unconscious agent of the Council to the safe house of a non-Council, unregulated entity."

"Esther is . . ."

"And *left* him there."

"I . . ."

"Did you, Agent Delacruz, file a report with the Council in regard to the incident?"

I hate being interrupted. "I left a message."

"Excuse me?"

"I don't have two-way telepathy, Chairman, because I'm not fully dead."

Botus widens his smile. "Of course."

"So the Council has generously set up a phone line that I report to, and I left the information on the machine." I wonder if the sarcasm is gushingly obvious. Then I decide I don't really care either way.

A moment passes. Botus is probably confirming this information with some other party.

"And did you know, Agent Delacruz, that this house ghost in question—"

"Esther."

"—has been known to harbor and give aid to various non-Council entities?"

"Esther is the most proficient ghost healer I know. She personally attended to—"

"That wasn't the question."

I let a few seconds slip past. "The Council's healing services would not have been administered in a timely enough fashion, giving the circumsta—"

"Also not the question, Agent Delacruz. The question was, did you know—"

"That Esther had non-Council ghosts up in her library sometimes? I did know that, yes. Found that out that very night, in fact."

My face burns with irritation. I want to lunge forward and throttle this ridiculous Botus person. Instead I stay quiet while some more murmured conferences go on around me.

"Interesting," Botus finally says, although at this point it's not at all clear what he's referring to. "Your case will be reviewed by the committee. Your complicity has been useful in our understanding of the situation, Agent Dela-cruz."

Cock. Time grumbles along like a limping beggar as I

wait in a side room. Suddenly, I'm not so good at patience anymore. I can't stop pacing, and the feeling that nothing's happening rankles my brain. After a grueling hour, they beckon me back in and explain that they're issuing me a verbal admonition for breach of protocol and will be keeping a sharp eye on me. They add, almost reluctantly, that I'm receiving official commendation for saving the life of a superior officer, and that I'll be taking over as lead agent on the case. None of it means anything, of course. It's all empty words and paperwork. I'm just glad to be out of that damn place.

I leave in a cloud of vague humiliation. I'd hoped, by the end, to at least storm out after some righteous speech. Or maybe go all stony and silent as the frustrated committee buffeted me helplessly with their idiotic questions. I wanted some tiny triumph amid all that unseemliness. Instead, it just sputtered out and I felt probed and abused and mostly empty.

Riley doesn't look so hot. It could be worse, given what he's been through, but still . . . it's hard to watch my friend flickering on the edge of existence. He's in a tidy little room the Council has set aside for injured ghosts—just a cot and whitewashed walls and Riley, all splayed out and muttering to himself. His eyes are closed. The room is charged with some kind of ghost-healing shit the Council uses, something like a hyperbaric chamber for the dead. The shit's relaxing, whatever it is; as soon as I walk in, a general easiness enters me, washes out all the lingering irritation from my hearing. Underneath that, though, there is a sadness, and the happy healing shit can't even touch that sadness; it's not going anywhere.

I don't think he even registers me walking in. I crouch against the wall near his cot and put my hand on his shoulder. It's so barely there I almost press right through him and touch the sheets. Riley makes a huffy noise and rolls over, eyes still shut.

CHAPTER TWENTY-FIVE

It stopped snowing. The early-afternoon sky is pale with splotches of gray. Folks walk around huddled up into themselves, scurrying from place to place before the hypothermia sets in. It's practically April, and this is some bullshit.

I hole up in one of those twenty-four-hour Mexican bakeries to take stock of the situation. A happy little round guy with spiky hair takes my order, bows graciously, and disappears into the back. An accordion-driven hard love ballad *oompah-oompah*s out of the speakers, but I barely notice it; I'm too busy trying to see past the emotional Drano of the last two hours and get a grip on what's really going on.

I hadn't really let myself deal too deeply with the thought of Dro being gone. First it was the initial terror of everything, then the dire need to *not* think about it as I escaped into Sasha's arms, and then the hearing. Now the reality of it clamors around me; I can't help but think about that last longing glimpse of his family that I interrupted.

The coffee's not bad. Mexicans don't get all extra about it like most island Latinos do, but they can make a fairly serious cup when they're in the mood. I find a smile for the portly waiter, and he seems pleased with himself. At the only other table in the place, an ancient mustachioed man in a Yankees cap plays Uno against an eight-year-old girl with pigtails. A couple day laborers in big vests and faded jeans trade stories at the counter.

I wonder if Riley's gonna be okay. I wonder who Sasha really is, what secrets she's tucked away inside herself. Then my thoughts glide reluctantly over my own secrets. Which ones slip out when I'm not paying attention, hanging in the air waiting to unravel?

Trevor.

If I hadn't killed him, would everything be different? I've dreamed about that moment—the blade leaving my hand, that awful squish as it found its mark—more times than I can count. What, besides the nefarious Council bureaucracy, gave me the authority to so cavalierly snatch away that man's life? I try again to imagine a scenario where Trevor and I just have a pleasant chat instead of me slaying him. The truth is, I know he's wrapped up in this ngk mess, and I know he was about to vanish into Hell's impossible haze.

I squint into my coffee.

There was no other way. The Council sent me to do a job and I did it. I wonder if it really is that simple for some soulcatchers.

The question lingers.

I would've been able to tell Sasha everything.

My heart actually lurches at the thought, and suddenly I'm irretrievably sad. It's one thing to talk slippery to the Council—it's a given; a call-and-response game that keeps everybody grumpy but mostly above water. But to have to store away my whole strange existence from this woman who has swept into my life so gracefully and trusted her body with mine—that's another story. Even poor Riley doesn't know the full extent of what's going on with me. And now Dro's gone. That recurring thought piles another heavy rock onto my heart.

No one knows what's really going on with me. Not a soul. I only barely understand it myself, and my vision seems to get blurrier by the minute. To top it off, the first however many years of my life are gone, a total void. Without warning, this matters. My whole life. I don't even know how old I am. What century I came from. How long I was dead. Nothing. I'm empty. Empty of history, of genealogy. Devoid of family. An utter abbreviation of a person.

"Buen provecho," the waiter says, putting a massive pork sandwich on the table. Besides the pig, there's every vegetable possible smashed in there. It's delicious. The eight-year-old giggles every time her abuelo picks up a card. Her laughter rises to a joyous cackle and she crows, "Uno!" The old man fusses with his mustache, furrows his brow, and then picks a card. And then another. "Chingada madre," he mutters as the laughter continues unabated across the table. "Mierda." Finally, he puts down one with a sigh and the girl gets real serious, scrunches up her face, and draws a card, then slams it down, yells, "Uno!" again, and resumes laughing.

A hipster, all skinny jeans and big glasses, pokes his head in, tries to ask directions to the train station, and leaves disappointed. The Council, in their infinite smugness, has put me in charge of this investigation. I put some more sandwich in me. Without Riley to bounce my ideas off of, I'm not sure how far I'll get. No, that's not it. I'll untangle this shit, but I'm not sure I'll make it out the other end intact. And I doubt it'll lift me out of this preposterous mood.

Another ranchera blasts across the bakery. It's a swirl of horns and pounding bass drums, somehow both mournful

and ecstatic. Also, slightly absurdly loud. The ngks are
effectively undefeatable. If this tall hairy fellow's somehow the source of their sudden appearance, dealing with
him might be the only way to get them out of the equation. But the bastard just pulled my ghost-killing blade
out of his gut with barely a flinch.

The tangled equation resolves itself into the simple question of how. Perhaps a trap of some kind. The basic laws of
physics still seemed to apply to this creature. Didn't see
him walking through walls or flying. He was a solid body,
a halfie at the deadest. Certainly powerful in whatever old
sorcery he was up to, but not undefeatable. No one's undefeatable. I might just have to work out some cleverness.
What worries me most, though, is time. Now that all these
new ngks have scuttled out of the woodworks, there's no
telling how fast the infestation will progress. The Council
has soulcatchers out there, stalking up and down Franklin
Avenue with their sharp eyes out, but really, what are they
going to do? Alert me. And then we can all sit and brood
about it more.

I killed my one lead. Slept with my other. At this point,
all I got is whatever trail of Post-it notes Trevor left behind
at the library.

The driving ranchera grinds to a halt just as the little girl
finally defeats her grandpa and erupts into giggling again.
He shuffles the deck and deals, sighing heavily through
his mustache.

CHAPTER TWENTY-SIX

Riley found me on Mama Esther's stoop one afternoon during my recovery. I'd been alive again for a few weeks at this point and was getting some sense of my body back. I could walk around and talk to people without sounding like a total moron. I was beginning to get a feel for things, understand my own strange powers, and grow into myself.

Riley looked me over for a few seconds. "How you feel, Cee?"

I stretched my arms out and rolled my head around, cracking my still-achy joints. "I feel good. How you feel?"

"I always feel good, man. I'm dead."

"Right."

"Let's go upstairs. I want to talk to you about something."

I could already feel it then, the urge to hunt. The pulsing inside me that would start up at any old time and take over. I was still physically diminished, could barely move my bad leg at all at that point, but it was like I could see a fiery image of what I would one day do, a woulda-been version of myself tearing loose from this somewhat use-less body and launching gleefully into the night. That me, the hunter, would stop momentarily and take in all the wild, churning signs and hints that the city had to offer. He would sniff the air, feel the breeze on his face, and understand all the stories and implications of each tiny detail, each swirling plastic bag and scattering rat. The universe became an ecstatic puzzle to this hunter-me, a magnificent path fingerprinted across the night to some abstract moment of glory: the capture.

I'd been hungering like that for a few weeks. And then Riley explained what exactly the Council had in mind for me, and it sounded like an answer to my prayers. "It's a bureaucratic disaster, Carlos," he warned me when he saw that thirst in my eyes. "I'm telling you now so you don't get to act surprised later. It's a whole fuckpot of politics and ego and all kindsa bullshit. But it's gainful employment and some measure of stability with an occa-sional sense of being useful and doing something right in the world. And you don't have many options open to you with your chilly gray half-dead ass. No offense."

I nodded, still thrilled.

"All right, then. Here." He held a walking stick out to me. It was mahogany and elegant without being bougie. I reached for it. "Wait." He pulled the handle up and a shiny silver blade appeared, glowing gently. My eyes got wide. "It'll fuck up a living person too, but the steel's sanctified and specially designed to deal the Deeper Death to the already dead."

I nodded. I musta looked like an addict staring down a fix. Still, I willed my fingers not to grab for it again. Riley watched me carefully and then sheathed the blade back into the cane and placed it in my hands.

"When you're not such a disaster, I'll start showing you the ropes."

Most of these damn books are in languages I don't know. The one in English is the diary of some monk that went batshit in the sixteenth century. I skim the pages until I get to the parts where Trevor's scribbled-on Post-its get excited: "Wrath, borne unto me one miraculous and terrible night, now poisons my bosom with such a rage as I cannot describe." Splendid. I don't have time for this shit. "'Twas a time I remember not, but had to recatalog the events of my life as described in my own hand, through these many years, to retrace the arc of my own history." Now that I can simmer with. "A singular event, a single scrap of memory, is all I possess, and I suspect that without the guidance and support of my fellow Fathers of Christ, I would be lost, a heretic, exiled from myself even and cursed to wander like a Jew from town to town." Also unpleasantly resonant. "Still, I resign myself to these dark cloisters, like the suddenly empty recesses of my mind, and here I shall stay and dissipate in the waning years of my life. I suspect my end can't be far, for I am grown gray, deathlike in my countenance even as my energy and virility seem heightened with each passing day. Oh, Lord Father, help me to understand these cruel changes that have settled upon me!"

Another tormented halfie.

There's another book that Trevor seemed particularly Post-it happy with, but the damn guy went ahead and wrote his notes in Flemish, or whatever the hell language this is.

I pour a glass of orange juice and squint at the ancient

pages. Someone went through a lot of trouble to make this book ornate. Its swirling illuminations look like they've been encrusted with gold; each page reveals a whole new universe of vivid, monstrous illustrations. Here, right in the middle, is the part that obviously interested Trevor. His handwriting gets more frantic; things are underlined several times and there're explanation points all over the damn place.

The central motif is a black-robed figure on a horse. A monk kneels before him, his face all torqued with fear, mouth wide open as if begging for his life. Naked bodies lay scattered like fallen leaves around them. Their skin is pale, and most of them have been run through with spears, but all their eyes are wide open. Above them, the text wraps around a giant skull that levitates in the sky. I run my finger along the page, feel the thick texture of the paper, and trace a triangle from the top of the skull to each edge of the picture.

A wildly elegant border runs the perimeter. At first I think it's just ornate, golden vines snaking up a pillar. Then I notice something in the spiraling vegetation: an eye. I squint and get all close to the page. Then I almost fall backward in my chair. There's a fucking ngk in there. It's hiding in the damn foliage. I quickly scan the rest of the border and find at least six more of the little fuckers. Each one is mostly concealed; just their evil little faces peer out from behind leaves and branches.

I need to know what these damn words mean.

CHAPTER TWENTY-SEVEN

ⓖ∽ᎧᎨᎧ∽Ꭷ

ama Esther?"

"Hm?"

"You all right?"

A weighty pause. I wonder about all the different ghosts and near-ghosts that have passed through these walls, unloaded their troubles to this great mother spirit, got some sense of peace, and kept it moving. "I'm fine, Carlos."

"More lies."

"Perhaps. But what are you going to do about it?"

"I'm working on it now, but I need your help." I take out the massive book and lay it open to the illumination that Trevor was so interested in. Mama Esther looks it over without a word. "Can you translate it?"

She opens and closes her mouth, her eyes scanning the picture. Then she leafs a few pages forward and backward in the book. "It was written by a monk in the twelfth century. He's going on about death and the devil and all this for a little while . . ." She's a few pages back now, running her huge finger along the words. "'Oh take my soul, ye vast armies of the night, for I am unworthy of inhabiting this frail human flesh. I am but a meager spirit, a humble servant of the Lord,' et cetera, et cetera . . . and then . . ." She raises one eyebrow. "Blah blah blah, Christ Jesus, rejuvenate my tired soul, blah blah . . ." The other eyebrow arches up. "'The Darkness came over me on the same day I was overtaken by a stranger on the road. He was as one dead but still in a mortal skin. A wizard or warlock from the pits of Hell, I am sure. He's caused in me such a tremulous fear. I nearly collapsed before him as one before the altar does kneel. The stranger had no name and was clothed all in robes of black, torn and shredded and reeking of burned flesh. I know not from whence he came.' Blah blah blah, he invites the stranger into his house—smart—and . . ." She turns the page. "Whoop, big surprise—the guy puts him under a sorcery of some kind. And then . . . they do something that makes the giant skull appear. Not quite sure what. This whole page"—she points to the drawing with the ngks hiding in it—"is like a grocery list of sorts. 'A grounded spirit, long since known to reside in the sleeping chamber, the brethren infants, the stranger himself and I, the gatekeeper, now that he hath laid his cold hands upon me and made me a pillar of damnation. I shall play this role, for I am cursed.'"

"And then?"

Mama Esther flips to the next page, which just has a single sentence: "'Death is all I see.'"

"Damn."

"Mm-hmm."

We ponder the drawings for a minute. Then I say, "Well, clearly, the brethren infants are the ngks. We can agree on that, yes?"

Mama Esther thinks for a moment, then nods. "Would seem so, yes."

"And the stranger, let's say that's this other basement dweller."

"Fair enough."

"That leaves the bedchamber ghost and the monk himself."

"That's me."

"Who, the monk?"

"The grounded ghost," Mama Esther says. "That's what I am."

"What does that mean?"

She moves her mouth from side to side a few times, trying to figure out how to explain it to me. "I'm affixed to this building. It's part of me and I'm part of it. The building itself is me. I can't totally make sense of it to someone—no offense—but to someone in a flesh-and-blood body, because you guys have different ideas of space and boundaries than we do."

I wave a hand to tell her none taken.

"But you are around enough dead folks to get that we have some loose physical boundaries with things. I'm not just the spirit of one soul, but rather several powerful women from a few generations and families, combined into one."

"And they all lived in this house?"

"Or spent time here, yes."

I pause to let that settle in. I'd figured it was something like that, to be honest, but had never played out the thought all the way through. Mama Esther is a house ghost; that's all I really needed to know. "So you can't leave?"

"Not without taking the house with me."

"What I don't understand is, where's the grounded ghost in this picture? I see the ngks, the cursed monk, the stranger, the dead . . . Where's the grounded ghost?"

"There." Mama Esther points to the giant skull floating above everything. "That'd be me."

There's an uncomfortable pause. I'm tussling with the truth of how much a target Mama Esther is, and I'm pissed that it's taken this long to figure that out. "Wish you'd showed me this earlier," I say.

Then I feel like an asshole.

"Well, I didn't, Carlos. I already told you that's not how I do things. First of all, I had no idea that what that halfie had his nose in was gonna come back to bite me so."

"I know. I'm sorry."

"And second of all, I know neutrality is a myth, but I'm going to come as close as I can, even if it means pissing off certain foul elements upstairs at the Council."

"Botus."

"Mm-hmm."

"He mentioned you at the hearing today."

"I'm sure he did. They were none too happy when they came to get Riley. Apparently, the fact that I saved his life is of no consequence to them." Mama Esther rubs her face and then directs an angry gaze out the window.

"He's going to live?" I ask.

"If he does, it'll be because you got him here quickly and I did what I had to do."

"Thank you." It sounds lame, given everything that's going on, and she shrugs it off with a sigh.

"He knew about you, Carlos."

"Who, Trevor?"

"He thought maybe you could be some kind of . . . alternative? He was fascinated, entranced by Sarco, but terrified too. Especially right before he vanished. He wanted me to help him find you."

I rub my eyes. It's what I feared. The knowledge just sinks like a stone into my tired mind. "You didn't." I can't change what I've done. The only path is forward. And I don't know that means.

"Of course not, but I knew your paths would cross

soon enough. Who else would the Ignoble Seven send against a halfie?"

Someone's in my apartment. The atmosphere is all off, tainted with whatever vague vibrations the intruder let linger. I unsheathe my blade and creep forward, letting each foot settle gently on the floor, edging ahead inches at a time. The bathroom is clear. No one's in the living room. I put my cane ever so silently against the bedroom door and push.

Sasha stands there, looking about as distraught as I must've yesterday. There's no tear traces, just an over-whelming solemnness about her: slumped shoulders, face tightened, body tense like at any given moment she'll either pounce or shatter. We regard each other silently. My face tells her face I can see something's horribly wrong; she nods.

"Make yourself at home," I say quietly, opening the door for her to come out into the living room.

She semi-smiles. "I didn't touch anything. Didn't look at anything. I just needed to be somewhere. Besides my place." She walks past me, and I'm briefly put out of service by the rush of her scent and all the memories of last night that it carries.

"Nice place." She's looking around, and I'm suddenly self-conscious. It's not a mess, just oddly put together. There's a lot of exposed pipes and random furniture, the product of living in a somewhat renovated warehouse and shopping on a whim. Mostly though, there are books. It's like a mini version of Mama Esther's; bookcases line almost every wall, and the books themselves seem to topple out of them and gather in unruly clusters around the apartment. A wan smile passes briefly across her face as she takes in the view, and then it's gone.

"You want to talk about it?"

"Yes. No." She sighs. "Yes, I do actually."

"I don't have any tea. But I do have beer."

She smiles again, the sadness momentarily retreating from her eyes before crowding back in. "Such a dude. A beer would hit the spot, actually."

I pop the tops of two bottles and put one in front of her. "It's my brother," Sasha says, straining for evenness. "I'm pretty sure he's dead." She sighs. "All the way dead, that is."

CHAPTER TWENTY-EIGHT

T revor was working with . . . Maybe that's not the right word. He was working for this guy named Sarco. An old-time sorcerer." She looks at me intently for a second, reading how her first breach into supernatural territory is sitting. I nod at her to keep going. "Real shady character, if you ask me, but brilliant, unfortunately, and there's a certain"—she hesitates, searching for the word—"truth to him. To what he says. It's hard to explain, Carlos.

"He showed up more than a year ago, talking all kinds of what seemed like dementia at the time, both to me and Trevor. I pretty much brushed him off, but Trevor has a more curious, wide-open nature than I do. He heard Sarco out and pretty soon was doing work for him."

"Work?"

"Trevor was . . . is a historian. A morbid one, yes, but that comes with the territory of being . . . what we are. He's a master of digging up old sorceries and witchcraft, figuring out various incantations from the different realms of the dead. It's quite stunning when you get the filtered, nonboring parts recited over dinner and don't have to thumb through thousands of pages of drivel. But Trevor can sort through drivel like no one else out there. He's like a computer with it.

"We'd been running with a group of other folks like us." I look at her strangely. "You know, dead but alive. Inbetweeners." I nod. There's others. Folks like us. My whole body tingles with the thought.

"Go on."

"It was just an informal thing, a loose band of survivors, so to speak. That's what we called ourselves: Survivors. For obvious reasons. Anyway, I do work for them still, here and there, and at the time Trevor and I were both pretty heavily involved. It's supersecret, as you can imagine. A small, close-knit community, not necessarily harmonious, sometimes fraught with strife and bullshit, but still . . . a haven nonetheless.

"Sarco shows up one day talking big talk about the dead and the living and the space in between."

It doesn't have to be so far apart, Trevor had said. A quote perhaps. I keep it to myself.

"And people became somewhat enamored really. He does have a way of sweet-talking. We had our reservations—I still do—but Trevor went in headfirst, despite my cautioning him. He started unearthing all these old secret incantations and things for some project Sarco had him on. He'd tell me about it at first." She looks away, and for a second I see a sliver of memory slip through the barricade around her mind. It's the two of them, brother and sister, having breakfast early one spring morning. He's going on about some old file he dug up; she's looking skeptical.

Then it's gone; she's closed it all back away.

"Then . . . he started keeping quiet about it. I think Sarco had him on some real silent pact type of shit." I light up a Malagueña and hold one up toward her. She shakes her head.

"Coffee?"

"Please."

She pads into the kitchen behind me and I start washing out the steel cafetera.

"The more Trevor disappeared into himself and his research, the less comfortable I was with the whole thing. Finally, one day, he started talking about making a run of some kind. Whatever it was Sarco had him on was coming to a head. He was out all hours, sometimes gone for days. At first, my stomach twisted into knots each time. You have to understand, Trevor and I have been through everything together. He's the only person in the world who knows who I really am. We literally died together. Going our separate ways is one thing, but this . . . it was like Sarco was eating my brother whole right in front of my face and there was nothing I could do.

"The worst part was, he made some sense, from what I could gather. I mean, he wasn't totally insane. If he'd just been some fucking nut, I'da just taken care of him and Trevor woulda gotten over it, but . . . well, maybe you can understand this, Carlos: we live in between two worlds, not wholly part of one nor the other. Here comes this man, this force of nature, and he wants to do something radical to bring those two worlds crashing together. Something huge. A total breakdown of the borderline between the living and the dead. It's a terrible, beautiful thought. Galvanized the shit out of the Survivors. Tore us apart too. Infighting broke out pretty soon after Sarco showed up, mostly over the ideas he was talking about, and soon there was a faction and then we scattered."

She looks so sad. I want to wrap around her, but I know

the story needs to come out. The cafetera chortles out a
steady burst of steam. I click off the burner and let the
coffee settle before pouring it into two white cups. "Milk
and sugar?"

"Black and bitter, please."

I hand her the coffee. She breathes in the steam with a
smile and we return to the living room.

"I kept my eye on Trevor as long as I could. Followed
him to the Red Edge, where he was meeting with some
hipster kids. I just wanted to make sure he was safe,
but . . . of course he took it personally. Little sis trying to
play big sis. We argued and I backed off. He went out New
Year's Eve and has been gone ever since." She's stony
faced, holding back the ocean. I think she's done, but then
she says: "Sarco . . . came to me . . . a few days later."

"Oh?"

"He wanted me. To recruit me," she adds quickly. "To
the cause. I asked him where Trevor was and he said he
didn't know, that he'd been looking for him too. 'Scouring
the heavens and earth' actually, because Sarco can't say
anything plain. And he said he needed my help, that he
was so close to something. Sounded just on the edge of
that end-of-times hysteria but still somehow coherent. It's
so hard to explain, Carlos, the way that man is. He's got a
way about him, all at once repellant and charming. Not in
a sexy way, just . . . the way the truth can be intoxicating
after you've gone without for so long, you know?"

A painfully apt analogy. I nod.

"We were all there just trying to get by, struggling
through life in the intersection, and here comes the cat
with some big-ass ideas about life and death and yeah,
part of me is all ears even though there's a an even deeper
part that's horrified, that doesn't trust his ass at all whatsoever in any way, shape, or form."

She says it all so matter-of-factly, but she's plainly shaken.

I open my mouth and close it again. An epic saga sits on the edge of my tongue, and for a second the whole night seems to lean forward to see if I'll say it or not.

"You have your own stories, I know," Sasha says, "but what I wanted to tell you . . ." She stops and touches her lips like she's not sure whether she should let the words out. "The reason I came here tonight. I don't know how to explain it: after you left this morning, I . . . I understood, for the first time since January, that he's dead. I'd probably known all along, but I was trying so hard to fight it. Hoping some other truth would figure out a way to make sense. But I knew. I did. I just couldn't . . . face it.

"When you left, I lay there and felt so alive and so sad and so happy all at once, like someone had pulled the protective coating away from my heart and I was just *raw* for the first time in so long."

I must've made a face because she's smiling, putting her hand on my leg. "Not in a bad way, Carlos. I mean, yes, it hurts. I'm broken-hearted, and I don't think I've fully dealt with it at all. But in a way, maybe I was dealing with it all that time I was in denial, bit by bit. Who knows?

"But the reason I let you into my house. The . . . that night you showed up at the Red Edge, I was . . . I didn't know what to do. I'd been going there night after night, waiting for Trevor to show up. I'd stalked those stupid kids he'd met up with, all the way back to their stupid Clinton Hill apartments, and found no trace of him. I said no to Sarco that first night, but he kept reaching out to me, trying to bring me in, and that night I was just about to give up the ghost and go find him. I was . . . I was more angry than anything, at Trevor and whatever stupidity he'd gotten tangled in, at myself for considering jumping in after him, at Sarco, at the dead. Everything. The

Survivors are mostly scattered. Seemed like all that was
left for me to do was put in with Sarco and hope I could at
least find out what happened to my brother, if not get him
back."

I love and am terrified about where all this is going. I
sip some coffee and blank my face.

"I don't know who the fuck you are, Carlos, or where
the fuck you came from or why the fuck you walked into
the bar that night at that very moment when you did. But I
know that I had been asking, asking without even realizing, for God or the universe or someone to send me some
kind of reminder that there was life outside the stupid triangle of my missing brother, this wild sorcerer, and me.
Because that's all I've been able to be about for the past
couple months, and it's wearing me out. It really is.

"I woulda settled for a goddamn butterfly or something, you know just something small and momentary to
snap me out of it. But they sent me you, you ridiculous,
tall, beautiful man, cutting through the crowd of nobod-
ies at the Red Edge and sitting down at my table with a
glass of wine and a rum and Coke. I don't know where
all this is going, but I know you did something huge
without even meaning to." She moves closer to me; her
hand's on my leg. "And I know you held me in all the
right ways last night."

I'm hard as a rock.

"And I know you're like me in a lot more ways than
just the obvious one." I'm laying her back on the couch,
tearing her clothes off.

No, I'm not.

I'm letting her nearness wash over me, sinking into the
bliss of the moment. Letting go . . . "And I know I want
you . . ." She's hovering over me, levitating for all I know.
We're barely touching, but she's all around me, her face

millimeters from mine. ". . . inside me." My hands are on her shoulders, peeling away her blouse, sliding off her pants, she's lowering herself onto me. We're about to be one, about to once again . . .

"Carlos."

"Hm?"

"Stop thinking so hard and fuck me."

Gleefully, I comply.

CHAPTER TWENTY-NINE

revor stares at me. His eyes are soft, sleepy. We're in a mostly dark room; my heart beats heavy in my chest; tears streak my cheeks.

Trevor rubs a hand over his face. "What is it, Sash?" My screaming woke him up. Again.

I shake my head; a nightmare's tendrils still cling to me. Frozen faces, mouths open, reach out of the darkness. Trevor's always known how to be there for me. I know this instinctively more than anything else. In one of my few shards of memory, I had squeezed my little body into the back of our closet, lost in the forest of Mom's and Dad's long winter coats. Trevor squatted patiently outside, telling me stupid stories until I giggled and finally emerged, still teary eyed. Now he watches me for a few seconds and smiles, waits a beat, then asks, "You want to talk about it?"

I don't even have words. I'm just tired. My whole body shakes.

"You want some tea?"

"No." Voice gravelly; I try to push back the sound of irritation. He wants to help and, after all, I woke him up.

*But it feels like something's clawing up inside of me and
I have no strength to play nice.*

"Coffee?"

"No."

"Video games?"

*The smile opens across my face so fast I don't see it com-
ing. I hate video games. Trevor knows this. But he loves
them, and that mischievous chuckle of his has always been
contagious. It's one of the few things I remember from life.
A laugh powerful enough to survive the shredding of most
of my other memories.*

*I can't say no to that and even feel a glint of joy surface
as he scrambles to set up the game console. The blue
light of the screen throws his shadow back against the far
wall, and then he turns to me. His face is in darkness, but
I can still see his smile.*

I wake up dead.

I must be dead, because my blade has been shoved
through the right side of my abdomen and into the couch.
I'm literally stuck like a goddamn butterfly. And whatever life force I had is fading fast. I'm thinking it must be
a dream and then I remember my own dream, which was
Sasha's dream: a memory. Which means we both opened
while we slept.

And she must've had one of mine.

She knows about Trevor.

I gasp and then cringe as needles of pain dance up and
down my right side. Sasha walks into the room. She's not
holding anything in anymore. Rage dances a maniacal
circle around her head. She doesn't have to speak for me to
understand that she saw everything while I slept. Everything.

I groan, and pain radiates along my midsection. She's putting on her jacket, moving toward the door. There are words trying to come out of me, but even breathing feels like it tears the wound deeper. Nothing leaves my mouth but a cruel gurgling sound.

Sasha opens the door and someone's standing in the hallway. Someone tall, with long greasy hair. At first she looks terrified; then she nods at him and shoots me a glare that is two parts rage and one part regret.

And then she's gone.

The man that I watched cut open Moishe's head strides up to the couch and smiles down at me with long, rotting teeth.

"Hello, Sarco," I say.

"Hello, my son."

CHAPTER THIRTY

❦

et away from me." It doesn't sound very convincing coming from a man with a shard of steel in his gut, but it's all I got. Some supernatural entity types really respond well to basic instructions.

Not Sarco.

"They named you Carlos Delacruz. How interesting."

I squint at him, partially through the pain but also because it's such a cryptic and absurd thing to say. Yes, they named me Carlos. The fuck? "They named you Sarco."

He laughs, a hoarse and humorless gargle. "One of many names I'm known by, yes."

"What's so interesting about my name?"

"Who gave it to you?"

Ugh. I don't feel like playing twenty fucking questions with this junky while I'm all speared up. "I don't know, man. Riley, I guess."

He just nods, smirking.

Great. Now what? I try to relax into the moment. There is, after all, not a single goddamn motherfucking thing I can do to make my situation any better. But getting even remotely comfortable is out of the question. Sarco rolls within a sour cloud of dread. I can feel it all over my body like it's some contagion; the feeling grows as he gets closer. My muscles tighten involuntarily, and all my damn hairs stand tall. Everything inside me screams to run, rebelling against the obvious physical impediments. *Just fucking go,* my body begs me. *Blade in your gut be damned. Just go.*

"Stop fighting it."

"What?"

The man is full of surprising and random things to say; I'll give him that.

"Stop fighting. That feeling you have, it's not me; it's you."

I'm forced to squint at him again, because I don't know what else to say. I haven't quite worked up the nerve to be as rude as I feel like being, so instead I just make faces and pant. I'm pretty sure the blade has blocked off whatever major blood vessel it sliced. From what I can tell, I'm not actively bleeding, but I suspect that breathing slightly wrong or, God forbid, chuckling, would jostle it just so and lead to instant exsanguination. Which might be better than whatever Sarco has planned for me, but still . . . I'd like to live.

"I don't . . . understand what . . . the fuck . . . you're talking about, Sarco."

He flashes that toothy smile, and I seriously consider dislodging the blade and opting for the quick out. "That horrible feeling you have when I come near."

"What about it?"

"It's your resistance. Your fear, Carlos."

"I'm not afraid." I even manage to say it with a steady voice.

He laughs again. "Your body is. And you're in shock. Concentrate on calming down your body. I'm not going to hurt you. You may not believe me, but it would help you stop shivering if you did."

I am shivering, dammit, but I figured that was from the stab wound more than anything else. I take a deep, very careful breath and let it out. I believe he's not going to hurt me, not yet anyway, for the simple fact that he's already had plenty of opportunity. Surely down the road, I'm in for some torture, but for now, I'm probably relatively safe. Also, cringeworthy though it is, he's right: allowing the wretchedness to rule me is not helping. Another deep breath and I'm somewhat calmer.

"There," Sarco says in a chillingly soothing voice. "That's better."

I shake my head, very carefully, because nothing's really better. I'm just more prepped for whatever nefarious nastiness he has planned. Fine, so be it.

"Relax, Carlos. I have a proposal for you. Very simple. Very easy. I need your help."

"Seeing as I'm in a terrific position to negotiate, by all means, out with it."

"Excellent." I wish he wouldn't grin though, seriously. I remember Sasha's strange story about Sarco trying to recruit her, but then I get distracted thinking about how she stabbed me in my sleep and can't concentrate. "I'm sure you've heard many strange and terrible things about me, Carlos."

"Seen some too."

"Mmm, of course, we've had a few unfortunate encounters, yes. Well, I'd like you to understand the context of my actions a little before you write me off as just a mad sorcerer."

"Wonderful."

"But to do that, I'm afraid you'll have to come with me."

I almost laugh but remember it might kill me. "How would you like me to accomplish that? I'm slightly indisposed."

"Your body, yes. But I don't need that part of you. You will be quite safe here, I can promise. The blade has successfully prevented a complete hemorrhage, and your body is remarkably proficient at survival."

"You're going to take my soul."

"Not take, Carlos. Merely borrow." When he laughs, I hear some chunk of phlegm get dislodged in his throat and he sputters and coughs a few times to clear it. Then he swallows loudly, and I throw up a little in my mouth. "With your permission, of course."

"Of course. And what makes you think I would ever give you permission to separate my soul from my body, Sarco?"

"Because I've already done it once, my son. I created you."

CHAPTER THIRTY-ONE

I think about Russell Ward and his divine infiltration theory. I have no idea what's in store, and I don't know how convinced the old wizard will be by me playing along, but I don't have much choice. Also, there's a part of me that's truly curious. It's almost a relief to stop resisting and give over control. As I come to my decision, I realize another thing: Sarco was right. The rational weighing of options distracted me from being terrified and yes, the feeling of sudden rot has subsided.

"I'm listening." Trying to ignore the sense that everything I say has been pre-scripted and plotted out by Sarco, from my trembling doubts to my grudging acceptance. He closes his eyes, magnanimous enough at this small victory to not gloat.

"I was once like you."

"A pincushion?"

He chuckles. "Well, that too, but that's another story. I mean I was destroyed and resurrected, occupied that same uncomfortable inbetweenness as you, my son." I suppress a shudder. "I was twenty-eight, a soldier of fortune roaming from massacre to massacre in the mess of fortified city-states and marshlands that later became Europe. I had dabbled in sorcery, of course, but they were burning witches at the time, and I figured there were better ways to die than as a mound of charred flesh." He scrunches up his face in disgust and then gazes down at me. "Do you believe me?"

I honestly don't know what to believe anymore, so I just stare back at him. Sarco shrugs. "The head of a small province north of Padua wanted to swallow up all the surrounding battlements and form them into a protective ring around his own castle. A recluse living in a tower just outside of the realm returned all his messengers as dead bodies slung over their own horses. I had just barely made it out of the Florentine Black and White wars. My whole body was a festering wound and I couldn't see straight, but war was all I knew how to do. We launched our attack on the tower, drunk, cocky, and reckless, as always. The ground started shaking, and before we could grasp what was happening, a hooded army rose straight out of the earth and routed our assault. It was over in minutes. We were torn from limb to limb, tossed aside like rag dolls, slashed, crushed, and beheaded. I landed in a heap beneath three of my fellow mercenaries."

Deep lines stretch across Sarco's face. Two crease his forehead, cross each other, and then break off into tiny tributaries that disappear beneath that mane of greasy black hair. His cheeks are sunken in, speckled by dry patches and ingrown hairs. "You died," I say.

Sarco nods. "Mostly." He opens his eyes, gazes down at me with something I can only call empathy. "The Tower-master came out at dusk. I sensed him. Even from the edge of death, I sensed him, sniffing through the corpses like a hellhound. He stopped over me—an enormous ancient man with no pupils in his eyes and hands like slabs of meat. Power radiated off him in heavy, nauseating waves. He pulled me from under those bodies—me and three others. Worked some sorcery on us and threw us in a dungeon to either rot or recover. I was the only one who made it. The others . . . I ate to stay alive. I was his slave and then his apprentice." Sarco smiles. "And then his killer."

"And me?"

"I wandered around the world like that, like you, for more than a century before it became tedious. I progressed. Half dead isn't all there is, you know."

"Imagine my relief."

"But it is a necessary beginning. A first step, so to speak. So yes, I did this to you, or had it done, I should say. And you survived. And yes, there are others. I gave you this gift, life, and turned you loose in the world. You didn't know; you can't ever fully understand what that means, of course, but now I'm here to ask something of you. You don't have to decide now. All I want is to show you what I mean."

The truth is: I want to know what the hell he's talking about. Even if it's all lies or insane ramblings, he seems to know a thing or two about who I am. More than I do even. And it's becoming more and more important that I figure that out. What was once a simple acceptance of the void grew suddenly and steadily into a curiosity and now a hunger.

I look up at Sarco and nod. "Okay," I say through clenched teeth. "Do it. But don't think I trust or believe anything you tell me."

Surprisingly, he doesn't laugh again. Instead he furrows his brow in concentration and places his long fingers on my chest. And then I black out.

I wake up light-headed. No. It's not just my head. My whole body. I'm floating. I'm barely there. I scuttle backward, dizzy with these new strange physics. A wave of nausea rises, but I get a handle on it before anything drastic happens. Sarco stands in a far corner of the room, looking smug. And I . . . No, my body is lying on the couch, still impaled, looking grayer than usual. A dark red splotch has formed on my shirt where the blade sticks out. At first I think I'm dead, that the bastard hoodwinked me somehow, but then my de-almafied body takes a shallow breath. I live, however tentative that lifeline may be.

"You see," Sarco's voice says from the absolute wrong part of the room. I whirl around and find myself face-to-face with a devastating void. Something like an empty television screen—just nothingness. Its shape is tall and gangly like Sarco but somehow . . . different. A twisted face glowers out at me—it's too blurry to identify, but I can see it's frowning something fierce. I realize the body in the corner is an empty husk, a mannequin. The guy knows what he's doing if he can leave his physical body behind in a standing position, on a whim apparently. From what I've heard, that's usually the kind of slick move that takes hours of preparation.

I have now established beyond a doubt that Sarco does not fuck around.

The rain doesn't land on my not-flesh. It sears right through it and leaves a tingling trail of sensation in its wake. I'm still marveling at the lightness, the dizzying freedom of being only spirit. Sarco is all business now that he's secured my go-ahead. Once I'd gotten my shit together enough to move around, he shot me a quick, "Come with me," and slid out the door into the rainy midnight streets without looking back.

We're moving fast, blazing through the darkness like plastic bags blown by the wind. I get the hang of it pretty quickly: thought controls movement. You want to go somewhere, you point yourself in that direction and propel forward on the engine of your own desire to arrive. Our long, translucent legs lunge with graceful steps just above the pavement. We brush past some night walkers, a few crackheads, and a security guard on his cigarette break, and they each shudder and look around as we slither by.

This is what Riley deals with. This is death.

"Where are we going?" I ask as we round a corner past a deserted lot.

"You'll see."

Asshole.

We head steadily south. Bed-Stuy passes in a blur of brownstones, corner stores, and Chinese joints; everything else is shuttered up at this hour. Even the Junklot is deserted: no old men malign one another over the domino table; the monstrous yard dogs are huddled away in their little tin shelters. Sarco slips across Atlantic Avenue without pausing, and I don't want to show fear or hesitation, so I do the same. A tractor-trailer plows right through me, all climaxing shushes of rainwater and grinding engines; I cringe even though I know better, open my spirit heart to accept whatever traumatic death awaits, but of course nothing happens. The truck is not one of those objects that can reach out of the physical world and into the spirit one, and as long as I'm not putting out that special effort to manifest myself onto some real-life object, it's like we never touched.

I saunter-float along behind Sarco, marveling at the many mysteries this phantom sorcerer holds. My life, my death: I do want to know. I can't pretend I don't. I want to know everything. About my life, my death, the Council, what would drive a man to throw so many lives to the wind. I won't like him, or the answers I'll get, probably, but I have to know. I'm done with not knowing. Then I'll realize it's all bullshit and walk away content. And then I'll fuck his operation up. But first I have to know.

I shudder as we pass Mama Esther's. The block is sleeping, oblivious to the terrible ticking clock that has been born in their midst. Oblivious to the fury of the ngks. I wonder, briefly, where those young lovers from back when have gone to. I wonder if Mama Esther's up there stewing in her confusion, or perhaps plotting some elaborate scheme to set things right. I've seen more of the real Mama Esther in this past week than I had in the whole time living at her place. And then it hits me: this area's probably crawling with soulcatchers.

I make a hissing noise at Sarco to let him know, but he's already ground to a halt and is waving at me to do the same. We hover just above the pavement for a minute, panting and taking in rain. Nothing moves on the block besides the windblown oaks. The streetlights show ugly orange splotches of the never-ending drizzle. And there's the soulcatcher: a tall fellow, all cloaked and helmeted, hunched forward and strutting toward us.

"Back!" Sarco hisses into my mind. I hurl my body behind a building and wait. The soulcatcher bristles with the knowledge that someone is lurking. I can feel his sudden focus from around the corner. And then it dawns on me that I'm hiding from one of my own soldiers. I know why and how I got here, but still, the thought is jarring. If he stumbles on us, there'll be a horrible moment of recognition and then . . . Sarco will probably kill him.

We wait for a few minutes, breathing heavy breaths

into the night, and then the soulcatcher wanders off. *"Come. Quickly."* We dash across the street, long spirit legs carrying us through the rain, and then move fast down Franklin Ave. and hook a right on Eastern Parkway. And then I realize where we're going.

CHAPTER THIRTY-TWO

᠅

Y ou're taking me to the entrada."

"The entrada is only a means to an end, Carlos."

"You're taking me to Hell."

Sarco smiles for the first time since we left my place, a gaping empty grin across his static-laced visage. It's better when he's just serious-looking, actually. "There're things you must see there."

"Why? What's this about?"

"It's about me having a chance to explain myself. I told you, I need your help. And I know your mind is already poisoned against me. Fine. Just see things as I do for a moment and then do what you will."

The park is all darkness tonight. Those lamps and their dim haze are a joke. We enter, and immediately I feel that pulsing of supernatural park life. It's even stronger now that I'm fully spirit, as if I've somehow tapped into a vast, swarming network of otherworldly creatures and undead souls. Every move I make sends a tremble along the weblines, and the park fluctuates and exhales on the whims of all its haunted guests.

And then we're standing in front of that hovering emptiness in the shadows of the trees. I realize that Sarco's

staticky void is probably made up of something quite
similar to the entrada; he becomes almost invisible standing in front of it. And then he's gone. And I know he
wants me to follow. I'm full of dread—an unnatural feeling for me until pretty recently. Everything in me wants
to turn around and float back through Brooklyn to where
my body lies pinned to the couch. I stand there, perched
on the brink of two universes, gazing dreamily into this
hypnotic gate of Hell.

I have to know.

I have to find out what's going on. For Riley, for me,
for Dro. For Sasha, in spite of everything. The only way
to end this is to get to the bottom of it, even if that means
walking into obvious damnation. I take a deep breath
and feel my barely there body flap gently in the wind like
laundry on the clothesline. Then I step into the entrada.

Most afterlifers spend their time in the Underworld. The
Council does its best to keep it that way, but of course,
there are always stragglers. Life has that certain magne-
tism; it draws death in even as it repels it. They chase each
other like high school sweethearts, now loving, now fighting. Teasing explodes into full-blown warfare, which leads
to great make-up sex. The sun sets and the moon rises; the
cycle begins again. The dead will always strive toward living, and the living will always cruise inevitably toward
death. What keeps things stable, as Mama Esther pointed
out, is that divine inexplicable balance.

Sometimes it's nostalgia that keeps a spirit swinging
back up into to the sunlit earthly plane. Could be an open
thread or some unanswered question. Or the perception
of one. The dream of a memory can go on haunting a
soul well past the grave, can reap supernatural havoc for

ages; it drives many a glowing shadow to late-night wanderings through the Brooklyn streets.

Besides a few notable exceptions, the living tend to wait till their time has come before going downstairs. I mighta passed through during my however-long-it-was period between death and resurrection, but if I did, I have no memory of it. Since then, the closest I've come is the Council's wide-open misty warehouse.

Until now.

First it's just darkness. Gradually, shapes waver into existence around me. They're abstract, though, and don't really seem sure whether they exist or not. Far off in the murkiness, swirling misty towers jut into black skies. Is there a sky in the Underworld? Whatever it is that surrounds me, it's splashed with grayish clouds and seems to go on forever. What's gone is the striking contrast between my own semiexistence and the solidity of the physical world. Here, everything is vague and ethereal and at first it's disconcerting as shit.

Sarco stands a few feet away, staring intently at me. He's excited. I can feel it bristling in the air around both of us, see his body panting up and down with anticipation. He's gotten me this far—some massive check on his to-do list for fucking up the planet, I'm sure. And now gears are turning for the next series of steps.

"Welcome to death." Sarco's voided face breaks into another grin. He loves this shit.

"All right, man. Show me what you brought me here to show me and let's get this over with."

"Why the hurry, Mr. Delacruz? Your body surely has a few more hours before it begins to decompose. Enjoy yourself. Few mortals have been where you stand."

"Charming. I'm charmed. Now, if you please."

There are shapes congregating around us, fluttering

shadows, hunched over in vague humanoid forms. They
lope toward where we stand, humming with curiosity. I
start to feel suffocated, like the gathering swarm of ghosts
is hoarding all the oxygen in the place. But then, I probably don't even deal in oxygen in this state. Either way, the
feeling is not pleasant. Sarco draws a blade and waves it
in a great semicircle. The wandering ghosts fall back with
murmurs of shock and anger. A wide berth has been cleared
around us, but I notice that the shadowy crowd keeps growing exponentially. Death seeks out life like a drug.

"Come," Sarco says, and for the first time, I detect a
hint of something off in his voice. Is it fear? Frustration?
I have no way of knowing. Either way, maybe all is not
going quite according to the plan.

"This way." He sweeps his arm again, clearing a throng
of whining, whispering shrouds. "Stay close. I would hate
for you to get caught up in the swarm. You know how the
dead love to make things their own."

He sounds somewhere in between genuine and mocking. I don't even care which it is anymore. The thickness
in the air is making it hard to concentrate. I try to focus
on his towering form as it glides on those long legs through
the clearing of ghosts. The shadows close in behind us,
reach out with long, icy fingers. They're hungry, lonely,
aching with wrath and desire but otherwise empty. Empty
and they sense something else, something full and alive,
even if it's just the torn-out soul of a living man. Still, it's
different, an anomaly in this place of death. And they
want some.

"The whole Underworld is like this?"

Sarco is a pretty wack Virgil, but he does seem to
know what he's talking about. Even if I can't trust a word
he says. "No, this is like the first sight of any third-world
country. These are the neediest that clutter around the

airports and train stations to get a glimpse or grapple a shred of the world they can never have. A sickening horde." He swipes his blade again, grunting with irritation, and the ghosts cleave away like windblown leaves. "Always wanting something. Wanting, wanting, wanting. Their whole essence is neediness. Tragic, really. Tragic and disgusting."

My whole flimsy body goes cold suddenly and I can't move. Sarco sweeps on ahead, not realizing I'm detained, and I watch as the shadows close around behind him. They're all over me, sliding in and out of my feeble existence, merging cruelly with my shroud, wrapping cold tentacle-like arms around and around me. I try to call out, but nothing happens. Try to project my mortal terror across the telepathy waves toward my enemy and savior, but all I hear is the silence of death and the occasional moans of these ghosts.

I can make out their faces now, feel their hot, dead breath against my face, on the back of my neck. They're old mostly; their skin once hung in curtains off their decaying faces; drool puddled in those hung-low mouths, unseeing eyes rolled back as machines clicked and chattered and beeped somewhere nearby. The endless tyranny of prolonged life. The restlessness left over from their slow rot hangs all around me.

Existence is so fragile when you're only a soul. I feel it slipping away in just a few short, terrifying minutes. I'm fading, my life essence splashing in prickly waves across the masses of dead that hem me in. And then I see him. His long arm reaches out of nowhere, clasps a few ghosts across their chests and flings them away. I gasp, my vision clouding over. Sarco's empty face appears, towers over me. He reaches a hand down and I take it and feel myself rising from the muck of spirit.

They're on him too. Those hungry fingers sliver up his tall body, envelop him in their starved wrath. For a terrible second, I'm pretty sure all is lost. Panic seems to grip Sarco. He lets go of my hand and slashes frantically at them with his blade. They're relentless, but they shy away from his sorcery and finally disperse. He pulls me up and there's a fury in him I hadn't seen before.

"Come quickly now," he whispers in a harsh, chipped voice. "This way." His blade waves out in front of him, clearing our path once again. The moaning ghosts clamor forward and swing back. I stay as close as I can to his shadow without being enveloped by it. It seems endless, this two-soul parade through the desperate masses. A few more times I think we won't make it; exhaustion creeps over my body in crisp waves, seems to pull me toward the uncertain ground. But I won't give in.

Finally, finally, finally we reach some kind of sanctity. The ghosts have gradually faded off and returned to their aimless wanderings across that misty plain. The vague towers loom closer now, and I realize they look familiar. It's like a crude projection, more hallucination than anything else, but I can make out the outlines of those fancy row houses that line the edge of Prospect Park. The angles are all off; it's only a cruel funhouse rendering, but still, there's no mistaking it. Farther away I see the ghost of Brooklyn's clock tower, an eerie red glow against the darkness.

CHAPTER THIRTY-THREE

Now what?"

Sarco seems to be taking a moment to collect himself. He wavers, rolling his neck back and forth like an athlete with sore muscles. "Now," he says when he's got himself together, "we continue."

"Sarco, tell me where we're going."

"You want to know about your life, Carlos?" His voice lilts with derision. I want to slap him, but he just saved my ass, and he's probably my only hope of getting out of here. Also, I want to know about my life. Desperately.

"I do. But I also want to know where we're going."

"You died nobly. Fighting."

"That a fact?" I keep my voice even, reminding myself over and over that these are surely lies. Absolutely, surely lies. And still . . .

"A truth teller, right to the end."

"You're gonna stay vague and keep hanging this over my head, aren't you? I still have no reason to believe you know anything about me, Sarco, so . . ."

He puts his hand on my head very suddenly, and there's the reason, plain as day: it's me. Me when I was alive. I can tell because my skin is the full shade of brown that it's supposed to be, not tinged with gray. My eyes sparkle with a vitality I've never known in them. I'm alive. The disembodied soul of the half-dead man that I've become shudders with recognition, hunger. Is this what those old invalid spirits felt as they mobbed us? I want. That life. Back inside me. I want it like a drug. Nothing else matters.

But the living me is upset. The image is shaky like a home video and a little too grainy. I watch myself swerve out of the way of something, turn a fearsome face toward the sky, and then lunge forward. Then it stops and replays again from the beginning: it's just a spliced-up, several-second clip, looped on an infinite repeat in my brain. I yell and wrench myself away from Sarco's grasp, away from the living me, and sink to the floor.

"Who was I?"

It doesn't matter to me if he's lying. At this point, I just want an answer. As long as it sounds believable enough, I'll take it. I'll take anything. I need to fulfill this craving.

"A murderer."

"What do you mean?"

"Come. I'll explain presently. Come." I look at him in disbelief. "Carlos, come with me. We can't just sit here waxing nostalgic. Your body only has so much time, remember."

We stumble on through the haze of ghost Brooklyn. Some things are the same, some are completely wrong. The dead have their own sense of architecture, apparently, and it doesn't look kindly on straight lines or finished products. Occasional ghosts glide around us through the streets, but they keep their distance.

We stop at what I figure to be the corner of Eastern Parkway and Washington, just past the Brooklyn Museum. There's a park there, in the living Brooklyn; a little grass-

and-benches type joint where old guys sit around for hours beating one another at chess. But here it's gone; it's empty like the entrada. I feel a chill come over me as we get close. "What is it?"

"The Underworld of the Underworld."

"The Deeper Death." I peer into the void, imagining Dro's sad form languishing away along with the all the shattered souls I dispatched here over the past three years. "This is where ghosts go when they die."

"No," Sarco says. "This is where they stop. It's the end of existence. An infinite ocean of utterly nothing. There's no one in there. No one and no thing. It's the incinerator of souls."

"Nice."

"Come on. We're almost there."

The trees reach in uncomfortable angles toward the sky like cursed yoga masters, frozen forever in the wrong pose. The whole place just seems like a dreary reflection of the living world, and I can imagine Riley saying, "Why the fuck you think I bang around up here? Fuck all that."

I'm not surprised when we stop outside Mama Esther's house. Of course all this sinister bullshit would lead back here. What does he have planned? I try to shake off this thick daze I've settled into, but it hangs all around me— the atmosphere is poisoned with it.

Sarco smiles down at me—never a good thing—and ushers me inside.

It's all different in here. The air is crisp. My faded feet scrape on real floorboards. The world has become physical again. It pulses with the life blood of existence.

Sarco starts up the stairs.

"Mama Esther . . ."

"Is sleeping. She will not see us."

I don't like this. The thing I don't like the most is that

I feel propelled forward, anxious to see it through, what-ever the hell it is. I can't tell if it's some nasty magic Sar-co's using on me or if I really just want to know what's going on, what mysteries he holds about my own life and the spirit world. Sasha, of all people, seemed to trust him. She didn't know the half of his treachery, I'm sure, and I probably don't either. Still, something pulls me along, beckons me forward. I step uneasily up the stairs after him.

"What's . . . ?" I'm tired of asking questions that don't get answered. I let that one die half formed, and all I hear is our feet creaking up the stairwell and the occasional groans and clicks of the house settling. We pass the second- and third-floor landings, pause briefly on the fourth, and then scale a ladder up onto the roof.

It's raining in the Underworld. A cruel wind has whipped up around us, and it buffets my body; I have to concen-trate not to swoop away off the roof with it. Sarco is exultant—he throws his arms up to the storm and laughs. "Can you feel it, Carlos?"

It's a rhetorical question, apparently, because he just keeps laughing instead of waiting for an answer. I can, though. The air is pregnant with tension the way it gets just before a hurricane. "The missing piece!" Sarco yells into the sky.

I just wait. Obviously, asking questions is useless. The guy will explain or he won't, and if he don't, I'm out. Matter-of-fact: I take a step back toward the ladder.

"You can have whatever you want, Carlos!" Sarco says. He's suddenly very close to me, horribly close. "It's you. I thought it was Trevor. Sasha maybe. But it's you. The missing piece."

"The fuck you going on about?"

By way of an answer, Sarco puts his hand on my head again and I see me, thrashing an arm at someone, my eyes desperate. I swing again, take a hit across the face, and stumble backward. Blood pours from a gash on my forehead. I launch forward, mouth open, and disappear.

"They don't need you, Carlos. They use you happily. But they don't need you." The dead sky rages around us with the coming storm, but Sarco's voice has dropped to a rancid whisper. "They don't even really know what you are, your true power." I know he's talking about the Council, and I'd be more comfortable if I didn't partially agree with him. "You're much more than some wretched intermediary. You're more than alive and more than dead, not just a poorly constructed halfling. You are complete."

I look around. The building is real beneath my feet. Mama Esther is somewhere inside, in the living world, maybe sleeping, maybe drugged. Ngks are crawling through the ghostly buildings around us. Out in the misty Underworld, I see the hordes of hungry, dilapidated souls that met us at the entrance. They're swarming toward us; there's no mistaking it. It's a sclerotic, gradual swarm, but it's definitely headed our way. I think about the list of ingredients, as Mama Esther called it, and look back at Sarco. "You're building an entrada."

"Fuck an entrada! I'm tearing a hole in the very fabric of the life-death continuum! Don't you see, Carlos?" He's almost pleading now, and it's damn awkward. But, suddenly, I do see, all too clearly. Ghostly threads stretch from the dilapidated buildings nearby. They're wispy and barely there but pulsing with energy. They all join together at a point in the center of the rooftop.

"The living and the dead don't have to be so far apart.

You are the living embodiment of that truth. It's a farce, this barrier, this wall between us. It's a lie." Lightning crackles across the sky. Black rain drizzles in wild circles around us.

"The cursed monk," I say.

Sarco nods. "You followed Trevor's paper trail."

"The stranger on the road. That was you, all those hundreds of years ago?"

"Hm, one familiar to me—let's say a distant uncle. The Towermaster introduced us. Masenfel, plague-bringer. A sorcerer of almost godlike powers. Taught me many things, that old one." He looks lost in thought for a few seconds and then turns his empty face to me. "What do you want to know?"

"Why?"

"Why destroy the barrier between the living and the dead? You know that already, Carlos. You may not understand the depth of it, but inside yourself, you know it's the natural way. Civilization took a turn, tore us from one another. There was a time, long forgotten, never recorded, when ancestors walked freely among the living; there was harmony. Carlos, the living world becomes more powerful for this. Do you see that?

"I destroyed the Towermaster because he wanted to hoard all his necromancy and world-shifting arts to himself and his select few. All these mystical arts don't need to be hidden away, the earth-shaking weapons of the powerful few. When this is done, when the gate is open, this magic will be at the hands of the whole world. We will enter a new age."

I just look at him; his staticky, impossible form trembles in the hellish wet wind sweeping across the rooftop.

"Carlos, do you have the foresight to understand that

what's happening here today is much greater than the petty casualties of the moment?"

"You killed my people, Sarco. That soulcatcher, Dro . . ."

Sarco sighs, the disappointed patriarch. "The soulcatcher was about to ruin everything. Yes, I killed him. My plan will not be ruined. Yes, I took one life to bring a new world order, yes. And Washington and Arroyo, they should not have fucked with ngks. Everybody knows that. The ngks are a part of the equation. They purify. A space must be purified before any sacred work is done there, cleansed and left alone. The ngks form a barrier against the meddlesome dead, and then they are pivotal in opening the gateway. They don't have to hurt anyone if people would only stay away from them."

"Easy for you to say."

Mama Esther's tired, unconscious face appears at the focal point of all those tingling threads. Slowly, grudgingly, her massive body begins to rise up from the ceiling.

"The ancient Romans had a god called Janus," Sarco says in my ear.

I step away from him. "Two faces. Watched the gates."

"Yes! Janus was a part of both worlds. His faces looked inside the gates and outside at the same time. Divinity, Carlos. The Divine Doorkeeper. This is the gift God has given humanity in the form of the inbetweeners. The missing link. Resurrected. You have a role to play in this great struggle between life and death, and it's not just as a busybody catching runaway grandma ghosts."

Again, uncomfortably close to home. I don't know what my role is in the grand scheme of things, but the sting of feeling underused is sharp.

"What will happen?"

"At first? Chaos. The hungry dead will pour through the

gate, scatter out into the world in their vast multitudes. The living will wander in. There is always a painful period of absolute crisis at the pinnacle of any great change."

Mama Esther has cleared the roof now and hangs a few feet up in the air, her body limp and leaning forward like she's dangling from a string. The threads that are converging on her tingle and twitch. There's ngks at the other end of each thread, I'm sure of it. Mama Esther is the focal point of a huge phantom spiderweb.

"The Council?"

"Ha! The Council will be obliterated. Probably first to go."

The thought has a certain charm to it.

"Eventually, balance will return to the world. The equation will even out, because that is the natural way of things. Except this time, the dead will exist in harmony with the living, not confined to some supernatural detention center. The living will feel a companionship with their lost loved ones, know the soft touch once more of those who passed. There will be a coming together, a palpable shift. The war will be no more, the barriers collapsed. The occult sorceries will be released like a wave of light across the world; living humans will be capable of powers they never imagined."

"And me?"

"The world begins and ends with one thing, Carlos: the gatekeeper."

"But aren't you just gonna tear it open and let them swarm through? What do you need a . . . ?"

"It's part of the equation, Carlos, part of the magic. To make a gate, one needs a gatekeeper. The ngks play their role, I play mine, and you play yours. The Council is a thing of the past. You will take up your rightful position as the living guardian of the crossroads, a warrior priest of unimagined powers, Carlos."

Sheets of rain cascade around us, sweep across the roof in Hell's untamed wind. I stare into Sarco's shifting void and smile.

"What do I have to do?"

CHAPTER THIRTY-FOUR

❧

Sarco looks me up and down. I'm just a flickering shroud, but I sense his gaze penetrating me, searching out my innermost secrets. "You have to take up the mantle," he says carefully. "It begins right here. I will rent open the gateway. The change will commence. There will be trouble, like I said. It won't be easy. A mad rush of souls will begin. Already they swarm, keen with the sense that something gigantic is about to happen." He seems suddenly tired, as if now that he's closer than ever to attaining his goal, he just wants to collapse and be done with it. He waves a lethargic hand toward the masses of ghosts closing steadily on us. "I can't force you to do it. If you say no, you can leave. I swear to you. But mark my words: it will be done. One way or the other. You would do well to be on the right side of this great moment." He pauses, maybe to catch his breath. The rain claps against rooftop around us; the clouds swirl overhead. "Will you help me, Carlos?"

"I will," I hear myself saying. "I will."

Sarco doesn't smile. Instead he drops his head, panting. For a second I think he's just going to collapse right there and become the most anticlimactic fatality of a grand world-changing scheme ever. Instead, he turns around, raises both hands, and lets out a howl that sends a tremble through me. The sky convulses in response. Thunder bursts out, and seconds later a shock of white lightning breaks the clouds. "Then step forward," Sarco whispers. He nods toward where Mama Esther hangs in the air like an overripe pumpkin.

I take a step toward her. The ngks have begun shimmying up their ghost threads toward us. The mass of hungry dead stretches out for miles to either side of the building. They're writhing and frothing, desperate to get to this strange new freedom. They can smell the living world, suddenly closer and more palpable than it's ever been.

I step forward, just an inch or two from my sad old friend the house ghost. The energy crackles and trembles around me. "Yes!" Sarco whispers. "Yes." The first ngk crosses onto the roof and stops its manic shimmying beside Sarco. It doesn't look at him—Ngks aren't big on direct eye contact—but its long mouth stretches all the way across its face and tiny sharp teeth appear. Sarco shakes his head, mumbling something under his breath. The other ngks have paused just shy of the rooftop. "No," Sarco says. "This is the one. Yes."

Are they negotiating? Can one negotiate with an ngk? Sarco's massive shadowy form sags. "Fine, then," he mutters, and the ngks all move as one toward Mama Esther.

Sarco responds to my unasked question. "They are not interested in humanity or magic. They care nothing for matters of equilibrium. They are fiercely loyal to one another and no one else."

"That much I gathered."

"That is always first and foremost for the ngk: its fellow ngk. Beyond that, they care only about one thing."

"Sexy lady ngks?"

"Food."

"Come again?"

"The ngks are scavengers. They appear every few centuries, feed off the festering souls of the dead and dying, and vanish back into the shadows of time. They know I'm on the brink of changing the world order. They are nothing if not strategic, dedicated. When the gateway is opened, the ngks will begin a feeding frenzy. They agreed to take part, but they want to be sure they can continue their runs when things settle down."

"Why don't they just feast on all these dead geriatrics heading our way?"

Sarco gets very close again. I suppress a shudder. "Because ngks like their meat fresh, Carlos, and they have long game. They're not just wild animals, eating anything that's in their path and then dying of famine. Ngks are the spiders that meticulously build their traps and then lie in wait, for centuries if need be. They serve their purpose—cleansing the ranks of death. And then they get out of the way. Their presence here means that they believe in what's about to happen. The future. Soon you'll understand. Now step forward, Carlos. Stand with us."

When I enter the space within Mama Esther's shroud, the first thing I feel is a shock of pain course through me, and I wonder if the whole thing was some cruel joke. Within seconds though, the pain turns to something else: power. A surge of crisp, living energy runs from my head to my toes, a vitality I've never known or imagined. I gaze from side to side, aghast at this sudden burst of potency, this life in my veins. This power. The ngks are all around me, grabbing at the folds of Mama Esther's cloudy edges and pulling outward. She flickers as she expands: an impossible darkness appears inside her that I realize is the

night sky in the living world. Soon the opening will cover
the whole building and then stretch all the way out to each
of the ngkified surrounding ones.

Power. It's the collective energy of all those frothing
souls; it's the bursting of history and lunacy and culminating sorcery, and it belongs to me. I can swish my right
hand and collapse a city block. I am life and death incar-
nated, so much more than the bumbling manservant the
Council abuses for their dirty work. The hungry dead surround me, base and pathetic little creatures, and I know in
seconds they'll swarm forward, through this brand-new
gateway.

"And so it begins!" Sarco yells.

And then I jump him.

CHAPTER THIRTY-FIVE

∽᪗ᦇ᠅

How to explain combat physics in the realm of the dead? Those phantom bodies are like watery sacks; they hold weight but only in the most slippery, translucent kind of way. You can feel the dead as a kind of dull, tingling pressure, the pressure of the spirit. They can rise up into the air as if buffeted by a supernatural wind, but it wears them out; flying is exhausting. The closest comparison would be an underwater fight that isn't in slo-mo and with a touch more gravity.

It takes effort for a soul to rise, so I make sure to catch Sarco nice and off guard before I ram him. He really is shocked—I hear a horrified gasp as our bodies connect and I heave us both forward over the edge of the rooftop. About halfway down, he seems to recover himself and I feel the sudden pressure against our plunge. It's too late though—I already have momentum on my side. I tighten my form and thrust us hard into the murky ground below. A crowd of old ghosts scatters languidly out of the way and we land in a heap.

They won't stay scattered for long.

As Sarco scrambles to recover himself, I make a grab for his blade, the only real chance I have. He darts away, waving his arms, but not before I wrap my translucent fingers around the handle and yank it away from him. "No!" Sarco yells. I slash him once, twice, and then stab forward, tearing his loose spirit flesh into shreds. Then, for good measure, I kick him backward into the swarm of hungry ghosts.

I don't wait to see what happens. There's no time. Between me and the entrada there are hundreds of starving souls and more on the way. I slash out cruelly, slicing a few that got too close, and begin cleaving a path back up this shimmering, hellish version of Franklin Avenue. They're furious, these ghosts—already been held at bay once, and now here comes another swashbuckler to tempt and then thwart them. A few times I feel them close in on me, but some well-placed slashes hold them off.

By the time I reach Eastern Parkway, I'm exhausted. I wonder, vaguely, whether my physical body is even still alive and what the hell would happen to me if it expires while I'm running around the Underworld. Then an icy hand slaps across my shoulder, pulling me down. I swing Sarco's blade over it, chopping it at the wrist, and when I turn around, there he is, towering before me and howling as the hungry ghosts clutter over him like ants. He reaches out again, and I stumble backward, almost lose my balance, and then turn and run, cutting ghosts out of my way as I go.

I pass the emptiness of the Deeper Death. Up ahead, haunted treetops glower over the fog of Prospect Park. The ghouls are thick and enraged on all sides of me, and I'm losing my strength fast, but . . . I'm so close. I brace myself and dive forward. Sarco's probably still behind me, grappling with the masses. I think I hear his scream carried on the howling wind, but there's no time to bother checking.

The park. Everything becomes a frantic blur as I slash and slice my way toward the entrada. I close on it, shoot a last glance behind me at the ghost riot—no Sarco to be seen—and plunge through, gasping for air.

My frail spirit body screams at me to rest, but I can't.

I can't.

Not with that creature on my trail. Not with the chance of him somehow making it through that hellhole alive. No. Just the thought of his empty face coming through the entrada is enough to get my distraught ass up and staggering in the direction of home and my poor, skewered body. The rain stopped, but the air is still wet and the streets are slick with its aftermath. I've never felt so blessed to be outside in the beautiful world, the world of the living, where things are real, you touch them and they stop your hand from going any farther. I'm alive, I think, somewhere and somehow, even if divided and exhausted and damn near dead.

I will make it home. I will get my body back. I will get that damn sword out of my gut, and I'll recover, somehow, and then I'll find Sarco and finish him off completely.

One way or amotherfuckingother.

PART THREE

❧

I slip my knots and garments,
utter the first no.
It begins where it ends.

Memory
Ignites like kindling
The time when I filled the sky.
Parting brought death.
Now, I drum on the carcass of the world
creating crises to recall my name

—Gloria Anzaldúa

"Canción de la diosa de la noche"

CHAPTER THIRTY-SIX

❧

I might be one of the last people in Brooklyn to have a landline. It's a source of endless amusement to Kia, but I'm glad of it tonight. Who knows where one of those ridiculous little cellular phones would've ended up in the course of all that fighting and fucking? I don't have it in me to go searching for shit right now. There's about ten seconds of life force left by the time I barge back into my apartment—just enough to grab the phone off the cradle and leave it by my barely breathing body. The number I need is in my jacket pocket. My jacket is draped over the couch, thank God.

I collapse over my own body, partially because I'm spent and partially because I have no earthly idea how to get back into it. Turns out, that's pretty much the deal: after a confusing jumble of physicality meshing with spirit, I'm staring up at the ceiling again, exalting in the searing pains running along my midsection and gasping for air. I grab the phone, very, very carefully, hunt the paper out of my jacket, and dial.

"Hello?" A groggy female voice.

"Victor . . ." All I can do is gasp. It must sound horrifying. "Victor . . . Please."

She's irritated. "Hold on. Babe . . . Babe! Some asshole's on the motherfucking phone for you, babe. *M*y phone." I hear a rustling of bedsheets. "Victor! Wake the fuck up."

"What?"

"You gave some freak my phone number, and now he's calling at four o'clock in the morning. Handle it." From the chaos that ensues, I deduce that she just brained him with the mobile. A few curses later Victor gets on.

"What? Who is this?"

"It's Carlos. The guy that isn't dead."

"Oh . . . shit. What happened? You sound horrible."

"I need . . . help."

"Jenny's kind of in a mood right now, Carlos. Maybe this isn't the—"

"Not . . . fucking . . . Jenny, Victor. I need a doctor. I'm . . . impaled."

"You're what?" He sounds a little more excited than horrified. Bloodthirsty paramedics.

"There's a twelve-inch blade pinning my gut to the couch. I . . . need . . . help."

"I'll be right over."

He takes down my address and hangs up. Just before I pass out, I remember that there's supposed to be a long-haired junky standing in the corner.

But there isn't.

"Well, damn," Victor says when he walks in the door.

"Can you stop gawking and do what you do, please."

He walks up close and stares in utter amazement at the blade. "It's just . . ."

"Victor, I'm dying!"

"No, I know, Carlos, but this is out of my . . . You need a doctor, Carlos. A surgeon."

"Then find me one. Please."

He looks puzzled for a minute. I can't tell if he's flipping through some mental Rolodex or still just entranced by my wound. Then he snaps his fingers. "I know just the one: this crazy Haitian motherfucker. A resident trauma surgeon at King's County. Renowed across the world apparently. Yes. Dr. Tijou will be perfect."

"Can Dr. Tijou keep a secret?"

"I guess we'll find out. Lemme make a phone call."

"Victor, wait. Get at this guy too." I pass him Baba Eddie's card. "Ask him if he could make a house call."

Baba Eddie shows up while Victor's out tracking down Dr. Tijou. He's dressed head to toe in white and looks more serious than I've ever seen him. Kia comes in behind him carrying a few heavy boxes, also in her whites. She disappears into the kitchen and starts mixing things up while Baba Eddie takes a long hard look at my situation.

"I don't know where you've been," he says finally, "but there's death all over you. It's like you took a bath in dead people."

"That pretty much sums up my night."

"It's not good. A limited amount of exposure is one thing, but you are covered in it. It's corroding you."

"There's also the small matter of the blade."

"Bah—not my department. Let the surgeon handle that. What good is getting unstuck if you've got death pervading every fiber of your aura?"

"Fair enough."

He shakes his head. I feel like a kid that stayed out too late binge drinking and now has to clean up the mess. "Kia," Baba Eddie yells over his shoulder. "Add some more basil."

"Whatchya cookin'?"

"Shush. You need to conserve your energy, so stop wasting it on boberías. Try to sleep."

When I wake up I'm once again being gazed at curiously, this time by a small, serious-looking dark-skinned woman. By her face you'd think she was young, too young to be a world-renowned trauma surgeon, except for the alarming streaks of white that run along either side of her otherwise pitch-black hair. She frowns at me, cocks her head to one side, frowns some more. Victor comes up beside her.

"What you think, Doc?"

Dr. Tijou considers, ponders, sighs, frowns some more, makes a *hmm*ing noise, coughs, and then shrugs. "Not bad."

"Word?" I say.

"Don't speak."

"What's the plan?" Victor asks.

"We pull it out."

"Just like that?"

"Of course not. You're going to start two large-bore IVs, and then we're going to prep the site with disinfectant and give the patient a prophylactic dose of amoxicillin. We will set up all the surgical tools necessary in case he decides to exsanguinate."

"Decides?"

"Don't speak, I said. And *then* we will pull out the blade." Victor nods. "Sounds good."

"Are you sure that's the right way to do it?" I ask.

"I am sure that's not the right way to do it, actually," the doctor says matter-of-factly. "Are you sure you don't want to go to a hospital?"

"I can't."

"Well, then, we are both sure of things. Now, be quiet."

They work with startling efficiency. Victor wraps rubber tourniquets around my arms and stabs me with two very large needles. He attaches a bag of saline to each site and hangs them on the lamp next to the couch while Dr. Tijou scrubs her hands and prepares some medications.

Baba Eddie comes in from the kitchen and says, "Oh, you guys go ahead."

"Ah," Dr. Tijou says. "Dr. Voudou!"

Baba Eddie opens a wide smile. "Dr. Bonecutter."

"It is a pleasure to meet you, sir."

"The pleasure is all mine." They shake, both grinning widely. I don't think anyone knows whether they're kidding or not. Probably not even they know.

"Would you like to go first?" Dr. Tijou asks.

"No, no, ours can wait till after. Body first, then spirit. You go right ahead, my dear."

Are they flirting? Mocking each other? I can't tell. I don't really care as long as I don't die.

"Very well," the doctor says with a courteous smile and a slight bow.

"Anyone want coffee?" Kia calls from the kitchen.

Everyone wants coffee except Dr. Tijou, who prefers tea.

"You ready?" she says a few minutes later when everything's in place.

I nod. "I guess so."

"I was talking to Victor."

"Oh. Right."

"I'm ready," Victor says, putting down his coffee mug and standing over the makeshift surgical table they set up.

"Then pull."

"Me?" Victor says.

"Him?" I say.

Dr. Tijou laughs. "It doesn't take any special medical

knowledge to pull a sword out of someone. It's what happens after that matters. It seemed like something you might enjoy doing, as a medic. If you want, I could—"

"No, no," Victor says, a little too hungrily. "I would love to. I just didn't know . . . Yes." He takes a deep breath, gloves up, and puts both hands on the blade handle.

Dr. Tijou nods. "Straight out, Victor. No twists, no turns. Just pull."

"'Kay." Victor's sweating. So am I. He braces himself and then pulls. I groan as sharp blasts of pain explode through my abdomen. Then it's gone and Dr. Tijou is peering gingerly into the hole it left behind.

"Bon Dieu!" she whispers.

"What?"

"The blade. She passed through your entire abdomen and out and somehow managed to miss every major organ and blood vessel, some by fractions of millimeters." Her eyes are wide. "I have never seen anything like that in my life! There are many . . . There are so many organs there, and the blade simply . . ." She dabs some gauze around the wound to stave off a little pool of blood that's formed. "Incredible."

"I'm going to live?"

Dr. Tijou takes her face out of my abdomen and straightens her back to alert the room she's about to say something important. "Either you, sir, are a very lucky man, or someone has gone out of their way to keep you alive."

CHAPTER THIRTY-SEVEN

〜◦◦◦〜

The doctor instructs Victor to take my vital signs, listens intently as he lists off the numbers, and then tells him to do it again. "And you say this is more or less baseline for the patient?" Her Creole accent seeps out even more now that she's alive with the thrill of a well-placed blade.

Victor nods. "Slightly lower than usual, but yes, that's what he tells me. That's how I first found him, actually." He starts in on the story of how we met, Dr. Tijou punctuating with little *hmm*s and *ooh*s. I can't focus on any of his words though. They just seem like vague amoebas floating above our heads. It occurs to me I've been holding on tightly to my life force, keeping it close to my core the way I did my secrets when I was around Sasha. It's wearing me out. "I think . . . I think I . . ." I hear myself saying. I'm probably trying to tell them I'm about to pass out, but then I just do it instead.

I wake up to the sound of an R & B joint bursting tinnily through someone else's headphones. The bass is so loud that whoever's listening to it will definitely be hearing impaired in about ten seconds. It's raining out. Those pitter-pattering footsteps slosh steadily against the window, and a mellow blue-gray light filters into the room.

Kia.

Kia's the one blowing out her own eardrums. She's tinkering around in the kitchen. "Coffee," I mumble. Of course, she can't hear me because some preteen is trying to seduce her point-blank at four million decibels. I grab something off the little table by the couch and launch it across the room. Turns out to be a small potted plant, which explodes against the far wall and sends Kia flying up into the air with surprise.

"What the *fuck,* Carlos!"

"Sorry, I didn't realize it was . . ." I stop because saying so many words has worn me out. "Coffee . . ." I mumble.

"No, man. Both Baba Eddie and Dr. Tijou said no coffee for you. You have to recover. Your pressure's low even by low-ass Carlos standards, and you lost a lot of blood. Coffee'll fuck you up even more."

I'm slightly alarmed by the brush of maternal tenderness that comes over Kia's voice. I must be truly messed up if she's actually deigned to be concerned.

"Okay. No coffee. Fuck."

And I'm out.

First I hear humming and the gentle swish of water. A voice I don't know; a large, older woman from the sound of it. It's a melancholy call-and-response, each line repeated, but she's doing both voices.

Then I hear Kia say: "Like this?"

The older woman grunts an approval and keeps humming.

"That's the song for the herbs?"

"Mm-hmm."

"It makes them happy?"

"It makes them work," the woman says. "Prayer puts the world to work. The action you take is your expression of intent. The world listens. And then works. Go get me some more iced tea, baby, okay?"

"All right, Iya."

I keep my eyes closed.

Kia's sitting in the easy chair next to the couch when I come back around. She smiles—not the fuck-you, I'm-winning smile I'm used to from Kia but a real one, full of warmth and . . . what's that? Kindness. She's still in her whites, a long skirt and button-down shirt. Her hair's wrapped up in a white head tie, and a million multicolored bead necklaces peek out from behind her collar. She looks like a whole other person. It's still raining, and I have no idea how much time has passed.

"How do you feel?"

"Better. A little. Don't think I can move though."

"Don't. We haven't done the cleansing yet. Baba had to run out to take care of some stuff. It's better you get a chance to recover some first anyway."

"Who was the woman?"

"Oh, from earlier? Iya Tiomi. One of Baba's people. We were making some herb washes for you."

"Figured something like that."

"Apparently, you're some kind of medical freak. Dr. Tijou was really amazed. She kept running around the place squawking about how she'd never seen anything like it in her career." Kia affects a pretty on-point Haitian accent. "'Even in Port-au-Prince! Sacrebleu!'"

I chuckle, which hurts but feels good at the same time. I haven't laughed in far too long.

"She was actually pretty cool with all the spiritual stuff too, even though she still calls it voudou."

"Well . . ."

"She even said she'd come back and help us do the cleansing."

As if on cue, Baba Eddie, Dr. Tijou, and Iya Tiomi come through the front door, shaking rain off their jackets and chuckling about some inside joke.

"How's the little dead guy?" Dr. Tijou asks amiably.

"He's awake!" Kia says. I'm still not used to this nice person that replaced her.

Baba Eddie clasps his hands together. "Excellent. We can begin." He lights up a fat-ass cigar, and everyone gathers around me. "Close your eyes, Carlos."

I hear words—very old, beautiful words. They come out of Baba Eddie in an endless stream with occasional pauses in which he mutters, "Um . . . coño . . . ah sí sí . . ." and jumps back in. There's a call-and-response part where Kia and Tiomi answer him with a mix of Spanish and some other language—Yoruban, I presume— and then I hear the *ftz-ftz*ing of lighters and the tiny crackle of candles coming to life around me. Something wet gets sprinkled on my face and then all over my body and, as more chanting begins, I drift off into a pleasant, dreamless sleep.

CHAPTER THIRTY-EIGHT

❦

Sometime in there I got good at being patient again. Life became a blur of sleeping and waking, mumbling senseless shit, passing back out. At one point I think someone bathed me, but I have no idea who. I remember smiling a lot, enjoying all the banter without understanding a word of it. Dr. Tijou seemed to have taken a liking to me, or at least to the peculiarity of my wound; she started showing up regularly and sipping her tea while Victor told wild ambulance stories and smoked cigarettes with Baba Eddie.

Despite the wealth of healing arts in the room—a doctor, a medic, and a wily Santería priest—it was Kia who ended up making sure I stayed on point with my medicines and herbal remedies. The others kept an eye out, checked vital signs every now and then, but basically yukked it up. Of course, laughter has its own healing properties, and their ongoing debates and zings kept my mind from lingering on Sasha for too long.

Then one day I start planning. It's not a conscious choice; it pretty much just happens. I wake up, lie there for a minute, and then my mind immediately drifts toward Sarco and his treachery. He's not dead. There's absolutely no way I would believe that he didn't somehow make it out of that swarm. His physical body being gone is proof enough of that. Anyway, the guy obviously has some severely advanced supernatural powers. If he could survive that barrage of stabs I dealt him with his own blade, well . . . I gonna need to see a body before I believe it's over.

And if he's still alive, that means he's still plotting. No madman in his right mind would go through all that trouble, have a whole plan in place, ready to go, get inches, seconds literally, from completion, and then just cast it away because the first halfie he tries for sticks it to him and storms off.

No.

Sarco will try again. And again and again until he either gets what he wants or gets obliterated trying. I set my mind toward making the latter happen.

Kia pokes her head in from the kitchen. "You want some water, Carlos?"

"With rum, please."

"Right."

If the ngks could be spoken to somehow, reasoned with, perhaps his whole plan would unravel. I know they're a crucial ingredient, but they don't or won't speak. We can barely get near them without spawning more or getting all kinds of casualties inflicted upon us. And Sarco will be looking for another halfie, once he recovers, and I have no doubt who he'll turn to first.

"Here. Water." Kia sets a glass on the table along with a little orange medicine vial. "And your pills."

"Gracias." I gulp down the pills. "You having fun?"

"I am, actually," she says seriously. "It's nice to get a break from the store for a while." She pauses, looks away. "And home."

It's one of those moments. Do you ask about all the

heaviness she inflected the word "home" with or just let it sit, let her get to it on her own? Kia's a pretty private person, so I opt to nod and let her continue if she wants to. She doesn't, but it's all over her: someone close is gone, has been gone for a while. A brother, cousin maybe. He's tall and lanky, young. His face stares defiantly out from the haze around Kia. He's probably dead, the way she carries him enshrined so.

Kia's staring at me. I exit her private thoughts and make myself smile. "It means a lot to me, you helping me out like this." I'm really not good with saying things like that, so it comes out all off rhythm.

"Ha—don't worry about it. I said I'm having fun." She smiles an awkward teenager smile and heads back into the kitchen.

If Sarco goes to Sasha . . . I don't know what I would do. In part because I don't know what she would do. She's a total unknown entity at this point, a wild card. On the one hand, she showed a healthy distrust of him when she was telling her story; on the other, she shish-kebabed me to the couch and summoned that asshole to my house. Then again, I killed her brother. But she also didn't look that happy to see Sarco when he showed up. And that face she made at me just before leaving: could that have been remorse in her eyes?

"Hey, whatever happened with your lady friend?" Kia yells over the clatter of dishwashing.

I hate it when she does that. "Which one?"

"Oh please. Don't act like you got chicks climbing over each other to get on that dick."

"Well, damn."

"The one that had you all frowny a few weeks ago."

"Oh yeah, that one. Seems she's the one that put the blade in me."

"Oh. So not so good, then."

"Well, she may have had somewhat of a justifiable reason."

She appears in the doorway, arms akimbo. "What the fuck did you do, Carlos?"

"No . . . nothing. To her. Nothing like *that*. I mean . . . it's complicated."

"No fucking shit it's complicated."

"You got a boyfriend, Kia?"

"Man . . ." she scoffs. "There's this one dude Renny I kinda like."

"Renny?"

"Renard."

"Is he eighty?"

"No, Carlos, he's sixteen. Just has an old-ass name. But I dunno. Mostly, I don't have time for these children that're tryna throw game my way. Seriously, these idiotic little boys come with some true stupidity, and quite frankly I got better shit to do."

"I hear you." Of course, I don't a have an adolescence to hark back to, but from what I've witnessed in the street, her assessment sounds about right.

"All right," Kia says, putting down the dish towel and sitting at the table. "Stop distracting me. I got homework and shit."

A murderer.

Sarco's voice wakes me from a delirious dream and I jolt up, throwing my glance around the dark room. Nothing stirs. Victor is knocked out in the easy chair, snoring loudly. The moon is strong tonight, sends bright beams in to illuminate the edges of my furniture. Outside, passing cars slosh through puddles and the rain still soft-steps through the night, against my windows.

No Sarco.

I lie back down.

Murderer.

That sickening whisper. He knows who I was. Or he said he did, anyway. My creator. He seemed to have the memories to prove it, but I suppose there are ways of faking such things. I roll over, scowling at my tender abdomen and impossible thought lines. I want to know. I couldn't give a fuck for three years and suddenly it matters. Because now the answer is a reality, somewhere, in someone's mind, even if it's a near-impossible, almost-definite lie of a reality. There's still a glimmer there, and a glimmer is all I need to get agitated.

Fuck.

I roll over again, squirming with pain.

Ass.

What happened immediately before that moment of me? What happened after? I took it to be some part of my death struggle, but who knows? If Sarco's telling the truth and I was a murderer, I suppose I could've had many moments like that.

Fuck.

This means that when I finally do find Sarco, I can't just ruthlessly end him for good the way I'd like to. I have to find out a few things first. And this complicates shit. The hunger for knowledge always complicates shit.

And I hate complicated shit.

Fuck.

CHAPTER THIRTY-NINE

⟨∾⟩

My brother."

I've never been so happy to see Riley in my whole entire life. Ever. And it's not a dream. I grin up at him like an overjoyed idiot and he rolls his eyes.

"I'll take that stupid-ass smile to mean you're feeling better."

"Yes." And it's true. I feel . . . cleansed. That fresh feeling, like when you've just taken the best nap ever. Yes. "How long have I been here?"

"Damn near two weeks, man."

"What?"

"You had a lot going on, apparently. Meanwhile, the ghost world keeps turning. We gotta talk."

"No shit we gotta talk. Are you okay? Cuz last time I saw you, the tables were turned."

"Yes, I recall," Riley says ruefully. "I'm good. Still a little shaken, I admit, but the COD dickheads actually have some pretty serious stuff they working with up there, and combined with the wonders Mama Esther worked on me in the immediate afterthefact, I gonna be fine."

"I'm so glad to hear that. Mama Esther?"

Riley makes a noncommittal shrug. "She's hanging in

there. Sarco put some nasty spell on her that had her all
narc'd out for a while, but she's conscious again. The COD
guys actually sucked up their old rivalry and sent some
cats over to work on her. She's recovering."

My mind lurches in frantic circles. Probably because
Riley's here—it's impossible not to slide into strategy
mode around that guy. "Sarco . . ."

"Yeah, well . . ."

"They haven't found him?"

Riley shakes his head. I hadn't really expected them
to, but the information still sends an unpleasant ball of
dread rising up my throat.

"I thought they'd . . ." I don't have the words because
I'm too busy imagining Sarco's shadow reaching out at
me through the gates of Hell.

"Nope, and the Council's none too happy 'bout everything."

"The fuck else is new?"

"Pretty much. But they're keeping you as lead on the
case, if that makes you feel any better."

I'm both relieved and embarrassed. Riley's got senior-
ity on me; he trained me. He's something of a legend
when it comes to tracking down spirits and putting them
in their place. There's no way I should be running a case
he's . . . Oh. "They took you off the case?"

"I'm on *light duty*." Accentuated with two little bunny
ears from his ghost fingers.

"Which means?"

"Technically, I'm a paper pusher for a few weeks, till I
get clearance. But I could give a fuck what it means, Carlos, and you know that. It's a bureau decision, which
means it's meaningless, which means I'll be helping you
out on this one, even if it's somewhat on the hush-
ity-ho-hush. But you're in charge, my brother. This is your

baby now. I just gonna be your pain-in-the-ass henchman for a change."

"Fair enough." Then I look away as my mind goes into overdrive again. Sarco, the ngks, Sasha, Mama Esther's . . . Lines stretch across a makeshift city map I have stashed in my subconscious. The park, the park, the park . . . "He's trying to tear a chasm into the Underworld. Release the dead."

"So I hear."

"And there's more. Not sure what, but . . . there was a lot he wasn't telling me."

"I would imagine."

I shake my head. And then an odd memory resurfaces. "Riley?"

"Oui?"

"Who named me Carlos?"

He chuckles. "I did. I found you. I figured I should get dibs on naming you."

"Why Carlos?"

"Oh. Cuz you looked Puerto Rican."

I roll my eyes. "And?"

"And I knew this ghost Lalo that has a son named Carlos. He runs a bodega over by the Junklot in Bed-Stuy. I had to send Lalo back down under but he asked me to keep an eye on his boy, so I check in now and then. And he was Puerto Rican. I think. Maybe Dominican."

"How charming. What about the Delacruz?"

"Oh, Baba Eddie came up with that actually."

"From the cross."

"Yeah, but you gotta ask him. I don't think he was talkin' 'bout Jesus."

We sit there quietly for a few moments. Then I say, "I know I've never asked you this before . . ."

Riley rolls his eyes. "Hold on. Lemme put some coffee on."

"You didn't even let me—"

"Why bother? You wanna know about the night I found you."

Stupid-ass mind-reading-ass friends.

Riley sets two steaming cups of coffee on the counter. "I was on a stakeout, keeping an eye on some dumbass ghost that wanted revenge for some shit that hadn't even happened to him. I don't remember. Some political imbroglio, I think. It was pouring rain. I was with Dro. Shit . . ."

We both just sit there dully for a second, letting the ghost of Dro's ghost pass over us and depart. I bristle, trying to direct my thoughts away from his family. "Go on."

"I remember!" Riley says it a little more excitedly than necessary; he's trying to get away from that emptiness too. "We were waiting on this fuckin' city councilman guy who had passed some bill that got some fuckin' old ghost's favorite house obliterated on one of those imminent domain heists. You know?"

"Kinda."

"Fucked-up thing was, the ghost hadn't even ever *lived* in the fuckin' house when he was alive. Didn't even haunt the motherfucker when he was dead. He just *liked* it." We both shake our heads and drink our coffees for a few moments. Ghosts can really be out of line sometimes. It's one thing to come back for true love and cause a little hubbub. Or some unresolved revenge bullshit, fine. You're wrong, blah blah blah, but I get it. At least you have a good reason.

But every now and then you get these real entitled-acting blowhards wanna come back around and raise a roof just because—perfect example: because they like a house. Ugh. Can't even roll my eyes far enough back into my flesh-and-blood head to express how out of line that shit is. So you like a house. Fucking stay your dead ass downstairs and paint a picture of it. No one wants your house-loving ass wandering around pestering some city councilman, even if he does deserve it.

I'd say as much to Riley, but he already knows. One or the other of us usually goes on that exact rant every couple months or so.

"Anyway," Riley says once enough time has passed for us to both have run through the whole spiel in our heads, "the ghost would come out the park every night—surprise, surprise—and go fuck with the councilman while he was walking his German ridgeback terrier or whatever."

"Did you just make that up? Cuz I really think it is in actuality a breed of dog."

"I don't fuckin' know, Carlos. I think Dro called it that." Another pause, shorter this time. "Shit was three years ago."

I just grunt.

"Fucking . . ." Riley says by way of a space filler while he finds his spot in the story again. "Oh! So we waiting by the archway, right, and it's raining and shit, ghostly-ass night, blah blah blah, and just, I mean *just* as Harley Q. Orenson or whoever the fuck he was comes a-strollin' out the motherfucking park, I notice something odd 'bout this pile of garbage that was scattered 'round the legs of the archway. I mean, first of all, it's weird that there's trash there in the first place, because especially since the white folks started really staking out they territories; Parks and Recreation does not slack on the pickup around there. You do not see piles of refuse around no Grand Army Plaza. But lo and bemotherfuckinghold: basura!

"So I squint at the shit through the rain some, think I see something that don't quite fit—that was your ankle—when suddenly Dro's tugging on my sleeve, like 'Agent Washington, Agent Washington!'"

"Oh, this was back when he still called you Agent Washington. Hilarious."

"Well, that is my title."

"Right. Go on."

"And, of course, the ghost is emerging, the councilman ridgeback-walking, all kindsa culmination is culminating in front my very eyes. Now, Carlos, we've already been through the fact that I'm really not a motherfucker who goes checking for situations that don't pertain to me. Not my style." He frowns like he just ate something really foul and shakes his head. "I don't."

"I know."

"Ever. Very rarely."

"Riley, I know that."

"So it was . . . odd, that I should insist on seeing what the fuck this situation was about. Especially because I didn't fully trust young Dro to know how to really bring a case to its final resting place, so to speak."

"Understood."

"But nevertheless, I sent Dro to deal with Orenson, and I went over to your crumpled ass and took a pulse."

"On my ass?"

"No! Your neck, dickhead. And you had none. Fine. If you'da just been dead, which I thought at first, I'da just walked the fuck away and someone woulda probably found you in the morning and hucked you over to the morgue right quick and called it a day."

"Right."

"But then you groaned."

I get us two beers out the fridge. Moving feels good. "Did I?"

"Rolled slightly over and moaned, I believe. Something creepy and zombielike, whatever it was. And I realized, something extremely motherfuckin' odd was going on."

"Correct."

"Then I left."

"You left?"

Riley shrugs. "Carlos, you were just some dead dude. So you were moving. It's weird, but what are you gonna do? I had a new guy about to fuck up a high-profile job, and I'm not gonna stop and play doctor with every damn near-dead guy that falls across my path."

"So why'd you come back?"

"I helped Dro sort out the house-loving homeboy. He really just needed a firm talking to and made himself scarce by his own accord. Then we headed to Mama Esther's, as a matter of fact, cuz I was a little spooked by the whole night and pissed about something—some Council bullshit, I'm sure—and I told her about what I'd found."

"And?"

"And she threw a shit fit and made me go back and get you."

"Did she say why?"

"Just went on about our brethren and not leaving 'em out for the wolves to chew on. It was all pretty cryptic, but you know how she can get when she's moody."

I nod, but I'm thinking about something else. An idea is gestating somewhere in me and I can't quite articulate it yet. Apparently, Riley recognizes the face because he takes one good look at me and stays quiet.

"All right." I look around. I've been cooped up in this house for who knows how many days. My midsection still aches where the blade went in and where it came out too, but I'm mostly healed up. The cleansings, the herbs, Dr. Tijou's wonder pills all musta done some pretty serious work on me. Baba Eddie had laid down his heavy-duty spiritual blocks on my place. I briefly entertain the image of Sarco's shadow, hovering just outside my door, claw raised. Then I shake my head. "Let's go," I say.

"Where?"

"Grand Army Plaza."

"What, now? It's three thirty in the morning."

"I know. I have a hunch about something."

"Carlos . . ."

But I'm throwing on my coat and heading out the door.

CHAPTER FORTY

❧❧❧

Feels good to roam the streets with Riley again. It's a certainty that travels with us, that I have his back and he has mine, and if some mess should go down, we will go down with it, cursing and stabbing all the way to Hell. Also, it's nice out. A warm wind blows my overcoat as we slip through Bed-Stuy, pass the colossal Marcy Projects with their ill hospital lighting and scattered characters stoop sitting through the graveyard shift. We pass the hustle and bustle of Fulton Street, still alive with crackheads, drunks, and occasional hipsters even at this late hour, and reach Atlantic Avenue. I realize we're retracing the steps I took with Sarco not long ago, and so instead of taking Franklin, we cut over to Washington and then Underhill, which drops us onto the parkway within sight of the brightly lit plaza.

Civil War soldiers glare out at the darkness from their frozen battle positions at the top of the arch. Traffic speeds around the rotunda where Flatbush Avenue smashes into Prospect Park and then divvies off into about six other streets. The Brooklyn Public Library looks on solemnly, a vast square structure with ornately carved front pieces and an elegant open-air entrance. The arch itself is a dazzling,

European-type structure, pale against the night sky with
dark statues of horses, angels, and warriors bursting like
lichen on either side and along the top.

"What you looking for, man?" Riley wants to know.

I stand beside one of the huge legs of the thing. My eyes
are closed, and all my sensory satellites are fully charged.
I shush Riley and hear him shrug and scoff and then stroll
around to the other side. A memory, a smell . . . anything
to trigger my mind to what happened here, to the last scrap
of life before my death. But all I hear is the late-night
wind, the passing traffic, the soft buzzing of streetlights.

And then there's something else. Something dead. Of
course, the surge of spirit activity writhing around in the
park fizzes along in an endless drone, but this isn't that.
This is . . . much closer. Much larger. Much older. And
still vague, somehow.

"Riley," I whisper-shout. "You feel that?"

"What?" he says; then he shuts up. "No. Yes! What the
ever-loving fuck?"

"Shh!"

It's growing, coming closer. It's fuller in the air around
us, a sensation more than anything else, a heaviness, a
presence. And it's peaking. Riley's beside me, and we're
looking at each other with our what-the-fuck faces. "Did
you know there was something here?" I whisper. I don't
even know why I'm whispering; it just seems appropriate.

He shakes his head. "I don't really fuck around in the
plaza unless they send me here."

And then it's on us, all around us, arrived. A humon-
gous pale face blanches the darkness between the two pil-
lars. It's looking down at us, or pointing down at us, I
should say, because the eyes are closed. That huge mouth
is twisted into an unmistakable frown, and canyons stretch
from either side of the nose past the edges of its lips.

The mouth opens and I crouch a little, thinking it might swoop down and gnaw on my head. "Dreams of tales untold," the ghost mutters.

"Excuse me?"

"The dreams, the dreams of tales untold, the weak empty-handed can defeat the bold."

"That a little poem you wrote?" Riley asks.

Those great big eyes squint open the tiniest sliver. "Just a thought."

"Who are you?" I say.

The ghost doesn't answer, just hangs there above us, flickering slightly.

"Yo!" Riley shouts, and the eyelids open all the way to reveal cloudy, cataracted pupils tainted by a labyrinth of squiggly veins. "What's your name, ghost?"

He seems to consider this for a moment, sighing deeply. I'm about to get really annoyed because I can't stand it when people ignore me, when the ghost says, "Pasternak."

Riley makes a face. "Pasternak? The fuck kinda . . ."

"How long you been here?" I ask.

Pasternak squints into the night. "How long have you been here?"

Riley looks at me. "This guy's really irritating me, Carlos."

"Me too."

Riley turns back to Pasternak and points at me. "You ever see this dude before?"

Pasternak swivels his giant murky eyes toward me for the first time and I shudder. A moment passes, during which Riley probably considers just slicing the fool and being done with it, and then the head nods slightly and Pasternak says, "Mm-hmm."

My heart jiggles. "When have you seen me? What happened?" I have to physically restrain myself from vomiting all my swirling questions out into the night.

Pasternak looks back at Riley, frowns, and then closes his eyes again.

The fuck, I want to yell. But I don't. I hold back. Because I want to know, and I don't think bullying it out of him will do any good.

"The fuck?" Riley yells. "He asked you a question."

"Hm?"

Riley throws his arms up. "I can't with this dude. I just can't. We want to know about what happened here, three years ago, to my friend. I was here. I found him. He was dead. It was raining. Do you remember? Anything?"

"So many days, so many nights. Rain, water, ocean, water, life . . . water. Dreams and daydreams. Nightmares." His eyes still closed, Pasternak seems to suck his face inward for a moment, suddenly becoming all sharp lines and creases, and then relaxes again.

I'm almost at breaking point. "Enough poetry! Tell us what happened, man."

"There were seven of you, but only five survived."

"That night? Here?"

"There were seven of you, and none survived. And then"—melodramatic pause in which Riley and I both consider many acts of violence—"there were five."

I had thought the ghost was frowning before, but turns out that was just his face, because now the edges of his mouth slide even further down, the lines etch deeper, and his eyebrows raise toward each other. "There were seven of you, and none survived," he says again. "And then there were five."

"Who? Who were the five?" I say. "Who was here?"

The eyes open wide again, suddenly terrified. Little spasms run along the side of Pasternak's face like lightning against the night sky. "Sarcofastas!" the ghost wails.

His eyes roll back in his head, and when he speaks again, it's in Sarco's voice.

"I release you, my children, into this rain-soaked night. You are free, for now. But one day I will again come calling. You will fear me, but you will be drawn to me too. I have given you life and you are indebted to me. It may be in a year or ten. I will call upon you, and together we will alter the course of the world.

"Now scatter."

Pasternak blinks. His eyes are watery and dart around. He glares at me for a good ten seconds, and then the darkness envelops him and he's gone.

The night seems very dark. Even those bright plaza lights only barely hold off the endless black sky. And inside, I'm empty once again. On the edge of knowledge and then lost. "Let's go," I say. "He's not coming back."

Riley looks around warily. "The fuck was all that about?"

"My rebirth, apparently. But let's get out of here. I don't like any of this."

We're about to walk away when something snaps into place. "Gah! Of course!" I yell, stopping short.

"What?"

I walk quickly around to the front of the arch and stare up at it. "The oil-covered dead man with the mustache!"

"The fuck you talking about?"

"Sasha! Her last memory. She said she saw a man, frozen as if in death, with a mustache and his body all slick like he was covered in oil." I point to one of the statues reaching out from the edge of the pillared leg.

Riley raises his eyebrows. "I'll be damned."

"We died together," I say.

"How sweet."

CHAPTER FORTY-ONE

❦

Mama Esther looks smaller than I've ever seen her, like the whole traumatic experience deflated her. She's backed into a shadowy corner of the library, surrounded by stacks of old books and half-empty coffee cups. A sad cello solo wails out of the old speaker box.

"Ahh, boys," she mutters when we come upstairs. "Boys, boys, boys."

"You all right, Mama Esther?"

She gazes up at me, her lids half closed. Dark moons circle beneath her eyes and she's trembling. "I wish I could say I was. Take a seat. You want a book? Looking for anything in particular?"

"No, Mama," Riley says. "We just came to see how you were doing."

"Ah." She waves us off with a huge, flickering hand. "Mama Esther'll be all right."

I take a step toward her and the old ghost's warmth embraces me. "Mama Esther."

"You lost her, huh?"

I nod and twist my mouth up to one side of my face. I imagine this is what it must be like being a little kid, confessing to your mom that you've done something stupid.

Mama Esther shakes her head. "I can't help you, Carlos."

"Can't or . . . ?"

"No." It's not even sharp, how she says it, just sad. "I don't know. She betrayed you to Sarco, no? Well, if she's not all the way dead or gone to ground, she will be soon." She ignores my flinch. "Sarco will be looking for her too. You know he needs a halfie."

"Sasha wouldn't—"

"Wouldn't what? You don't know a damn thing about what that woman would do. Did you think she'd stab you? When a necromancer as powerful as Sarco is in play, folks will do all kinds of shit you'd never expect to stay alive. All bets are off. She'll let you know how to find her when she's ready to be found."

I open my mouth to explain the real reason Sasha betrayed me, but Mama Esther cuts me off. "I understood something about the ngks when all that mess went down. Those threads they use—it's like they have a physical manifestation of a hive mind, yes? That's how they're able to materialize so fast around each other. One has a thought or notion, a tinge of fear or rage, the rest of 'em have it too. Instantly."

Riley and I shudder. I'm sure the memory of Dro succumbing to that sudden onslaught burns through both of us.

Mama Esther pays us no mind. "It's the same spiritual technology the Council uses to get in touch with you, same fibrous interconnected threads, but the ones the ngks use are about eighty times more powerful and they can construct and manipulate their web like it's a living part of them. When they want something heavy done, they fortify that web. The Council's is just weak and stagnant, like the rest of the Council's shit."

She peers down to see if either of us will take the bait.

We don't. Mama Esther exhales loudly. "The ngks' thread-web is powerful enough to rip that hole Sarco wants between the living world and the Underworld, but it needs a puncture point, like a thread needs a needle, yes?"

"The house ghost," Riley mutters.

"And a halfie is the final ingredient," Mama Esther says. "A doorman to manage the chaos, shape it into whatever sick fantasy Sarco has schemed up. Without all the ingredients, the whole plan collapses. You know he'll be back for me too. And there ain't that many house ghosts around these days . . ."

"We got guys all around the place," I say. "Twenty-four seven."

"He'll be back though. He'll wait till the city thrashes amid the collective energy of a thousand revelers and then he'll unleash his foul designs again, Carlos. You'll see."

The pronouncement sends a shiver through me. "I don't think he'd walk right into so many soulcatchers' waiting arms," I say. It sounds forced though. "Plus, I gave him a few scratches to think about while we were tangling downstairs."

The old house ghost shakes her head, eyes closed. "'Course he'll be back. If you didn't think so, you wouldn't have them boys out there waiting for him."

"We're gonna do whatever we can to stop him, Mama Esther," Riley says, straining his voice toward sincerity. It's not hard to see we're both in over our heads.

Mama Esther makes a sad attempt at a smile. "I know you will, boys. I know."

It's daybreak when I walk out of the diner on Vanderbilt. I head south, past the plaza with all its shadowed memories,

through the still-gray park to Flatbush. I find a comfortable stoop out of sight and perch there, sipping the dregs
of my to-go coffee, and ponder.

Sasha appears after the sun has fully risen and pushed
long shadows across Ocean Avenue. The air smells fresh,
the promise of a warm day ahead. I tail her to the Q train;
keep one car back and hidden within a crowd of morning
commuters. We switch twice and then rumble out of a tunnel and up over the Brooklyn skyline. We're at a stop near
the shipyards when she steps onto the platform and then
disappears down some stairs. I slip out just as the doors
are closing, earn some scowls from a group of old Russian
women, and follow Sasha to the street level.

There are so many words inside of me. They bristle
and burn in my throat, beg to be let out. Usually, when
I'm trailing someone, it's to send them back to Hell. If
the mark swings around suddenly, I just skip to endgame
and that's that. But this . . . I step out of the station just as
Sasha crosses the dirty street beneath the tracks. If she
turns around, I don't know what I would do. There's no
script. Probably, all these words would tumble out, these
stupid, useless words I've been carrying everywhere like
a bouquet of delicate, beautiful, stupid, useless flowers.

If she turns I may crumble.

A car screeches its brakes and swerves around me, but
Sasha doesn't look back. I'm almost disappointed. She
shoots a glance to one side, eyes squinted, and then turns
down an alleyway. I wait a beat, then lean my back against
the corner and peek out. Halfway down the block, Sasha
talks to a bearded man in a fedora. His skin is ashen, a
deathly pale that lets me know he's one of us. The Survivors, they call themselves. She hands him a package. I
duck back out of sight.

I need to know more about this man, but Mama Esther's

right: Sasha's bound to vanish at any given moment, especially if she's exchanging strange packages with strange men in some strange backwater Brooklyn alley. I hole up behind a concrete pillar beneath the tracks and wait.

And wait.

And check back around the corner. The street is empty. I curse. Walk halfway down it, curse again. Storm back out. And wait.

The sky grows dark.

CHAPTER FORTY-TWO

❦

It's been going on every night for the past three or four weeks." Mrs. Overbrook squints up at me like I might have something to do with it. I don't.

"Just bumping or other noises too?"

"No, singing, clapping. Tambourines." Her hands wave small circles. "All kinds of things."

"I see."

"Are you going to file a report, Detective?"

"Sure. Any recent deaths in the family, ma'am?"

"What's that?"

"Deaths. Have you lost any family members recently?"

"Come." She takes my cool gray hand in her warm little brown one and walks crookedly beside me into the next room. I'm still getting back into the swing of things, tidying up these sad little crinkles in the life-and-death continuum. Sasha hasn't shown up for more than a week. Sarco's shadow waits for me around every corner. And my wound itches every time I think too hard about either of them. Mrs. Overbrook hobbles along through the forest of old newspapers and random knickknacks cluttered to the low ceiling. It's too hot in here. Outside the window, the sun does glorious things to the Manhattan skyline. "Pretty, right?"

"Beautiful," I say. Then I realize she's not talking about the view, which she's probably more than used to at this point; she's talking about a small shrine set up in a wooden bookcase beside the window. Four adorable little kids smile out of a framed picture in the middle. Around it, Mrs. Overbrook has stapled some squiggly marker drawings and a short thank-you letter written in careful, looping script. A fake gold necklace hangs off one shelf, and a tiny ballerina music box sits on the bottom.

"They died in a fire, down south."

"How long ago?"

"It'll be two years in June. Their stupid cow of a mother was smoking in bed. She lived, her drunk-ass son-of-a-bitch husband lived, and all my little angels passed away." She looks for a second like she might break down crying, but then she gathers herself and smiles up at me. "I'll never understand why the Lord does what he does. Nothin' to do but accept it. But it pains my heart, Detective. It really does."

"I cannot even imagine."

"It's them, isn't it—been pestering my sleep so?"

"I think so, yes, Mrs. Overbrook."

"Thought so." She looks at me with that penetrating gaze of the old and wise, squinting through two solid inches of glass that magnifies her eyes into giant, wandering splotches. "You're not like other cops I've met."

"I'll take that as a compliment. Do you want me to deal with your situation?"

She considers for a moment, staring thoughtfully at the shrine. "No."

Our eyes meet again, and I feel an infinity of understanding pass between us, one so deep I don't even completely grasp it. So I nod. "Okay, Mrs. Overbrook."

"I think it's rather comforting. I just wanted someone to come take a look. Someone who would know what to do."

I'm a little startled by how much her words mean to me. "Glad I could help."

Unfounded. That's what I'll scrawl on my paperwork for this one. I've already half written it in my head as I step out of the pee-stained elevator and walk through the lobby. *The investigating officer has determined that there was no supernatural activity in the apartment in question. Further review is unnecessary.* I've written those words so many times now, I can't even count. You'd be amazed how many folks get attached to their ghosts.

Elton Ellis, the tactless miniature messenger ghost, is waiting for me outside Mrs. Overbrook's public housing project.

"Yes?"

"The Council has a message for you."

"Why didn't they just blast it to me the way they usually do?"

"The system is down."

"Excuse me?"

"Something happened. A glitch or something, and they can't get through. Or not every time anyway. So they send me."

"How convenient for you."

"Well . . . in a way."

"Out with it."

Elton Ellis clears his throat, then says: "The crack house off Fulton Street."

"What about it?"

"That's it."

"The crack house off Fulton Street. That's the whole message?"

"Word for word. What'dyou think it means?"

"Guess I'll go there and find out."

"Maybe there's something there they want you to see."

I glare down at the little ghost. "Is that what you over-heard somewhere, or are you being speculative?"

"Maybe I heard one of the chairmen saying that to one of the soulcatchers."

"Maybe you heard something else too?"

Elton Ellis shrugs. "Maybe."

I fish through my pockets for a little toy or candy for him, but I'm all out. Figures. I tell him to wait right there and fast-walk it to the bodega across the street and back.

"Here," I say, handing him a fistful of assorted penny candies.

He eyes them hungrily. "That oughta shut it down."

"Who said that—Botus?"

"Maybe."

I throw him a sharp look so he knows he's not getting any more candy out of me.

"Okay, yeah. Botus. He thinks the case's a waste of time and a useless runaround and wants you back deal-ing with other things."

"But I am dealing with other . . . Oh, never mind. Any-thing else?"

"Agent Washington wants you to meet him at the Bur-gundy when you're done. Where you going?"

There's actually a couple of crack houses off Fulton Street, but I'm pretty sure I know which one they mean. It's a big brick building with a long history of unfortunate fires, ODs, kidnappings . . . I'm sure Victor's seen his share of living hell at this spot. Spiritually, the place is a disaster. So much ruined life attracts the ruinous dead too, and I have to shoulder through a crowd of muttering shadows just to get to the front door. They're dripping with regret, bitterness, all the sloppy leftovers of a life poorly lived, and I want nothing to do with it.

"Shmash'ema," one of them moans as I hurry past. "Shmash'ema, ohhh da li." The old tattered spirit's thrown himself in my path and I don't want to touch him.

"The fuck out my way."

"Shmaaaa-aaa!" he gurgles. "Car . . . los!" Ugh. I hate it when they know your name. There's no reason for that.

"Move!"

He slithers and writhes, an almost formless mass of wayward hair and tentacular slabs of fat, and finally gets in a position that I can easily step over, which I do.

"Shmlaaaaa Carlo-os!"

I walk into the dim building, step past a few sleeping-or-dead bodies in the front foyer, and eye the shadows for Sarco. But he's not here. He's nowhere. I've stared into how many shadows these past weeks? Scanned how many empty streets? It seems never-ending. I keep waiting for the shivering dread to pass, for my old reckless self to come back, unsullied by fear. But it won't. Far as my mind is concerned, Sarco waits around every corner. He slides along alleyways, slinking out when I've turned my back and vanishing again when I spin, blade drawn, to confront him. I can't go on like this, chasing my own shadow.

I march up a flight of rickety stairs, brush past a guy in his underpants, drooling, all scratchy beard and flimsy, tracked-up arms, and find another room full of human desecration. I knock my cane a few times on the wood-paneled floor. "Anybody seen a tall, pale dude with long, nasty black hair?"

A few guys look up at me and then look back down. One nods his head toward the back of the room, and I gingerly step over a few huddled clumps to an empty spot of floor. Balled-up rubber gloves and blood stained bandages lay scattered around like someone just turned over a hospital garbage can. Then I realize that whole part of the floor is a shade darker than the rest.

Blood.

"What happened?" I ask no one in particular.

"Dweezo crapped out," a grizzly old man offers. I recognize him—Delton Jennings: one of the regular homeless guys who make their night rounds through the city.

"Dweezo?"

"The guy you lookin' for."

"Was he a Muppet?"

"Naw, man, that was just what they called him. I dunno."

"All right, how'd it play out?"

"Nah, he was just all fucked-up-looking when he showed up this morning. Blood kept trickling out his eye and shit."

"His eye?"

"That's what I said! And then he started coughing. He was up here and he started coughing and then he threw up and it was bright red, yo, and then, well . . . that." He nods at the sizable stain stretched across the wood floor.

"EMS just left a few minutes ago."

"You know where they took him?"

"Woodhull, I think. It was all kinda rush-rush."

I thank Delton and work my way back downstairs and out the door. The same phantom nastiness tries to get in my way again, cooing his horrible song, but I step past before he can really become a nuisance.

"Shmloooo," the thing gurgles as I walk away. "Car-lossss . . ."

———

Woodhull looks more like a prison than a hospital. The hulking cement monstrosity sits at the geographical moment where Bushwick, Williamsburg, and Bed-Stuy converge. Three massive towers jut out from an aggressively plain block of nondescript windows. One concrete ramp loops around into a parking lot and another peels off from the street into an awning-covered driveway, where ambulances idle outside the ER doors. A series of grumpy-looking surgeons, security guards, and EMTs share cigarettes and horror stories on the curb directly in front of a NO SMOKING sign.

I wait, blending with the passing bums and street riffraff, until an ambulance crew rolls up and unloads a screaming bearded guy who appears to be velcroed to the stretcher. A couple cops jump out, looking exhausted. "Fuck ya mothas!" the guy yells. "Fuck all ya fuckin' fuck mothas. Twice!" Perfect. "I will"—he bangs his head against the stretcher—"fucking kill you all!"

Hospital cops are running everywhere, looking for restraints, trying to appear competent. It's a mess. I slip in on the current of that chaos, veer off down any old hallway and find an elevator. The morgue is all bright lights and bland colors. We have a guy down there, Mortimer, who lets us pretty much roam free when we need to. I don't know if he knows what all is going on, or if he just takes whatever handout the Council has for him and forgets what he sees. Either way, he nods his jowly old head as I strut past and mumbles: "Row seven, bin A."

I walk down the aisles, peering at the numbers like I'm using the damn Dewey decimal system for the dead. The little silver doors seems to go on forever, and I try not to think about dozens of bodies decaying around me, many unclaimed, unnamed. Death is one thing. The moment of the release of the soul, all that: fine. But the physical body after the fact? Get it away from me. That smell of rot, that festering, bubbling transition into mold and then dust? Hell no. Good night. I don't like dead bodies.

But apparently there's one I have to see, so I put my hand on the cold steel handle and roll out bin A in the seventh column. It's Sarco, all right. His mouth hangs open in that particular dead-guy way, rotten teeth jutting out in all kinds of unseemly directions. Ugh. And he's naked, his pale skin even paler now and lacking in all the stretch and shine of life.

"Bled to death."

"Jesus Christ!" I jump backward, reaching for my blade, before I realize it's only Mortimer. The guy should really know better than to sneak up on a man in a morgue. Surely there's some protocol about that.

"Odd case really."

"Oh?" I say when I recover my composure.

"The EMTs were so used to bringing him in for some bullshit OD or another night of binge drinking, I think it caught 'em off guard that something was actually wrong with him."

"That and he was bleeding out his eyes."

"Well . . . yeah, that too."

"Anything else?"

Mortimer digs in his lab coat pockets, retrieves a flask, and tugs on it brazenly, making loud guzzling noises. When he's done, he wipes his mouth, smacks his lips a few times, and says: "Nope."

CHAPTER FORTY-THREE

⚭

"They're what?"

"That's what they said."

"But, Riley . . ." I let out a sigh that's full of my dull hatred for the Council. Then I give up trying to finish the sentence, because Riley already knows what I was gonna say. "Fuck."

"Word."

We're in the Burgundy Bar. I'm trying not to think about Dro not being here with us. I'm trying not to think about Sasha too. I had been getting good at that; she's vanished as predicted, after all. But Sasha keeps creeping back into my thoughts.

"I'm so . . . ugh!" I don't even give a fuck about all the surly drunks that're making faces my way right now. Least of my damn concerns. That crazy guy in the corner? I'll be that. I am that. I'm done pretending shit. "Riley. The fuck we gonna do?"

"Honestly?"

"Honestly."

"You need to consider the possibility that the dude done died and that's what it is."

"But I . . ."

"I know you don't like it. But that's what you looking at right now."

"I said, I wouldn't believe he was dead till I saw a body."

"And?"

"And I saw the body and I still don't believe he's dead."

"Well, the Council does. And they say there's no record of him becoming a ghost or nothin'."

"Like they never miss a spirit."

"Right. Well, regardless. Case closed."

"But no." I down another shot. "No. We keep going."

Riley does too. "Carlos, it doesn't bother you that the homey checked out in damn near the same way your boy from New Year's did?"

"It does. It does. Of course it does."

"Well, what does that tell you?"

"That some sinister shit is at play."

"No! Well, yes, but besides that . . ."

I put my head on the bar and then lift it up again. "Indeed. Quiñones, dos más por favor."

"It tells you there's someone else workin' things. Pullin' strings. A third party."

"Fuck. Well, that's not case closed then. It's case wide the fuck open."

"Right, but the Sarco chapter of the case is closed. Anyway," Riley says languidly. The alcohol seethes through his words now. He pauses, squints up his face like he's trying to remember what he was about to say.

"Anyway?" I drink my shot; he drinks his.

We both let out that satisfied, holy shit *aaaah!* noise, and then Riley goes: "Oh yeah, anyway, the Council wants to tell you about how they're shuttin' down your big case in person."

I bust out laughing. Not really sure why. "When?"

"You were sposta be there about fifteen minutes ago."

I stop laughing. "What?"

Now Riley's cracking up. "They said ASAP about forty-five minutes back, so . . . I figure that means about twenty minutes later. So, yeah."

"Who told you?"

"The little guy. Erfin. Orifice. Orifice Eddie."

"Elton Ellis."

"Right."

"Why didn't they just . . . ?"

"The system's fucking down."

I let out another exasperated sigh. "In so many more ways than one."

There's a somber pause, and then we both break out laughing again.

Botus seems unpleasantly victorious today. He doesn't simmer in the shadows with the rest of the committee like at the last hearing. "Agent Delacruz," he says, sliding forward so the bright overhead lights shine right through him and throw drastic shadows down his face. "How wonderful that you have recovered so well."

"Mm-hmm."

"We really quite enjoyed your report, although we were dismayed to see how much trouble you went through and, of course, that you proceeded into the realm of the dead without first obtaining permission for said activity from the Council."

Assery! My mind bumbles through the big clunky words I have to say to justify said activity, but I'm still a little tipsy, so I know they're not going to come out right. "The situation," I say, very slowly, "was sufficiently urgent . . . as to require . . ."

"Of course," Botus says with a pay-no-mind swipe of his hand. "We're just glad you made it out okay." This is when I realize something must indeed be very wrong. I've never heard of him being this magnanimous. "What's . . . ? How shall I put it? Ironic? What's ironic, Carlos, is all that trouble you went through and still were not able to fully thwart the conspirator Sarco."

"Hm, ironic, right." Trying not to roll my eyes.

"Fortunately, he was found dead, as you know, yesterday afternoon. Perhaps even brought low as a result of some of the damage you inflicted on him during the foray into the Underworld?" I want to stab Botus. But I won't, partially because my aim would be a little off right now and I don't think I'll have more than one shot. He's going somewhere with all this, enjoying it thoroughly too. "So we are going to close the case, but only partially."

"Partially?"

"Well, of course, ngks are still there, infesting several buildings around the rogue entity Esther." Besides calling Esther a rogue entity, this is the first thing Botus has said that I agree with, possibly ever. "And many tantalizing, unanswered questions remain: Who was this character? Where did he obtain the spiritual technology to do what he almost did? What is the nature of his alliance with the ngks? How exactly did he finally meet his end?"

I'm nodding, dazed more by the shock of agreeing than by the alcohol.

"And finally," Botus finishes elaborately, "who was he working for?"

I stop nodding. "Come again?"

"We have reason to believe, Agent Delacruz, that the conspirator Sarco was actually in league with another entity . . ." I'm not tipsy anymore. My mind is sharp with despair. "One besides the ngks, that is."

And then my stomach plummets. I know exactly where this is going. And as I think it, Botus is sliding Sasha's picture across the table with his icy fingers. "Pretty little thing, isn't she?"

And I'm raging across the room, overturning carefully placed furniture and growling my inhuman wrath as I wrap my hands around Botus's shimmery neck and plunge my blade through his chest. No. No, not that. I'm nodding. Looking with disinterest, a touch of disdain even, at the picture Trevor showed me those months ago, ignoring the fluttering sensation in my chest. I shrug. Don't want to overdo it. Just a shrug.

"We believe this person to be, in fact, the mastermind behind the conspirator Sarco's operation. Or should I say . . . mistressmind?"

That cements it: Botus gotta die. He looks at me for a shared chuckle, but I just stare.

He shrugs. "Anyway, we believe she has designed and carried out numerous breaches of the Council code and may have even manipulated this Sarco into performing her bidding. Perhaps with some form of mind trickery or hypnosis."

Lies. Impossible, ridiculous lies. "I see."

"We also have reason to suspect, Agent Delacruz, that she is, like yourself, an inbetweener, probably related somehow to the unsavory fellow you dealt with so proficiently last New Year's Eve. Well done, by the way."

I nod. Some of my best work, actually. Completely fucked up my life. *You're welcome.*

"Anyway, it's fitting, in a way, that you should lead up this part deux of the investigation, so to speak."

"Where can I find her?"

"We don't know, I'm afraid. May take a little reconnaissance work. But all your operational considerations regarding Sarco should be transferred directly to this new target, considered extremely lethal and a vast threat to the Council and all that we stand for. From what we can figure, an attack is imminent."

An attack is *always* imminent, but I don't have it in me to get slick.

"We want her dead. Deeply dead. Gone. *Extinct.* Is that clear, Agent Delacruz?"

"Crystal. When do I start?"

"Immediately, of course."

My voice sounds cold and a hundred miles away. "Excellent."

"Well," Riley says. "We both knew this was going to happen sooner or later."

I shrug. We're back at the Burgundy, but I don't even feel like drinking anymore. "It's true, but damn . . ." A horrible thought occurs to me and I try to put it away.

"Spit it out, man."

"I just . . . you don't think . . . the Council's somehow . . . you know?"

Riley sighs. "I know, and no." I'm almost disappointed. In some twisted way. This whole mess'd be much easier to swallow if I could just blame it on a vast Council conspiracy and call it a day. "I've had that thought many times, Carlos, believe me. The sheer amount of complete fuckery that goes on over there is astounding, but it's just that: fuckery. There's no logic or rhythm to it. There's no underlying genius or cover-up. They just overdo everything and get bogged down in all that supernatural bureaucracy, and somehow it manages to fuck up the rest of our lives again and again."

"Damn, that does pretty much sum it up."

"Let me ask you a question."

I nod for him to go ahead.

"Y'all fucked or you made love?"

My face says, *I have no idea what you're talking about*, so that I don't have to.

"Did you pound that pussy, or did you softly caress it until the morning's first motherfuckin' light?"

"Um . . . a little of both, I guess."

Riley puts his face in his hands and sighs. "Oh, Christ Jesus, Carlos. That's bad."

"Why? What's that mean?" Riley and his damn relationship theories. I really think he spends this much time thinking about it because he hasn't been in one since he's been dead. I'm not even really sure if he . . . can. The few cryptic shards of his life he claims to remember always magically happen to be when he was getting it on. It's gone well past the realm of credibility at this point, but I don't really mind.

"I'm just saying, when you . . ." He pauses, tries to arrange his thoughts. "I'm trying to establish the degree of entangled that you've gotten yourself. Because when it comes to women that are involved with investigations, it's one thing to have a one-off, like you were on the brink of with that white chick, Christina."

"Amanda."

"But it's a whole other situation when you're talking about, you know . . . the heavy-duty shit. *And* you killed her brother? Damn. Tangled-ass web you weave, son."

"Indeed."

"So you gonna go after her?"

I nod.

"What you gonna do when you catch her?"

I dismount the barstool and drop some ones on the counter. "To be honest, I don't have a fucking clue."

CHAPTER FORTY-FOUR

ind Sasha.
   This is, after all, what I do. When I returned, when
I woke from the groggy, infinite sleep, my body already
knew how to cast this fibrous, tingling net around me and
then cull it back and digest the wealth of information it
brought. I knew how to interpret each flash and glimmer,
the droll tides of sorrow and flash-pan bursts of joy. Lying
there in Mama Esther's guest room, I perfected the push
and pull. Found the outer reach, contracted just so and then
released again, inching this web of mine farther and farther until the entire neighborhood around me gave up its
pulsing secrets, and I had to stop from sheer information
fatigue.

And now, standing in the center of an open field in
Prospect Park at dusk, I throw farther out into the reaches
of Brooklyn than I ever have before. This is my second
night of searching, second night of standing perfectly still
in the middle of this park, projecting and retracting, coming up empty. Clouds cover the moon; a breeze passes,
whispering of autumn's approach. The amphitheater of trees
around me shivers.

Ignore the park spirits—no anomalies ping out from

the darkened slopes to either side. The surrounding neighborhoods tingle with life—Brooklyn braces itself for something. Hearts race, preparations in full swing. Even the
cops know it's coming; they shift their weight and mutter
to one another.

But *what?*

I draw back in. Breathe. Breathe again and then release,
wider this time, beyond the park, beyond the projects and
massive ornate apartment complexes, past Empire Boule-
vard and Eastern Parkway, deep into Bed-Stuy, Crown
Heights, Flatbush.

Sasha.

Thousands of pings, heartaches, fears, great sweeping
torrents of love and doubt, explosions of rage and the glib,
monotonous landslide of depression. Honking horns and
flashing lights, a thrusting motion, sudden death, slow im-
possibly slow decay, the birth of a new movement, a ritual
repeated again and again, the gathering tide of generations shifting repeating changing vanishing a pinprick a
temper tantrum a gas leak a nail clipping a regret a scrap
of lined paper scribbled on in long frantic letters a puff of
steam a journey a bike helmet playing cards *Sasha* an
engine a pair of scissors a— It was just a wisp. Circle in,
circle in—train tracks domino tables chairs the night sky
regret a swallow a crack in the sidewalk a tunnel an old
hand, shivering, turns over another card a trash can a
wheel a pigeon two pigeons an iron bridge over the tracks
a chair—

"Again?"

What?

"Yes?"

I open my eyes. The glimmer of a soulcatcher helmet
clouds the night sky. The threads release, a last flickering

glimpse of Sasha vanishes amid the avalanche of information, and then there's nothing.

"Sir?"

I blink. I'm lying on my back.

"Sir, you don't look well, sir."

No . . . shit. Information overload. Never cast the net that far before.

"A hand, sir?" The soulcatcher reaches a shimmering glove toward me.

I shake my head.

"We came for orders."

Orders. We. A few shadows stir in the corner of my eye. Right. Hunched on my elbows now, I take in the squad of soulcatchers. Those battered, horseshoe-crab helmets and long hooded cloaks. Ornate face guards like some elegant skullsmile.

"We brought you coffee, sir."

Bless them. I gather myself, roll onto my front, then heave up to a crouch, and finally stand. "Black?"

"And no sugar, just like you like it." The soulcatcher nods to where a blue-and-white to-go cup sits in the grass. Protocol junkies. There's no one around, no one to see the cup float and then pass to me by an invisible hand. They probably whispered in some poor drunk's ears till he stumbled into a bodega for it and then distracted him and whisked it away, vanishing it with some Council magic as they made their way through the streets into the park. And then they put it on the ground for me. So the empty park and midnight sky wouldn't see them pass it.

Protocol junkies.

I pick it up, pop the plastic lid opening, and take a sip. It's thin bodega trash water, but I let out a satisfied *ahh* sound anyway. "You've done well, fellas."

"Thank you, sir. Do you have orders for us?"

"Orders?"

"Regarding the apprehension of Sasha Brass."

"Queens," I say.

"Sir?"

"Got word she might be in Queens."

The shrouds flutter uncomfortably. "The borough? Anything more . . . specific?"

"Is Queens too large an area for you to cover with your 'catchers?"

"No, sir."

I look up at the cloudy sky and sip my coffee. "Then happy hunting. I'm following up with some leads over here."

For a few seconds, the soulcatchers just waver in the night wind. I turn to look at them, very slowly and with death in my eyes. They turn and slip silently across the field.

I know I'm an asshole for that. They'll be searching the backstreets of Corona and Rego Park until next Tuesday, but I need them out of the way, and if I just send them home, it'll raise too many eyebrows.

Once again in silence, I close my eyes and strain, poring over the jumble of meta- and microdata. A wrinkled hand overturned a card onto a velvet cloth. It's a cloth I've seen before, a hand I know.

I open my eyes and then run.

CHAPTER FORTY-FIVE

～ ❦ ～

Old Ginny is not a fortune-teller I put much stock in. Nice lady, but as far the future goes, she's useless. Still, when she looks me dead in the eyes tonight and scowls, "You, sir, are fucked," I have to lend it a little credence. I've never seen her predict with such certainty; usually she's all waving hands and *hmm*ing it up to seem more authentic.

"Well, thanks for the vote of confidence, Ginny."

She looks up at me from her little cubbyhole storefront. "I'm just saying."

"Maybe keep it to yourself next time. I didn't ask for a damn reading."

"Sometimes I give freebies."

"How charitable. You seen a—?" How to describe Sasha and not sound like a twelve-year-old asshole discovering poetry for the first time?

Ginny raises her eyebrows at me.

"A beautiful . . ." I wave my hands around.

"I seen her," Old Ginny says. "Stopped by a few hours ago." She flips over another card: Death. "Oh boy."

"You turn over that card every time I come around, Ginny. I'm not impressed."

"Well, maybe that should tell you something."

"The woman. What'd she want?"

"Weed."

"Excuse me?"

"She asked me if I knew where to get some weed."

"Did you . . . did you tell her?"

"Sent her to TiVo."

"The fuck kinda street name is TiVo?"

The old fortune-teller shrugs. "He likes to have his shows recorded while he's out selling, I guess."

"Whatever. Where does he sit?"

"Ocean Ave.," Ginny says. "A few blocks down from the park."

I close my eyes. *She'll let you know how to find her when she's ready to be found.* Mama Esther's words whisper through me. "Thank you, Ginny."

"Be careful out there, Carlos."

Brooklyn's beautiful tonight. I stroll down a quiet residential block, enjoying the warm air on my face. I can almost ignore the nagging sensation that Sarco looms in every tall shadow. A wrinkled old man sits on his stoop, enjoying a cigarette like he's done every night before bed for the past forty-something years. He's dying and he knows it, better than his doctors even, but he could give a shit. It's been a long and glorious life, full of hard work and good love and he's pretty much ready to go. So he sits there grinning out at the night and tips his battered baseball cap as I pass.

"Evening," I say. A few cars go by. The trees swirl and gossip quietly above me. No ghosts, no Sarco. No one at all, in fact, once I pass Old Dying Guy. Then I turn a corner onto Ocean Ave.; the block is alive with mommies and children, teenagers flirting, street vendors selling knickknacks. Smoke billows from those big barbecue vats, and you can smell jerk chicken getting brown for blocks and blocks and blocks. The whole neighborhood is celebrating another day of life.

I'm pretty sure Sasha had no interest in buying weed, but just in case I'm wrong, I walk up to the dude with a baseball cap and puffy jacket on the far end of the block.

"TiVo?"

"Who the fuck wants to know?"

"I do."

He sizes me up, squinting through whatever calculation makes me coplike or not. "Come," he finally says. We walk between two apartment buildings, past a trash dump, and into a small back office where a little white guy sits typing on a laptop.

"This dude came looking for you, T. Want me to pop him?"

I'm working out my own calculations—how fast I can unsheathe my cane-blade and slice both these mother-fuckers—when TiVo waves a hand without looking up from the screen. "Nah, it's cool, Melo. Thanks. Hang on one"—he types one last thing and then looks up at me—"sec. There. Hey, what can I do for you? You want some weed? Meth? Red? Purple Haze? P-funk? I got it, homeslice."

"No," I say. "I'm straight. Did a pretty girl come through today, looking for weed?"

Melo wiggles his eyebrows. "Did she! Ay . . ." I shut him up with a glance, look back at TiVo.

"She did." He smirks. "Sold her a dime bag."

"She say anything?"

I'm wondering when it'll kick into TiVo that I could be

a cop, a rival gang member, anything . . . but he just shrugs. "Nah, just bought the dime and peaced."

"See where she went?"

"Nah. You sure you don't want some weed, man?" His eyes drift back to the computer screen.

I shake my head and see myself out.

CHAPTER FORTY-SIX

⟋⟍

I stand perfectly still across the street from Sasha's building. It's another of these giant, antique-looking beasts that fill up Flatbush with their vast lobbies and rickety old elevators. I'd given up staking the place out when it was clear she'd vacated the place. Now she's let me know she's back and I have no idea what to do. There's a little Mexican kid sitting outside wearing a Spider-Man outfit and talking to himself. I'm trying not to see myself in him.

This is supposed to be fun. I was born to hunt, dammit. But instead, for the first time, I am that creepy guy that people so often mistake me for. I'm a stalker. And my stalker's mind is cluttered with endless irritating debates about what will happen next—a hundred hypotheticals, none of which do me any good whatsoever. I could walk right up there. We could have it out, settle our differences, have amazing sex, and then fuck up Sarco's plans. In whatever order makes the most sense, of course. But then I could walk up there and find Sarco waiting instead of her. Or Sarco waiting *with* her, infinite ughh, and then that'd be that.

Across the street, mini-Spider-Man is having a whole debate with himself in Spanish.

What if, he's probably saying, *Sasha really is behind the whole thing?*

Bullshit, he replies, shaking his head. *She's had every reason in the world to stab you without being a super-natural criminal mastermind.*

But she reeled you right in too, didn't she? Worked it just right. You think it was all just happenstance how sweet everything worked out?

I followed the footprints she left for me to see. She's not stupid, and she knew I'd be looking for her. She led me to her door. Mama Esther said she'd reach out; she reached out.

Mm-hmm. Bet it feels good to think that.

You shut up.

Okay.

The kid fishes some old crackers out of his little school satchel and chews on them, looking thoughtfully at nothing at all. I go for a Malagueña, realize I'm out, curse, and then limp from my stalker spot toward the bodega on the corner.

And that's when I realize I'm being followed.

It's like a jolt of pure life in my veins. The little hairs on the back of my neck stand up; the whole world around me springs into sharp focus. I'd been waiting for this feeling, that sweet thrill of the hunt, but when the target's all cluttered by emotions, well . . . the thrill keeps its distance.

This, though, is something else entirely. Someone has their eyes glued to my back. They're plotting from the shadows, improvising around any obstacles or uncertainties, planning ahead, setting up traps. Doing what I do. For a terrible second I both hope and fear that it's Sasha, but immediately, I know it's not. This is an altogether different feeling. The wind whispers in my ear, the subtle atmospheric changes, the faces passing by, the shushing trees—they all sound the subtle warnings of the universe. Something is coming. It's close. It's been with me for a while, too. I've just had my head too far up my ass to notice. Damn.

The old Yemeni guy behind the counter grins as he sells me another pack of cigars. "A beautiful night, yes?"

I'm forming a plan. I'll get this hidden follower somewhere where it thinks it can attack in safety, away from Sasha, and flush it out. "Yes, beautiful night." And then I'll find out what the hell's going on.

Clarity. My heart comes to life with the sudden awareness that I just decided what to do. All it took was a threat and a plan to make everything make sense. Maybe it doesn't totally make sense, but that's not even my concern right now. I'm sliding along the momentum of the night. I'm willing to take some hits if it means getting my swagger back. I will lead this unknown threat away, and then I'll take it out. Yes.

"Good night," the old guy says.

I nod at him, smiling for the first time in days, and then walk out the door. Then something huge gets up in front of me, eclipsing the streetlights, the passing cars, the whole world. Giant hands shove me backward into the bodega, and I hear the door slam and then lock.

It takes a half second before I recognize the face glowering down at me, now gray and lifeless. "Moishe?"

CHAPTER FORTY-SEVEN

⟳∾⊙∾⟲

His head and beard are shaved, his face is twisted with maddened intent, and he's not wearing his Hasidic blacks, only a tattered T-shirt and gray pants. But it's Moishe, without a doubt. And yet, at the same time, it's definitely not. Something's off. There's a nasty scar reaching across his forehead where Sarco shanked him. A million thoughts burn through me now, but I can't deal with them, because the dead giant is advancing with his long arms outstretched.

I scatter out of the way, upsetting a pyramid of canned soup, and dash to the back of the store.

"Stop this!" the old Yemeni yells. "Get out of here!"

The giant silences him with a well-flung can of soup. It ricochets across the counter, sends up an explosion of penny candies and chewing gum, and whizzes past the old man's head, thudding against the bulletproof glass behind him. The man shuts up and slides down behind the counter. I duck around to another aisle just as the giant turns back to me.

In three long strides he's crossed the store and is rounding the corner when I catch him across the face with a broom handle. The giant stumbles back a step and I follow up with some gut shots. He doubles over but manages to charge, pinning me against a wall of kitty litter and dog food.

"Moishe!" I yell. "Come out of it!" I should just save my breath. Whatever spell he's under or thing he's become, it's not letting up anytime soon. Anyway, he's got those huge hands around my neck now, and my windpipe is giving way beneath his grip. I summon all my strength and shove us both forward, delivering a few swats with my cane as he struggles to keep balance. He growls at me, lunges, and I realize I'm fighting for my life. I turn and run, upsetting everything off the shelves as I go. It slows him a little, but those damn legs are so long it's not much good.

Moishe died. I saw it happen. Sarco put my blade through his head. But here he is. And he's not a ghost. He's definitely come back, something like me, but those eyes, those eyes are empty. He's emoting. Rage courses through him as he charges toward me, but there's no life to him. He's an empty puppet.

The giant's full weight thunders against me, and we crash to the floor. I thrash my arms and legs, making myself as difficult as possible to keep ahold of. He's flustered, reaching out stupidly to keep me still but missing. I manage to turn over onto my back and immediately take a solid fist across the mouth. Feels like a cinder block just found me from a few stories up, and for a second I think I might pass out. I hold on, though, if nothing else because my life depends on it, and thrust my hips up, knocking him just off balance enough for me to squirm away.

Hello, my son. Sarco's hideous whisper echoes back to me. He's a resurrectionist. He did it to Moishe. He did it to me. He did it to Sasha. I know it's true as soon as it occurs to me. Sarco murdered me and brought me back.

Partially. No wonder he has stored-up memories of me before I died. He was there. He was there when I died.

I make a dash for the door, but I know it's pointless. It's locked, and there's no way I'll be able to get it open before he gets to me. Endgame has come much faster than I expected. I'm reaching for my blade when the shot rings out. It's ear-shattering, and the sheer shock of it throws me to the ground. I hear a monstrous clattering from behind me, whirl myself around, blade out, and see Moishe crash backward against the salsa and applesauce shelf, shattering half the bottles as he slides down to the ground. A continent of blood opens across his shirt.

The old Yemeni's face is tight and furious. He lowers the gun, one of those no-fucking-joke *Dirty Harry* hand cannons, looks me dead in the eye, and says: "Get out of my store. Now."

I start to say something, but what's the point? The police will be here any second, asking all kinds of unseemly questions. I'm halfway down the block, my brand-new cuts and bruises burning in the fresh night air, when a huge figure bursts out of the store amid shattering glass. I flatten myself against a wall. Another gunshot shatters the night. Moishe stumbles into the street, dodges a passing car, and then lurches toward the sidewalk. I can't tell what those wide, darting eyes take in, but I'm guessing he's spotted me. I throw myself into a crowd of folks moving quickly along the avenue.

Everything hurts. The night closes in on me. Too many people around. Witnesses, gossipers, hungry ghosts. I need to get somewhere safe, assess my damage, and start over. There's a new element in the equation.

I make it to a wide swarming intersection at a southern corner of Prospect Park. Tons of people fill the street;

their laughter dances into the sky amid the thrum of bass-boosted speakers blasting a relentless Caribbean beat. Did Sasha set me up? Is the whole thing a trap? I glance back and see the tattered dead giant standing in the middle of Ocean Avenue; cars peel to either side of him, honking and cursing. And then I notice all the cars have flags hanging off them.

J'ouvert. Carnival. That's what all these folks are doing out here. The West Indian Day Parade is about to erupt in a three-day festival through Crown Heights. That's what the city's been bracing itself for. *He will try again,* Mama Esther said. *He'll wait till the city thrashes amid the collective energy of a hundred revelers, and then he'll unleash his vapid designs again, Carlos. You'll see.* The Council wasn't kidding when they said an attack was imminent. The corpse that once was Moishe hasn't moved. Maybe I wore him out. More likely, he has some other business to attend to. Either way, I have to regroup. I turn and break out toward the parkway, ignoring the burning of the giant's eyes against my back.

CHAPTER FORTY-EIGHT

⟨∾⟩⟨∾⟩

You sure?" Riley says. We're on a rooftop watching Eastern Parkway fill with revelers.

"I am. It makes perfect sense: two million people flooding the streets of Brooklyn in full regalia, raging street parties all through the night and straight on past dawn. I don't think any supernatural mischief maker could resist such a distraction. Plus, it has the added benefit of culminating mere blocks from Mama Esther's and in the whole area surrounding Prospect Park's eastern edge."

"This is all true."

"Plus-plus: there'll be a hundred thousand spirits in the air, taking part in the festivities. And the people will be in masks and feathers. Even folks with the Vision will be confused between the living and the dead."

"Indeed. Of course, there'll also be a bajillion soul-catchers swarming through the crowd, sacking folks up and lugging 'em back downstairs."

"Bah." I wave the very idea away. "Sarco's not scared of soulcatchers. Doesn't mean a thing."

"And now the real estate Hasid is in play."

"That ain't him, man. Whatever it was Sarco did to

bring me and Sasha back, it's not what he did to Moishe. He's just a shell, Riley."

"He a corpuscle."

"A whobascule?"

"A corpuscle's like an empty body with an angry-ass spirit shoved in it. Rude as fuck thing to do to someone if you ask me."

"Sounds about right. Whatever it is, it . . ."

Riley's doing something to his face. "I'm listening," he says, but he's busy squinting and probing his fingers along his left eye.

"No, you're not. What'd you lose a contact or something?"

"Dammit, Carlos, the dead don't wear contacts!"

"Well?"

"Hang . . . the fuck . . . on." Suddenly, his fingers slide all the way into his socket and he makes a little *guh!* noise, something between a gasp and a grunt.

"Riley!"

"I'm okay. I'm okay." But his other eye tears up, and he's still squinting and writhing. Then, with a nasty popping sound, he pulls out his fingers. And, I realize, his eye.

"Gah!"

"Here." He hands me the eye.

"No! The fuck I'm supposed to do with this?"

"C'mon, man, don't be such a little girl. You put it in."

"Put it in?"

"In your eye, Carlos. I wanna try something." He waves the glowing sphere at me. "Take it."

He's not gonna give up. Plus, I'm almost as curious as I am horrified. I take the eye. It's nebular like him, just a gentle tickle against my fingertips and a little mushy. "Put it in?"

"Your eye."

"Ugh, Riley!"

"Look, we do it all the time ghost to ghost when one goes into the Underworld and the other's up top. If it works right, you should be able to see what I see once I go downstairs."

I look at the shimmering ghost eye. "Shouldn't I give you my eye if . . . ?"

"Carlos." Riley gives me a Riley look. "Don't act new. You should know better than to come at me with some anatomy and physiology bullshit. Save it for your living friends, okay? The dead don't fuck with those rules. We much more holistic than that. If I see some shit with one eye, the other eye gonna see it, even if it's in you. Intent takes you a long way in the Underworld. Anyway, I said I wanted to try it. I don't know if it'll work at all with your damn flesh-and-blood ass, but since we're splitting up and what I see will matter somewhat to your situation, I figure it's worth a shot."

I think I hurt his feelings. I brace myself and then turn the eyeball to face out and place it up against my own. There's a little resistance at first. I'm sure my body is screaming *What the everlasting fuck*, but eventually Riley's eye slides into place and all I feel is a slight pressure.

"There. Not so bad, right?"

"And it should work when you get downstairs?"

"Should."

"But I'll still be able to see up here with my right eye, right?"

"Unless you poke it the fuck out, yeah. You'll get the hang of it. You can kind of toggle back and forth by squinting once it starts working. You'll see."

"Great."

We watch the burgeoning mass of partiers gather beneath us.

"Okay," Riley says. "How you wanna play it?"

It's actually the day before the parade, but the celebra-
tions begin tonight. The NYPD has lined up barricades all
along Eastern Parkway and cops in riot gear stand around,
shifting their collective weight from one foot to the other
and waiting for some shit to go down. Their red and blue
lights pulsate across the block. Vendors are setting up
food stands, guys have tables draped with flags from every
imaginable Caribbean island and a few they mighta made
up. Young people wander in laughing droves up and down
the blocked-off street, carrying on, getting lifted by the
excitement in the air. You can taste all that collective
energy pointing toward a wild and terrific night.

And then, of course, there's the spirits: they're everywhere. Ghosts whip through the air in fancy, colorful piru-
ettes, shimmy up and down the street, cavort and converse
above the heads of the living revelers. They're tiny, flickering specks of light and they're gigantic, blimplike, floating
fatuously across the night. They're swarming packs of dwarf-
ish chattermouths, and they're long-legged, tall-walking
long faces, all serious in the face of coming celebration. It's
a joyous sight, so many spirits wandering free, and I wonder
briefly if Sarco isn't onto something marvelous . . . If it
weren't being masterminded by a sociopathic dickhead who
probably killed me and the woman I love, I might very well
be all aboard for figuring out a way to close the gap between
the living and the dead.

I head to a food stand, dodging a guy painted all blue

who teeters drunkenly across the parkway on ten-foot-tall stilts. Home-cooked rice and peas, spicy jerk chicken, and steamed cabbage—a beautiful thing. Fills me up just right, and when I'm done I toss the Styrofoam container and head west toward the park. The streets are already getting crowded. I see a few soulcatchers slip silently between passing bodies, watch them circle and then disappear like sharks, hunting down some petty offender, no doubt. I roll my eyes. Tonight is not the time to be chasing our tails. At least backup will be readily available if things get hairy. In theory, anyway.

Somewhere among this teeming, feathered mass of life, Sarco lurks. Moishe's tattered shell is out there too, I'm sure. And so is Sasha. I'll be so happy when I can think her name without shuddering deep inside.

Something horrible happened. People are running, crying. Cops have their visors down and their faces clenched; hands linger near service revolvers and wrap tightly around billy clubs. I swig from my flask and slide between the rushing crowd, flowing gracefully against the current. This might be something in my department, or it might just be some same-old street-festival bullshit. There's a kid in his twenties sitting on the ground, cursing. He's not wearing a shirt and a few superficial gashes crisscross his chest and shoulders. He stands up, wobbles, curses some more, and sits back down. PD is barging around nonsensically, trying to create their own brutal order out of the chaos. Some EMS guys work their way through the crowd, but neither one is Victor. The uniforms close in around the slashed-up guy, blocking him from view till all that's left of him are shouted curses and the bloodstain on the sidewalk.

———

At the southeastern corner of the park, a group of teenagers twists and grinds to some pounding soca music. The rhythm gets into you, beats against your bones, and finds you vibrating whether you want to or not. They're all wrapped around one another, pulsing in time. A light rain has started, barely more than a mist, and no one seems to care. They're all sweat-soaked anyway.

Past the writhing teenagers, I glimpse a tall shadow lurking in the parking lot of a twenty-four-hour pharmacy. Moishe's haunted shell. I make a point of not breaking into a run. Instead I vanish backward into the crowd, work my way down a side street, and reappear around a different corner, coming toward the empty lot from the side.

He's gone. He's gone, and now I wonder if he was even there at all or just another of my paranoid imaginings. I glance back and forth, but the crowd is tremendous, a vast, pulsating mass of revelers, and even a gigantic mostly dead white guy could disappear into it as long as he ducks down a little. I catch a flash of movement from the side street I just came down and swing my head around. Nothing.

I wait.

Someone staggers out into the lamplight, someone tall. I launch forward, not bothering to conceal myself anymore. He's a block and a half away and seems to fade back into the velvety shadows as I approach.

A few rats scurry around. Trash is strewn everywhere. The thumping soca rumbles along. He must be so close, watching.

"Carlos." Riley's voice in my head startles the shit out of me, and I almost drop my cane. *"You there?"*

Not like I can respond. I make sure to keep my concentration fixed on whatever imminent attack awaits and halfway listen to Riley. *"You were right. Sasha was at her place, and now your girl's on the move."* My girl. That jackass. He wouldn't say that if we were in the same room. Okay, he probably would. *"She just left her building and is going north on Ocean. I'm keeping a distance cuz I assume she can spot ghostly motherfuckers like myself."*

My eyes scan overflowing trash barrels, a rusty old Dumpster with two smashed televisions sitting in front of it like attentive manservants, a darkened streetlamp, a flicker of movement that turns out to be more rats, a whole repeating collage of colorful posters for upcoming dance parties, a dimly lit billboard.

"Something else . . ."

A little farther down the block, a piece of metal clatters wildly against the pavement and splashes into a puddle. As I whirl around toward it, I catch movement in the corner of my eye. It's very close to me—something stirring in the shadows. I'm unsheathing my blade as the giant rumbles out of the darkness, knocking me onto my ass.

"I don't really know how to tell you this, Carlos."

I have no idea what Riley's ambling on about, but I have more important things to deal with right now. I swift kick Moishe in the gut as he closes on me, but it does little to hold him back. He growls and drops forward onto his knees, his hands stretching toward my neck. I roll out the way just in time not to get strangled, but he catches my ankle.

"It's Sasha . . ."

I *fwap* my cane across his face and batter it against his arms. He holds tight. Fine. I unsheathe and chop off his hand. Moishe roars, a guttural, inhuman noise that chills my bones. I stumble to my feet and turn around. The giant's already up. Blood trickles languidly from his stump of a wrist. He looks at me and howls with rage.

"She's pregnant."

The giant charges.

CHAPTER FORTY-NINE

❦

P regnant!" I yell it so loud that I actually startle the giant for a second and he loses his momentum. Not that I'm in any position to take advantage. I just stand there gaping like an asshole. He lunges. I manage to side-step only just enough so I get shoulder checked instead of full-body demolished. I lose my grip on the blade, and it goes clattering off into a pile of garbage. The sound knocks me out of the daze—I stumble backward and clear out of the way of his swinging fists.

My blade is out of reach. Running is useless because one of the giant's strides equals four of mine. So I grab the nearest trash can and thrash him with it as hard as I can when he dives for me. It catches him full across the face, which stuns him just long enough for me to bring it down on his left knee. When he crumples, I hit the same knee again, and this time I hear it snap pleasantly. He moans, and I crack him across the face again.

Okay. (1) I need my blade back, and (2) pregnant?

What? I can consider Thing #2 as I deal with Thing #1, but still . . . it gives me pause. The giant groans and rolls over. I know he won't stay down long, even with the solid thrashing I gave him. Plus, I'm a little dizzy from

whatever damage he did on me. I stumble toward the
trash pile that my blade clattered into.

I think Riley said Sasha was pregnant. I'm pretty sure
that's what he said. It makes sense, I suppose. A season
has passed. She'd be showing. But where's my fucking
blade? Panic churns the emotional confusion that's already
prickling my brain. There's a million crumpled up soda
cans, shredded candy wrappers, Chinese food containers,
all devastated and scattered about like some decimated
city after a hurricane.

But no blade.

I hear something behind me and spin around. The giant
is gone.

*"Hey, Carlos. Sorry, man. Didn't mean to drop a bomb
like that and then disappear. It's just . . . there's a lot
going on out here."* No shit. I hate not being able to have a
two-way conversation. No blade. And Rasputin the Invin-
cible Giant that I just fucked up has already run off.

*"Yeah, anyway, I guess we'll deal with the preggo
thing later, cuz right now, ya girl is making her way very
quickly . . ."* Riley pauses to catch his breath, and for a
second all I hear is his heavy panting in my ear. *"Sorry,
she's fast. She's going to the entrada, Carlos. I don't
know . . . I don't know if Sarco's somewhere, or what the
deal is, but like it or not, what we gotta deal with right
now is that Sasha's making moves. Pregnant and everything. Sorry, man. Maybe it's not yours."*

I wish he would stop talking.

*"Anyway, when we get underground, the Second Sight
should kick in, and you'll be able to see for yourself, so
that's . . . nice. Ah, fuck. I gotta catch up with this chick,
man. I'll check in with you in a bit."*

Terrific.

Sasha's heading for the entrada. Which means she's

either meeting Sarco somewhere in the Underworld or . . . or she really is masterminding this whole fiasco. Or maybe some other wildly plausible explanation I just can't think of right now. Either way, she's surely heading for Mama Esther's.

I have to get there first.

As I think it, the dead giant lopes out of the shadows again. He's limping badly but otherwise doesn't seem nearly as worse for wear as he should. I don't have time to fuck around with Andre anymore. I got places to be. I hurl one last trash can his way for good measure and make a break for it.

CHAPTER FIFTY

❦

But nothing is ever simple. I am, after all, limp-legged. I'm fierce with it, of course, got it down to a nice rhythmic swagger, but that's *with* my cane. Without the damn cane, I just hobble. Still, the giant's leg is freshly busted and he hasn't gotten used to the shifting of weight, the trembling off-balance feeling with every step. Then again, he's huge. So we're about even, and must be quite a sight to behold, tearing through the crowded midnight streets.

If it wasn't Carnival, I'm sure we'd get even more stares, but as it stands, Brooklyn is bursting with strangely swaggering people. Moishe and I are both a little paler and a little more desperate than the rest, but otherwise, no one pays us much mind. There's a strip of Flatbush Avenue that's four lanes wide and surrounded by wilderness; the park on one side and the Botanical Gardens on the other. Hundreds of revelers crowd the street, dancing and yelling and carrying on. I push through, working my way north toward Eastern Parkway and trying not to hurt anybody or start a fight. Every time I look back, the giant is gaining on me. Halfway to Grand Army Plaza I'm already winded as hell. This no-cane-having bullshit is really not the way to go. I pause for a few seconds to catch my breath. The giant's huge pale head bounces above the crowd toward me.

Then, all at once, I'm in the Underworld, surrounded by ghosts. It takes me a second to realize that it's just Riley's Second Sight kicking in, and even then it's freakishly disorienting. Those same horrible, slow-moving ghouls crowd all around, and some kind of tumultuousness is erupting up ahead. The ghouls lurch forward as one and then a few of them back up suddenly.

"Carlos, can you hear me? Ugh! Stupid question, my bad. Anyway, hopefully this shit is working and you can see that I'm surrounded by your old nursing home friends, and Sasha's up ahead somewhere, fucking shit up. Gonna try to get you a visual. Stand by."

Just what I need: a visual of the woman who's probably carrying my baby tussling with a gang of ancient death creatures.

I squint my left eye so the real world around me comes back into focus and then duck into Prospect Park. Everything on the ground is useless twigs, but up ahead I see a felled tree. I limp over to it and snap one of the branches free, maybe a little more aggressively than necessary. This'll do.

I don't see the giant anywhere, so I pop back out onto Flatbush and, now with at least a semblance of a cane, make my way north with a quickness.

Sasha is in rare form. At first, all I see are ghost bodies falling over themselves to get out of the way. Then Riley shoves through the crowd and there she is: beautiful as ever and with a little paunch in her belly. She's got a blade in each hand, and there's no doubt she knows exactly what the fuck she's doing with them. This isn't some frantic slash-fest; she lashes out with precision, cuts down one ghost and simultaneously stabs another as it rushes up behind her. Every move is exactly as fierce as it needs to be; she never overshoots, doesn't even seem winded.

Suddenly, her presence at the Red Edge makes perfect sense. She wasn't just keeping an eye on her brother: she was his bodyguard. No wonder he was so terrified that night—his protector hadn't come along with him. But still, there was something else . . . The giant is waiting for me at Grand Army Plaza. He must've slipped ahead while I picked a new cane. The crowds are thicker and sweatier here. Eastern Parkway is the epicenter of the revelry, and it's kicked into full swing as we hurtle toward dawn. I duck into a passing crowd of revelers, trying to lose myself in the masses. The giant wades in after me. He's smiling.

"Carlos, you seeing this? Fuck, I keep doing that. I really wish we had two-way, my brother, because I would love to hear what the fuck you're saying right now. Your girl is killing them! Literally. I've really never seen anything like it."

She really is, too. I think about my desperate slashing while I was trying to get away from the same ghouls. That wasn't even swordplay, just me trying to stay alive and keep a clear path. Sasha's in her physical body, which makes them come at her even more voraciously, but none can get close. She advances forward in careful sidesteps, one blade pulled back at hip level and the other in front, pointed straight up. When a few ghosts try to get cute and slosh forward hungrily, she slices in a clean downward diagonal, catching three of them with one strike.

They fall back, and when two more come forward, she stabs them with her other blade, *pow-pow*, in quick succession and steps over their writhing forms. It's like a dance, the way she glides along, chopping and hacking as she goes.

The giant's disappeared again though, so I have to check fully back into reality and get my ass to Mama Esther's.

CHAPTER FIFTY-ONE

❧

Underhill Avenue is a small, relatively quiet street tucked in between Washington and Vanderbilt. It's mostly residential and white and the revelry hasn't spilled onto it much, so I hang a left off Eastern Parkway and make good progress for a block or two. Then I realize he's behind me. I feel the air shift as he lumbers onto Underhill from the parkway, feel the world call out its quiet warnings. He's teeming with rage and I can feel that too. Whatever shred of a soul he's got left has been corroded with the singular intent of destroying me—that much is clear. And me being elusive is irking the shit out of him. He lumbers down the block. His gait's still torqued from that kneecap I shattered, but still, the guy's fast.

I cut across a playground, all stretched out shadows and pools of darkness, and then wind around a corner toward Washington. If it comes down to it, I'll have to engage him again, but I really don't know how many more of these little throwdowns I can take. Perhaps his other kneecap will have to be my next target. When I check back, he's already storming through the playground.

Washington Avenue is bustling with a mix of celebrating West Indians in feathers and face paint, and drunken hipsters in, well, hipster clothes. I dash across the street, nearly get smashed by a city bus, and head down Prospect Place toward Classon. He's a half a block back and gaining. People are staring at him, this ungainly giant on my trail, but no one thinks to, say, stick out their foot and trip him, or arrest him maybe. I should be so lucky.

In the Underworld, Sasha's cleared herself some kind of space and is leaning against a tree, panting. She's also, I notice, clutching her belly. I wish Riley would tell me what the fuck is going on, but I guess there's nothing to say: she fought off the ghouls and is probably composing herself before the final assault on Mama Esther's. Or whatever the plan is. Riley seems to be watching from behind a corner, and suddenly the view spins and I'm looking back at the mass of hungry ghosts. I hear him say, *Oh shit*. There're hundreds of them and more gathering every second. They're all facing toward Sasha. Angry storm clouds converge in the murky skies of Hell.

The march toward life has begun.

Where is Sarco? I need him to show up so (a) I can stop worrying about where he is and (b) I can know Sasha's not really in charge of this whole nasty scheme. Okay, I'm in denial. I can admit that and still be in denial, right?

This ginormous, old building sprawled across a full block of Classon Avenue was once the Jewish Hospital and then a vacant, graffiti-covered ghost sanctuary, and now it's a bunch of luxury apartments. Go figure.

When I turn around, the giant is lurching across the street toward me. He waves a baseball bat that he must've picked up somewhere. I'm just trying to imagine how poorly my dead branch will match up against that Louisville Slugger when he gets plowed into by a passing livery cab. That huge body splays out across the windshield, spiderwebbing it, and then he slides down and tumbles off to the side of the street.

"The fuck!" the driver yells, jumping out. The giant's up in seconds flat and towering over him. The driver gets calm real quick. "Okay, buddy, okay." The giant grunts and taps his bat against the Crown Vic a few times, causing excessive damage and making his point very clearly. As I leave, the driver jumps back in his car and screeches off.

I can see Mama Esther's. It's two blocks down on the right. I'm not even totally sure what I'm going to do when I get there, but I know if the world is about to be overrun by throngs of hungry ghosts, I need to be on that rooftop to stem the flow. The giant grunts a few blocks behind me.

And then it starts to rain.

I pause at Mama Esther's doorway to catch my breath and check on Sasha. For a second, it's impossible to tell where she is because there're so many damn ghosts around. Then I recognize one of the towers that marks the entranceway to Prospect Park, just a crooked shadow of itself in the Underworld, and realize Sasha is much farther back than I had thought. Either the ghosts have held up her progress or . . .

"Uh, Carlos, I don't think ol' girl's heading for Mama Esther's." Riley has such excellent timing. If she's not going to Mama Esther's, there must be another target spot where they've set up to tear open the breach. Somewhere with ngks surrounding it, which could really be anywhere as long as they aren't reported. I step off the stoop and start fast-walking down Franklin, keeping an eye out

for the giant. Somewhere with a halfie, which is wherever
Sasha goes, really.

"Carlos." And somewhere with a foundational ghost.
"Carlos, she's heading for the plaza."

Pasternak.

Fuck.

CHAPTER FIFTY-TWO

❦

*T*he way I see it," Riley's explaining helpfully, "*that faux poetic dipshit Pasternak is a grounded ghost, just like Esther. He's the house ghost of the Grand Army Plaza, right? So that's that.*"

I'm heading fast down Franklin, pushing through the crowd past tattoo parlors and hair salons. Still no giant. Sasha's at the foot of the archway. A thick forest of hungry ghosts crowds around her, but they're keeping some distance now; either they know better than to fuck with her or they realize she's about to bust them out of Hell.

"*And the only reason we knew about the ngks around Franklin is because Mama Esther reported them, right? Right. So let's say this Pasternak fuck is in it with whoever, Sarco or Sasha, either that or they got him under some kinda spell, which would explain why he was such a babbling pain in the ass the other night, I suppose. Man . . . shit's devious, yo.*"

That's the damn truth. A middle-aged Rasta guy steps in my path to explain that he has flags for sale, all brightly displayed on this table right here. I nod and smile and sway out of the way and keep it moving. Cut a right on Saint John's Place, a left on Classon, and keep zigzagging street to street till I'm back on the parkway. The whole world is exploding with revelers. A warm, thumping ecstasy has settled over the crowd, and they're all boogying to the same syncopated beat that bursts out of the speakers.

"She's inside," Riley reports. *"I'm going in after her."* It's dark in the Underworld; Riley must be in the leg of the archway. A spirally metal staircase winds upward into the shadows.

Finally, I'm at the plaza, winded and sweaty but in one piece and the giant's nowhere to be seen. On the inner part of the arch there's a small door, locked tight by a heavy chain. There's a million people around, including cops, but they're all focused away from me, watching the endless party burst along the parkway, so they don't see me make quick work of the lock and slip inside.

I muddle around for a few seconds till I find the light switch, but it's pretty useless—a dim little bulb comes to life from behind a few stacked chairs, and I can only just make out . . . a snarling dragon face glaring down at me. What the hell? I glance around and realize I'm surrounded by grinning skeletons, old hunchbacks, perched crows. All frozen in that lumpy, papier-mâchéd eternity and gathering dust. Who knew? I start up the spiraling metal staircase.

Something's happening.

Sasha's on the second-floor landing—a crude metal platform, shrouded in darkness. But she's not running up the stairs. She's turned around. Riley must be right in front of her. She's says something and takes a menacing step toward me . . . him. Us. Riley's blade is out, pointed forward. I realize I may be about to watch my best friend kill the woman who's carrying my baby, or vice versa, and all I want to do is close my eyes and make it go away.

And then I notice something about Sasha. It's subtle.

At first I think I'm making it up—but no, it's that glint in
her eye. It's familiar. It's . . . Sarco. Yes, now that I see it,
I'm sure of it. Sasha takes a step forward, slashes out at
Riley, and there's no doubt: Sarco is there. He's with her.
In her. Sarco's taken over Sasha. No wonder we couldn't
find him all night.

Sasha's blade whips out at Riley again. He parries and
backs a few steps down the stairs. He's holding back; he
doesn't want to hurt her or the baby. Our baby. If Sarco's
inside of Sasha now, that means . . . the junky probably
wasn't his real body either. He's a parasite. Inhabits the
living and then leaves them shredded up inside and a few
days later, they hemorrhage and die. David. David just
up and bled out, not long after the whole mess. It also
means Sarco's not a halfie at all, not anymore anyway—
he's something else entirely. I tuck that information away
for my next bar fight or Council run-in.

Sarco/Sasha charges down a few steps and slices, first
with one blade and then the other. Riley blocks the first
cut, but the second catches his hand. The view gets all
jumbly as he stumbles backward down the stairs, then
loses his balance and clatters to the ground. I see Sasha's
feet running up toward the next landing.

Trevor was terrified that night, I think as I run up
another flight. He was whispering to me, like he thought
someone was listening. Because Sarco was there, lurking inside David the hipster's little body. Hiding in the
trees probably that whole time while Trevor died in my
arms. Then he moved on to the junky's body, leaving
David mortally ill and terrified. I reach the next landing,
push past some long-armed papier-mâché skeletons, and
start up the ladder toward the roof. And after Sarco got
stuck in the Underworld with me, he re-entered the junky
and then abandoned him a few days later. Then the junky

wandered out and died too. Then Sarco must've just free floated for a while, recovering, until he landed on Sasha. The thought of that demon being mortally entwined inside her sends a wave of nausea over me.

I reach the top of the ladder and push open the trap-door. I'm hoisting myself up onto the roof when a huge hand wraps around my ankle. The giant will not give up. I kick at the hand with my other foot, but it won't loosen. Then he pulls, and I'm wrenched off the ladder and fall straight down in a dazed panic. I swing my elbow out just before I crash, catching him on the crown of his head, and we both tumble to the ground. He growls and grabs for my neck with a hand and his stumpy wrist. I pull away just before he catches me, send a swift kick across his face, and then scatter back up the ladder, heave a massive metal plank out of the way, and hoist myself up onto the rooftop.

It's pouring rain. I know the legions of hungry dead are rushing toward this soon-to-be wide-open hole to the liv-ing world. Riley is painstakingly recovering himself and climbing the stairs, his wounded hand hanging limply by his side.

Pasternak is on the roof, floating just above the angel and her horses, and those ghostly ngk threads reach from him off into the surrounding buildings. He's got that lan-guid damn expression on his face again. He's flickering, and with each spasm of light that flashes across his huge body, I catch a glimpse of the murky skies of the Under-world. It's hypnotizing. I'm so transfixed I almost miss it when the giant's huge arm reaches up onto the rooftop, followed by his big heaving head. I have just enough time to lift up the wood-enforced metal plank they use to cover the roof entrance. I wait for him to hoist himself into the most awkward possible position and bring it down on his head. There's a horrible sound: splintering bone and the soft mushiness of flesh collapsing together. The giant lays still. That thick dead blood of his gushes languidly out from under the metal plank and gets speckled by falling rain.

When I look back at Pasternak, all I see is Sasha looking at me from the other side. A red tear runs down her face, and then she falls to her knees. I burst forward and then stop short when Sarco's towering shadow billows like a cloud of smoke out of Sasha's body. For a terrible second, we just stare at each other. Then Sasha goes limp and falls facedown, halfway across the gateway that was once Pasternak. I see something small scramble along the edge of the rooftop out of the corner of my eye. It's gone when I swing my head around to look, but I already know: the ngks are converging.

CHAPTER FIFTY-THREE

❧

Sarco steps forward into the world of the living. His hazy shadow arms stretch to either side and his head is thrown back with laughter. The sky explodes with rain, lightning, and swirling clouds. He picks up one of Sasha's blades, watching me the whole time, and then walks over to Moishe's crumpled body. I reach Sasha just as Sarco crouches down and disappears into the doubly dead giant.

Her chest is moving up and down. Which means she's breathing. Which means she's alive. I exhale, finally, although I hadn't even realized I was holding my breath. I lift her up into my arms and she looks at me. "Don't get all cute," she whispers. A little stream of blood trickles out of her left eye and I wipe it away. Then she hands me her blade. Sarco the giant trembles, convulses, and then tosses the metal plank off his head like it's a piece of cardboard. He's up, smashed, bloody head and all, and stumbling toward us. Ngks crawl along their threads from the edges of the roof. Then, as if on some secret cue, they all rush forward toward where I'm cradling Sasha.

I rise onto one knee and lift my blade up just in time to parry Sarco's downswing. The ngks are everywhere;

their little gray-green bodies shimmy with sinister laughter as they scatter toward the center of the roof. It's growing, the portal. Already it's almost larger than Pasternak,
and soon it'll cover the whole archway. I can see the
masses of hungry ghosts converging on the house, a
slow-motion riot of death. Sarco slices at me again, and I
fend him off. The giant's strength is still overwhelming,
but his body's been through it recently; I can tell Sarco's
struggling to make it work. Still—I'm not sure how long
I can hold him off.

I advance, stabbing forward and forcing him toward
the edge of the rooftop. With Sarco at least somewhat out
of the picture, I just might be able to close the portal. The
ngks close in on Sasha. I send a series of slices toward
Sarco, all of which he blocks easily. The first line of hungry ghosts has made it to the rooftop in the Underworld.
They stumble forward, collapsing on top of one another
and sliding along, arms outstretched. Sasha struggles to
her feet and throws herself out of the way just as the ngks
reach the edge of the portal and begin pulling it open,
snickering all the while.

"Don't you see how close we are?" Sarco yells. His voice
sounds clipped and awkward coming from the giant's
shattered mouth. "Don't you see?" He swings his blade
with unchecked fury. "I will not be stopped, halfie! Or are
you just worried about your pretty family?"

"This is where you killed us."

"Mm." He nods. "But I brought you back, didn't I?
You're alive, aren't you?"

I send him backward with a barrage of swipes. "Who
was I?" Blue police lights pulse below, but they're not for
us. An early-morning parade of partiers is swooping past
and heading down Flatbush.

"You'd love to know, wouldn't you? Well . . . Nothing is simple my friend."

He's getting tired. But even if the giant's body gives out, who's to say he won't try to jump into mine? "Consider that you're giving up a golden opportunity, Carlos, both to find out who you really were and to join me in changing the world. The world!"

He tries to grin, but it loosens his already mutilated jaw that much more. His mouth becomes unhinged and drops open inhumanly wide. Blood pours out and then slows to a trickle.

Enraged, Sarco renews his attacks with even more vigor. His blows come crashing again and again, and suddenly his huge foot is on my chest and then I'm skidding across the rooftop. Sasha's blade clatters out of my hand. I'm rising to get it, but Sarco's already bearing down on me, blade raised for the kill strike.

"Carlos!" Sasha yells. I turn and see an ngk flying toward my head. And I understand. I grasp the cool squirming body. Sarco brings his blade down, all full of that pent-up righteous rage, and I raise the ngk to meet it. The one remaining eye in his smashed head gets wide, but it's too late: the squealing ngk goes suddenly quiet as it splits into two pieces in my grasp.

Everything stops.

Sarco drops his sword and turns his broken face toward the cluster of ngks at the portal. They've all put down what they were doing and turned to look at him. It happens so fast: in seconds they're across the rooftop and on him.

Seeing the ngks' vengeful feeding frenzy happen to a ghost was bad enough. When there's live flesh involved, it's really a whole other story. The little monsters dig their claws into the giant's already dead skin, wrap their sharp

little mouths around his arms and legs, tear out chunks
and chew them up and keep going, burrowing like little
humanoid rats as Sarco screams and writhes. There's
nothing he can do, of course, but scream and deal with it.
I see one clamor onto his head and stick its whole upper
body *into* the gaping hole of his mouth. More blood pours
out, probably because the thing's eating his tongue.

Sasha stands in front of the portal. She's recovered the
blade I dropped and holds it out in front of her, pointed
directly at the foremost ghost on the other side. They seem
to recall exactly who she is and what she's already done to
their buddies—none of them moves a single inch. I pick
up the blade Sarco dropped, careful not to disturb the
massacre. Then I walk over and stand by her side. I'm not
sure if there's a point really. She obviously has this han-
dled, but I simply don't know what else to do with myself.

Sarco finally drops to his knees and then falls onto the
gravelly rooftop. The ngks are still feasting away mercilessly. What's left of the giant body shivers and the shadow
Sarco emerges. He's heaving, barely alive from what I
can tell, and the ngks are on him instantly, leaving behind
the flayed carcass of what was once Moishe.

Say what you like about ngks, but those little mother-
fuckers are efficient as hell. Sarco makes a pathetic
attempt to swirl up into the sky but they drag him down
quickly. He reaches a desperate hand out toward us, but
one of them leaps on it, digs its claws in, and tears it off.
He screams, a soul-shattering, last-gasp type of scream,
and seconds later Sarco is no more.

The ngks are done. They do their little tidying-up routine and begin to wander off into the night. Whatever
arrangement they'd worked out with Sarco, it was clearly
violated when he sliced one of them in half. The portal
begins to shrink. One dilapidated old ghost makes a

half-assed attempt to hurtle across before it closes and Sasha chops his arm off. And then the portal's gone, and it's raining, and Sasha's beside me, as radiant and mostly alive as ever, and, of course, pregnant. There's dried blood on her face and a new trickle slips out of her ear. She smiles at me sadly, and then her eyes roll back in her head and she pitches forward, unconscious.

CHAPTER FIFTY-FOUR

◦◦◦◦◦

Williamsburg is almost deserted at four a.m. this Tuesday morning.

Almost.

If you happened to be strolling down the darkened streets, you might see a crowd of surly-looking Hasidics blinking against the early-morning rain. They're wearing long black coats and rimmed hats and one in particular is quite old and quite magnanimous. You can tell by how the others show a certain deference to him, keep their eyes always darting back to him. He might have a century under his belt, but he stands erect and proud, an ancient oak tree in the shadowy Brooklyn night.

Victor parks his SUV in front of the Jews and shuts off the headlights. We glance back and forth to make sure no one's around and then open the trunk and heave out the enormous bundle. The Jews have a stretcher waiting, probably borrowed from one of their volunteer ambulances, and two of them stand on either side, bracing it as we lower the great weight down.

I hear a weeping sound over the falling rain and realize it's coming from a small figure sitting on a park bench a few feet away. Traffic rushes past on the Brooklyn-Queens

Expressway beneath us. The trembling woman stands,
escorted by a sturdy young man, and approaches the gurney. I don't want to see this, but I steady myself and keep
quiet. The man looks at us with an unspoken question, and
Victor realizes it first and indicates the side of the bundle
where the head would be. The Jew unwraps it gently. A
flash of horror crosses his face, but he controls it, forces
his expression back to neutral and steps aside so the widow
can look. Her wail cuts through the night, runs circles
through my brain, tears mercilessly down my spinal column, and shivers out in dim echoes down the block.

Two more men escort the sobbing woman away, and
then a short, stout fellow beside the old oak tree steps
toward me. Could be Moishe's brother or cousin, from the
look of him. "It is as you say," he says solemnly. "You
must tell us . . ."

"I can't," I say. "I told you I can't. I know it's not fair."

"We have other methods of compelling you to answer
our questions."

"I'm sure you do, but you won't find me. And it's not
necessary. Moishe saved my life. The . . . man who did
this to him has been destroyed. That's all I can tell you.
It's over." I pause, searching for words. "I'm . . . sorry."

The guy looks like he's about to say something rude
when the elderly man steps forward and silences him
with a glance. He regards the body with an unchanged
face, and then he looks up at me. Those ancient, squinty
eyes: his gaze is penetrating. I'm sure he instantly knows
all my secrets, but the trivial inner life of a half-dead
Puerto Rican is useless to this old sage. "There is no
point, Herschel. Leave him be." The voice is surprisingly
robust for such a withered little body. "This being is like
a diaspora unto himself, and he caused no harm to your
brother." He nods at me and with the tiniest of gestures

sets the whole entourage into motion, wheeling the gurney away and folding back up into the night.

"C'mon," Victor says when we're back in the SUV. "Let's go see about your lady."

Baba Eddie smiles at me. We're sitting at my kitchen table. I'm trying to ignore the sounds of Dr. Tijou tinkering away in the other room. Baba Eddie's smoking. Smiling. Smiling and smoking.

"I know you're feeling particularly like shit right now, Carlos."

"More or less."

"But you should know, you've done well."

"I don't think I have."

"I don't know the whole story, but I suspect you're being too hard on yourself. I can see it on your face."

I shrug. And then I remember: "Riley told me that you named me."

Baba Eddie grinds out his cigarette. "I did."

"From the cross?"

"Crosses have been spiritually important symbols long before Jesus died on one."

"Ah, yes, so I hear."

"Specifically, I had in mind the crossroads."

"Any in particular?"

"Well, in your case, the ones between life and death. For the Lucumí, for many traditions really, the crossroads are a sacred place. We have our own spirit to watch over them. It's about a turning point, the moment of crisis."

"I'd like a moment of noncrisis right about now though."

He's still smiling. "Of course, Carlos, but it doesn't mean you're in constant crisis. It means you are born from a place where opposites converge and you always carry that

with you. How you find harmony between them is your
own business."

So simple, he makes it sound. Still, it makes sense.

Dr. Tijou walks in suddenly and I stand up. She raises
her hand and shakes her head. "I have nothing to report
yet. We have some waiting to do."

I collapse back into my chair and try to harmonize life
and death.

Dr. Tijou is ecstatic. I suspect it's partially because she's
happy to be around our strange union of friends again,
but also, she's blabbering on about some crazy machete
massacre she had to deal with outside of Port-au-Prince
one time. "Once the bleeding stopped," she explains, "we
had a chance to try to replace the arm! Try, I said, because,
of course—"

"Dr. Tijou," I say as calmly as possible. "Sasha."

"Ah, of course!"

We're sitting at my kitchen table. It's raining again.
I'm sipping a cold cup of coffee and Dr. Tijou is on her
eighth cup of tea or something. She's been in and out of
the living room all day, checking things, adjusting other
things, fussing about in all kinds of remarkable, trauma-
surgeon ways. It's been nerve-racking as hell, but I've
managed not to get in the way and not to ask too many
questions, as requested. But I've had it. No more Haitian
war stories, no more pleasantries. I need to know what's
going on: The doctor seems to grasp my impatience. She
smiles. "I'm not an obstetrician, but it seems the baby is
going to be okay."

"And the mommy?"

"The mommy . . . is another department. Physically, she
is stable. I have stemmed the internal bleeding that we

detected, as best I can tell. I cannot speak for the other end. That is Dr. Voudou's department." She allows herself a small chuckle and then looks somber. "She is very strong though, that one. A fighter."

I nod. Sasha had swayed in and out of consciousness during the whole desperate flight back to my place. Whispered a few mostly meaningless sentences and then lapsed into a daze where she seemed to be trying to pull her own skin off, as if Sarco were still in her somehow. I tried not to think too hard about it, the haunting image of that demon crawling all up inside of her, but it's hard to shake. We made it here and I laid her on the couch and got Victor on the phone quick. When things started to slow down, I collapsed next to Sasha, after making sure she was still breathing, and didn't wake till Victor rang my bell with Dr. Tijou in tow. Riley came a few minutes later. He was scratched up and winded but otherwise all right.

"Dr. Voudou, he is on the way?"

"Should be here any minute," I say. *Patience, Carlos, patience.* Rushing things won't help. It's all out of my hands, but still, my insides squirm with desperation as another few minutes tick past with no Baba Eddie. Don't think about the decaying corpses of David and the junky, but of course that's all I can see. Shit. I sip at my coffee irritably even though it's only grounds and a dark trickle.

"¿Hola, mi gente?" Eddie. I jump up from the table, almost spilling Dr. Tijou's tea, and rush to open the door. Eddie's already halfway in. Apparently, I left it unlocked, and he's carrying a big cardboard box. Two younger guys and Iya Tiomi, all dressed in white, come in behind him, followed by Kia and Victor. "Sorry it took so long. We had to make some runs to get supplies."

"It's fine," I say, trying not to sound rushed. "She's in here."

Baba Eddie is all business. He sets down the box, takes a long hard look at Sasha, and starts giving orders. "Thomas, start boiling water. Chris, prepare the herbs. Kia . . ."

"The animals?"

"The animals."

"And, Iya Tiomi."

The older woman smiles.

"See what you can see."

She nods and, after some groaning and maneuvering, sits on the couch beside Sasha.

Baba Eddie turns to me. "Now, you, tell me exactly what happened."

CHAPTER FIFTY-FIVE

の~⊙

The santeros work late into the night. At some point, Dr. Tijou politely asks if I wouldn't mind changing the sheets for her so she can crash out on my bed. I don't even think she has any reason to be here anymore except pure curiosity. And maybe a doomed crush on "Dr. Voudou." She slips under the fresh covers and passes out with a smile on her face.

"So that's the magic stabbing lady that stole your heart," Kia says as we have coffee at the kitchen table. It must be getting near dawn by now.

"Indeed it is."

"You knocked her up."

I nod. "Indeed I did."

"Well, at least you got to sleep with her, then."

"Thanks, Kia. That's comforting."

"I'm saying, it's better to have loved and lost, right?"

"I think so. I'll let you know after this ordeal is over."

"Fair enough."

We sip in silence for a few minutes. In the other room, the babas chant softly. Iya Tiomi's voice rises above the others in a raspy staccato and then the men answer her. Someone's clanging away rhythmically on a cowbell and beneath it all is the endless swooshing of water. I'd be able to appreciate how beautiful it was if I weren't so worried about losing the woman I love.

"You love her?" Kia says, once again digging into my private thoughts without permission. One day I'm gonna have to speak to her about that.

I search myself for a second, even though I know the answer. Maybe so it doesn't seem as irrational as it feels. Then again, who ever said love was rational? "I do."

Kia nods solemnly. "Seems complicated."

"It is. Very."

The conversation's strangely comforting, for all its simplicity. Kia has a way of showing that she gets it without saying too much. And anyway, I couldn't deal with a lot of chatter right now.

A few minutes later, Baba Eddie walks in looking exhausted. He slumps into a chair and pulls out a cigarette, plops it into his mouth without the usual fanfare, and lights up. I raise my eyebrows at him.

"She's all right."

Thank you, universe. Thank you, stars, world, all of that. Thank you. Yes. "And the baby?"

Eddie puts his hands up. "Best I can tell, yes. We have spiritually deep cleaned her with everything we got. The spirits seem to be in accordance and have given their blessings, so on my end, all is well." He puts his hand on my knee reassuringly and then leans back into his chair and exhales a huge mountain of smoke.

"Thank you, Baba. I don't know what to say."

"De nada, Carlos. Just give me some coffee please."

I put a new pot on, and we sit listening to the clunk and clatter of santeros cleaning up and the gurgle of freshly made coffee.

"You almost died."

Sasha's smile is faded, but she's still somehow full of life. "I know."

"You saved my life."

She smiles again, but a second later it's gone. "You saved mine too. Thank you."

This is harder than I thought it'd be. But then, she's probably exhausted.

"Can you talk about it—what happened?"

She sits up a little, and it crashes down on me one more time how beautiful she is, even after all the hell she's just lived. All the pieces fit together just right. "I tried to contact you."

"Ginny," I say.

She nods. "Felt you looking for me that first night. You know fortune-tellers, even wack ones, got all that energy floating around the place. Figured that'd be the easiest way to ping you, and you'd put the rest together when she told you I was going to TiVo."

"I did!"

"Not quickly enough."

"I know. The giant jumped me while I was waiting for you to come out."

We sit in the silence of our missed connection for a few seconds. I try not to wonder if anything would've been different if we'd have managed to link up before Sarco got to her.

"Anyway, I knew he'd be coming for me," Sasha says. "And that it would be useless to fight him. I knew he'd have some other plan up his sleeve. I more or less had pieced together what he was up to from what Trevor had

told me and some of my own sources. I was gonna do a
Carlos." (Sad smile. I crumble a little inside.) "And go
along right up until I had a chance to come at him. But, of
course, someone like Sarco won't be caught in the same
trick twice. Even when he swarmed up inside of me, I was
still figuring eventually he'd have to come out, and when
he did, I'd figure out how to destroy him one way or the
other. I focused all of my protective energy around the
baby and just tried to stay conscious while that madman
rushed through the streets with my body.

"He knew exactly what he was doing, made right for
the entrada, and as soon as we got there, he relaxed his
hold on me some. Sarco knows I'm better with a blade
than he'll ever be, even with all that sorcery. And he also
knew as long as he was inside me, occupying me, this
baby's life was in his claws and I wouldn't try any kind
of slickness. And he was right, of course. As soon as I
had control of my body back, those old phantoms were
closing in and I had a blade in each hand that I knew
exactly what to do with."

"I saw."

"You didn't know I was a trained assassin? How do
you think the Survivors survive?"

"There's a lot I don't know about you, Sasha."

"Anyway, he was back in control as soon as we were in
the clear. And then once he left me, I had no idea . . ."
Her voice trails off, and for a second I think she might
just break down. Instead she rallies herself. ". . . just how
fucked up I'd feel when he was gone. It was like there
was a thousand-pound weight around my neck and a million razor blades hacking away at my insides. And all I
could think about was this baby inside me, this life that
I'd only just gotten used to having and suddenly seemed
so up for grabs, so fragile."

"It's . . . ours?"

She laughs. "Of course, Carlos. Who else's would it . . . ? Yes, it's ours. Yours and mine."

I nod, ecstatic and heartbroken at the same time.

"And, Carlos." Uh-oh. I feel the next two words closing in on me from a mile away. "I'm leaving."

"*Leaving* leaving? Where to?"

"I don't know." She thinks for a minute. "I can't tell you."

"Ah." A lump is forming in the pit of my . . . what is that, my stomach? My soul? I don't know. It sucks though. "But . . ." But what? I have no words.

"I can't . . . be with you." I nod, even though I don't really mean to. "You killed my brother, Carlos."

I was following orders! No. That won't do. *I didn't know he was* . . . No. *I'm sorry.* Sweet and true, but too little, too late. "You stabbed me." I didn't really mean to say that one; it just came out.

She actually smiles a little. "I know."

"I could've died. That doesn't make us even?" Ugh! Of course it doesn't. Why must I open my mouth and make sentences?

"I knew you wouldn't die. I made sure of it."

"Ah, I thought so." Sweet, but . . . I'm still losing. "I'm sorry."

"I know. Me too."

"We died together." I blurt it out like it's my last grasp at salvaging whatever we had. Then, like an asshole, I temper it with, "I think."

She cocks her head to the side. "At Grand Army Plaza?"

"Yes. I spoke to the resident ghost there a few nights back. He saw everything but would only give me cryptic answers. I think Sarco had him under some kind of spell."

"What'd he say?"

"That there were seven of us, and none survived, and then there were five."

Her eyes are far away. "Anything else?"

"Nothing worthwhile. And now, of course, he's been obliterated in the melee along with the only other guy that knows what happened."

"Maybe not the only one . . ."

"What do you mean?"

"I'll be checking on some things. Maybe I'll get in touch. I don't know."

"The baby . . ."

She looks dangerously close to tears. "I know it's not fair to you, Carlos. I know that. But it doesn't change . . . what happened. Maybe someday, I don't know. I don't even want to say that because it seems cruel. I just . . . I can't."

My whole body tenses and I almost overturn the coffee table. A fury hurls through me. It's not directed at one thing or another, just . . . everything. I close my eyes and will it to subside, force my mind back to somewhere semi-rational.

The fury simmers some.

"No. Stay." Something not quite pleading but not demanding either. But her face is steeled. I nod. "Okay. I see." What else can I say? I can't force her to stay.

"Go," she says. "Give me a few hours. I have some people coming to get me. I can't do lingering good-byes."

"So you're going to take my child and kick me out of my apartment?"

"Carlos."

"No, I don't want a drawn-out thing either." I stand up, suddenly very far away from her. My face tries to make itself into a smile but doesn't quite get there and it comes out as a grimace instead. "Good-bye."

"Bye."

I grab my coat and the new cane-blade that Riley brought me and walk out into the weird, drizzly morning. Halfway down the block, I put a Malagueña to my lips and light it, letting that thick rich smoke invade me. A few hours pass while I circle Brooklyn, thinking so many thoughts and then none at all, smoking and cursing and smiling and dreaming. I'm more like a ghost now than I've ever been—just a wisp of a soul slipping through the streets, barely noticed. Wrestling endlessly with myself.

Maybe when I return she'll be there waiting.

Quiet.

Maybe her smell will greet me as I walk through the door, her smile will find mine and my hand will rest on her full belly, and we'll settle into the couch and find that oneness we once slid so easily into.

Shhh.

Absurdly, I remember that little boy in the Spider-Man outfit, arguing with himself outside her building right before I got jumped. I'm almost back at my place, and I don't want to go in because I know what I'll find and what I won't find. I briefly consider just walking away and never coming back, walking south and south and south till something makes sense again. Then I crumple up the thought and throw it away and walk up my stairs.

She's not here. No one's here. I've never felt so much emptiness in my own house. I think maybe I'll collapse dramatically onto the couch and take a semi-infinite nap, when I notice something sitting on the coffee table that wasn't there before. A cassette tape. It has one word scrawled across it, and I don't have to read it to know what it says.

My hands don't tremble as I slide it into the old tape player and press play.

Okay, they tremble a little.

The first note is all I need to hear. I stop the tape, take a deep breath, start it again. When the voice comes in, everything, all that thinking, stops. The drums clackity-clack beneath and each note is a river that runs from the speaker into my blood vessels and through my heart.

When the whole thing crashes to a close, I rewind the tape and play it again.